First published in the UK in 2018 by Aria,
an imprint of Head of Zeus Ltd

This paperback edition published in 2020 by Aria,
an imprint of Head of Zeus Ltd

9 7 5 3 1 2 4 6 8

A catalogue record for this book is available from the British Library.

ISBN (PBO): 9781838930660
ISBN (E): 9781786692566

Printed and bound in Great Britain by
CPI Group (UK) Ltd, Croydon CR0 4YY

MIX
Paper from
responsible sources
FSC® C020471

Head of Zeus Ltd
5–8 Hardwick Street
London EC1R 4RG

WWW.HEADOFZEUS.COM

Heather BURNSIDE

Vendetta

HEAD of ZEUS

For Kerry and Pascoe

PART ONE

1990–1992

1

It was late evening and Adele was walking around the darkened interior of her brother's Manchester nightclub, the Golden Bell. She smiled as she listened to the lyrics of 'The Only Way Is Up' by Yazz and felt the throbbing of the rhythmic disco beat. The revellers seemed to feed off the energy from the music and the blue strobe lighting. Gazing upwards, she noticed the intermittent blasts of illumination from laser beams scudding across the ceiling, and the array of multicoloured overhead spotlights. She never tired of that sight. There was no atmosphere like it.

Adele had only been managing the Golden Bell for a couple of weeks and, despite her initial reservations, she was quite enjoying it. As she carried out her checks she was glad to see that most of the customers seemed happy. The only exception was a group of young women occupying a peripheral table.

It was the second time Adele had passed the young women, who were on a hen night. The first time the table had been full of chatter and laughter, and all had seemed well. But the atmosphere between them had now changed. They were bickering and Adele decided to stick around in case things turned nasty.

As she hovered close to the table she caught snippets of their conversation. It was a dispute over money. One of the women, called Trish, was running a kitty and some of the others felt they'd been short-changed.

'We should have had at least two fuckin' drinks out of that!' shouted a big, busty blonde with a ragged complexion, called Tina. 'And now you're asking us for another fiver? You can fuck right off!'

Tina's tight top clung to her large breasts, emphasising the outline of her ill-fitting bra by the surplus flesh that bulged over the top. Adele watched Trish's reaction as many of the others sided with Tina. Trish was a tall girl with bobbed hair dyed in a shade of black that was as severe as her acute facial features. Her expression bore a look of anger tinged with guilt.

'What are you fuckin' accusing me of?' she demanded, getting up from her seat and facing Tina head-on.

Then Tina was out of her seat too, her friends holding her back as she let out a verbal onslaught and tried to get at Trish. Adele felt the rapid rhythm of her heartbeat as her fight or flight response kicked in. She stepped forward.

Gazing around her, Adele was relieved to spot one of the bouncers, Barney, racing towards the crowd of girls, who were now yelling at each other. Many of the girls were trying to get at Trish, who responded by waving her fist at them.

Before Barney could reach the table, Trish pulled some money out of her handbag and slammed it down onto the table. 'Stick your fuckin' kitty up yer arse!' she yelled. 'See if I care.' Then she upended the table, sending a spray of drinks all over the other girls.

Tina screeched as the cold chill of ice-laden alcohol hit her. Then she looked down at her clothing, which was drenched with drink, forming a large cola-coloured patch on her skirt. 'You stupid bitch!' she yelled. 'This outfit cost me a fuckin' fortune.'

She dragged herself away from her friends and went for Trish but Barney stepped between them.

'Calm it, girls!' he shouted but Tina was beyond pacifying.

Unable to get to Trish, Tina aimed a venom-filled punch straight at Barney. As the force of the blow knocked him temporarily off balance, Adele waded in. She knew Barney was too much of a gentleman to trade blows with a woman.

Within seconds Adele had overpowered Tina and wrenched her arms behind her back, and she was now marching her towards the door. It wasn't the first time Adele had been grateful for her martial arts skills and the hours of practice she put in at the gym each week. Tina, like many others, had taken one look at Adele and underestimated her fighting ability.

Adele had a sophisticated demeanour, which belied her inner strength. Her attractive face was framed by a mane of dark glossy hair, her skin radiant and her eyes dark and sultry. Only her eyes hinted at the hidden depths within, but most people missed the clue.

Several bouncers ran towards the table of girls. Glancing over at the remaining party, Adele noticed that they were engaged in a full-on fight, dragging at each other's hair and scratching viciously.

'Get them all out!' shouted Adele as she heaved against Tina's bulky frame.

Barney soon joined her, his bottom lip now spattered with blood where Tina had hit him. Between them they managed to propel Tina towards the exit. While Adele opened the door, Barney pushed the girl out into the street.

'You can't fuckin' do that!' yelled Tina, hammering on the glass door panels.

'We just did!' shouted Adele. 'And don't bother coming back,' she added.

Turning back into the foyer, Adele noticed the bouncers leading several of the other girls towards the exit. 'Make sure they don't get back in!' she ordered the doormen who were standing guard at the doors.

Out of the corner of her eye she spotted the handsome, chiselled features of Glynn, her brother's number two, her former lover and now her nemesis. 'What the fuck's going on?' he demanded.

'It's OK,' Adele replied coolly. 'We've already sorted it.'

Adele didn't want Glynn to think she needed his help. He wasn't at all happy that she was running the club rather than him. Glynn had previously told her she was out of her depth and had vowed that she wouldn't get any help from him. Since then he'd gone back on his word; he couldn't resist making his authority felt within the club. But Adele was out to prove that she didn't need him.

She walked away from Glynn and headed for the sanctuary of her upstairs office, taking the stairs two at a time. Adele locked the door then let out a puff of breath as she leant against the back of it and let her shoulders sag. Thank God that was over!

But as Adele recovered from her brisk walk up the stairs and her breathing steadied, she noticed her heartbeat was still frantic. She looked down at her hands, which were shaking. Perhaps the incident had affected her more than she realised or perhaps it was the constant presence of Glynn that had unnerved her.

Adele strode across the office and pulled out the desk drawer from which she withdrew a half-bottle of brandy. She poured the liquid from the bottle into a mug then sat back and sipped. After a short while relief began to flood through her body, relaxing her primed limbs and calming her mind. It was times like these when she realised the extent of what she had taken on.

When Adele's brother, Peter, had asked her to take over the running of the Golden Bell while he was serving a stretch for GBH, she had baulked at the idea. She saw it as too big a risk, knowing that the nightclub scene was plagued by protection rackets, drug dealers and God knew what else. But then Peter had reminded her about all he had done for her in the past and she'd reluctantly agreed.

Adele would probably always feel indebted to Peter. He was the one who had helped her try to conceal her father's killing when she had beaten him to death in a violent rage. After years of abuse his vicious beating of her mother had been the last straw and Adele had just flipped. And with a prison record behind her, no one would employ her until Peter had again come to her rescue and asked her to work for him.

Now, as she was starting to get used to managing the Golden Bell, the task didn't seem so daunting. In fact, despite the many challenges, it gave her a buzz. She was responsible for the whole of it, until her brother was released anyway. And that level of responsibility gave her a certain kudos that she enjoyed.

But running a nightclub did have its downside. Adele had never before realised just how much trouble could occur inside a club and how quickly situations became inflamed once the alcohol was flowing. Normally the bouncers had things under control so quickly that the punters didn't even notice anything was amiss, but there was the odd occasion when things spilled over.

This was the first time Adele had had to get personally involved since she had been running the Golden Bell and, although she was capable of handling herself, she didn't like trouble. She'd seen too much of it in her life already, and preferred to keep a safe distance if possible.

But despite it all, Adele was still glad she had taken on the task of running Peter's nightclub as well as many of his other businesses, because, without her there, hen-party brawls would be the least of their problems. There was also Glynn to contend with.

She didn't trust him one bit and it was nothing to do with him being her former lover. Glynn had a ruthless streak, which she hadn't known about until she had been seeing him for a few weeks. He was ambitious and he'd made it plain to her that his ambitions extended beyond the right side of the law. Glynn was a murderer who killed as a matter of course if it suited his purposes.

But the main reason Adele didn't trust Glynn was because she was convinced that he had been behind her brother's arrest and subsequent incarceration. Peter had foolishly raided a nightclub that was run by a rival gang and, although Glynn was supposed to be involved in a simultaneous raid, he had backed out at the last minute.

Adele didn't believe Glynn's cover story about his sick aunty taking a turn for the worse even though Peter seemed to have bought it. There was no doubt in her mind that Glynn had designs on her brother's business empire, and putting Peter behind bars was just the first step to achieving that. Adele knew that she was the only person who could stop him taking things further.

2

Adele had now been managing the Golden Bell for several weeks. She was enjoying the challenge but it was difficult trying to keep up with the office work while also keeping an eye on things inside the club. It was late when she arrived at work on that Monday after another busy weekend. She walked up the back stairs carrying her cup of freshly brewed coffee, which she'd collected from a nearby sandwich shop.

On the way to her office she passed her brother's old office and spotted Glynn through the door that was slightly ajar. Not for the first time she felt a pang of irritation at the way he had made himself so at home in Peter's office. She wondered just what he found to do in there or was it perhaps just his way of making a statement?

'Morning!' he shouted sarcastically as she tried to creep past unnoticed.

Adele grunted in response then continued on her way. Yet again she could feel annoyance burgeoning inside her and regretted her decision to retain her old office. Initially she had planned to move into Peter's office but had then changed her mind when she'd realised the logistics of shifting all her files and computer. But the main reason she had decided to keep her old office was because the safe was kept there, and she wanted it where she could see it.

Adele hadn't been at her desk long when she received a call from Glynn to say that a lady had arrived to see her.

'OK, send her to my office,' she instructed.

'What's it about?' he asked as though he had a right to know.

'You'll find out soon enough,' said Adele, quickly replacing the telephone receiver.

Expecting a knock on her office door, Adele was surprised when two minutes later Glynn barged in instead. 'Hang on there a minute,' he said to someone outside the door. Then, looking across at Adele, he said, 'It's Margaret Jackson to see you.'

The statement sounded more like a question but Adele wasn't prepared to let him know just who Margaret Jackson was. At least, not yet anyway.

'OK, send her in, please,' she said frostily.

Glynn spun around but was stopped by Adele just as he was walking back out of the door. 'Oh, and, Glynn?'

she said. He turned back till he was facing her again, a look of annoyance on his face. 'Can you make sure Peter's office is clear and tidy, please? I'm going to need it shortly.'

'What d'you mean?' he asked, his tone aggressive and his eyebrows knitted together in anger. 'I'm working in there.'

'What exactly are you doing?' she asked.

He sidled up to her desk, leaning across till his face was inches from hers, then said in a low growl, 'None of your fuckin' business.'

Adele felt the first stirrings of fear as her heart rate speeded up. 'It *is* my business,' she said, trying to disguise the slight quiver in her voice. 'Peter's left me in charge so I decide who works where. You shouldn't need an office anyway. I mean, security isn't exactly an office-based job, is it?'

She didn't hide the cynicism she displayed whenever discussing security with Glynn. They both knew it was a glorified title used to describe what really went on. It was a protection racket. Glynn and his gang would offer to protect pubs and clubs from trouble, at a price. If the owners and landlords didn't buy into their services, Glynn and his gang would make things very difficult for them until they paid up.

Adele had a good idea of what their work entailed, and she wanted nothing to do with it. She'd agreed to run Peter's legal businesses but wasn't prepared to get involved in the shadier side of things, which Peter had left in Glynn's hands.

'I've got things I need to sort out and I need a fuckin' office to do it in,' he snarled.

'And what sort of things are they?' she asked, knowing he wouldn't want to discuss any of his activities with her.

'None of your fuckin' business,' he repeated, then he stomped out of the office, leaving Margaret Jackson outside in the corridor.

'Come in!' shouted Adele, realising that the poor woman would be bemused by Glynn's lack of manners.

Margaret Jackson strode into the office. Aged in her late forties, she stood tall and smart in a grey tweed fitted jacket and black knee-length skirt. Her hair was drawn back from her handsome face in neat layers. It was a face that spoke of experience and a no-nonsense approach, and Adele noticed a wry smile cross her lips and an amused twinkle light up her eyes as she approached the desk.

'Don't worry about him,' said Adele. 'Please, take a seat. What can I get you to drink?'

'Nothing for me, thanks,' said Margaret, who appeared unfazed despite Glynn's stroppiness.

Adele smiled across the desk at her, sure in her own mind that Margaret was the perfect choice for the job of bookkeeper and personal assistant. As she took in Margaret's cool demeanour she knew that this woman wouldn't let Glynn push her around. And she was the perfect age too. Adele had had enough of Glynn flirting with the bar staff downstairs; she could do without him playing up to the office staff too.

'So, Margaret,' Adele began. 'I explained to you in the interview that you would be responsible for all the accounts for the nightclub, the sunbed shops and the bookmakers. I'll be in as much as I can to help you but with the nightclub to run it won't always be early, I'm afraid.'

'That's all right,' Margaret assured her. 'If there's anything I'm not sure about I can always put it to one side till you're available.'

As Adele ran through the basic requirements with Margaret, she warmed to her more and more. Margaret had a confident, efficient air about her and Adele felt sure that she would be leaving things in capable hands. It was a relief because she was struggling to keep up with everything since she had taken on responsibility for all Peter's businesses, and it would be good to have a second pair of hands.

When she had finished explaining everything to Margaret, Adele said, 'Oh, there's just one more thing. Glynn runs a security business for my brother. You won't really find yourself getting involved in that side of things but the security staff will sometimes come to put the takings in the safe until we can take them to the bank the following day.'

Margaret nodded her understanding although Adele wasn't sure that Margaret knew what was meant by 'security'. 'I want you to have a spare set of keys to my office and the safe,' Adele continued. 'If I'm not around would you please make sure you count the cash and lock it up in the safe? Also, ask which of the businesses it relates to, whether it's one of the sunbed shops, the bookmakers or security. We bank the money for the security business but other than that you won't have to get involved.'

'Yes, certainly,' said Margaret.

'Right, well, I guess that's about it, then,' said Adele. 'The only thing that's left is for me to show you your new office.' Then she got up from her seat, walked past Margaret and said, 'Follow me.'

To Adele's consternation when she reached Peter's office Glynn was still sitting at the desk. He quickly slipped some papers inside a file as she knocked sharply on the door then stepped inside.

'Glynn, I think it's time for me to introduce my new bookkeeper and personal assistant, Margaret Jackson,' she said.

Margaret strode confidently across the room and grasped Glynn's hand then shook it profusely. 'Pleased to meet you,' she said, with a hint of sarcasm.

He glared at Adele, the shock evident in his pinched features. His hand remained limp, its only movement controlled by Margaret.

'I intend to get more involved in the running of the nightclub as well as keeping a check on Peter's other businesses,' Adele explained. 'So I need someone here to look after things for me.'

Glynn's jaw dropped open then he muttered, 'OK,' and withdrew his hand from Margaret's grip.

'Margaret will need an office to work in,' Adele continued. 'And as I wish to remain in my office, I thought that Margaret could occupy Peter's office for now.'

'No fuckin' way!' snapped Glynn. 'This is the boss's office and always has been.'

'Well, from today you can regard it as the book-keeper's office,' said Adele, noticing the amused smile on Margaret's face. 'The boss's office is further up the corridor and is occupied by me,' she added smugly.

Glynn glared from one to the other of them, incensed. 'You can't fuckin' do that!' he yelled.

'I think you'll find that I can,' said Adele, drawing comfort from Margaret's presence. 'In fact, I just have. And, for your information, Peter left no instructions that you were to occupy his office so I'm confused as to why you're here in the first place.'

Glynn stood up, grabbing the file that had sat in front of him. 'We'll soon fuckin' see what Peter thinks about this,' he said.

'It's OK, I'll save you the bother,' said Adele. 'I've already cleared it with him, but, in case of any misunderstandings in future, he's given me free rein to run the business as I see fit. Oh, and one last thing,' she added. 'In future all cash banked to the safe is to go through me. I'll want to know how much is there and which business it's for. You can keep a note of the security takings as Peter will want to know about them. In my absence Margaret will take care of things. And if I'm not around in the evenings, I'll leave the safe key and the key to my office with Paula. She can bank the nightclub takings.'

'You what?' he demanded. 'You're leaving the fuckin' nightclub takings to a barmaid?'

'Bar Manager,' Adele corrected. 'I've just promoted her. And, she won't be taking the cash upstairs on her own. One of the bouncers will accompany her.'

Glynn stormed across the office, stopping next to her on his way out. 'You've not heard the fuckin' last of this!' he spat at her before storming out of the door with his file of secrets clutched in his hands.

Adele could feel a cold shiver of fear as he passed her but she turned to Margaret and attempted to cover her trepidation as she smiled and said, 'Don't worry about Glynn. His bark's worse than his bite.'

Adele only wished she believed those words. She'd upset Glynn and he was a dangerous man when upset. But she'd had to do it. Adele had to let him know who was boss. Now that she was running things she would make sure everything was legal and above board. And if she had to risk Glynn's fury to do that, then it was a risk she was prepared to take.

3

David strutted into the Sportsman's and then into the small side room where his leader, Alan, usually met with the rest of the crew. In the room was a large table together with seating that ran along each wall and was fitted into the corner.

Despite being ten minutes late, David was relaxed when he saw Alan, who had taken up the corner space and was surrounded by his main men. Alan's arms were splayed along the wooden shelving that framed the upholstery, emphasising his toned pecs and his bulging biceps, and he seemed to be enjoying the adulation of his gang. He looked up when David walked in the room.

'You took your fuckin' time,' he said. 'We've been waiting to start.'

But David could tell by the slight smile on Alan's face that he wasn't annoyed with him.

'Sorry, boss,' he said, cheekily. 'My last collection took longer than I thought.'

'No mither. You can tell me about that later,' said Alan. 'We've got other stuff to talk about now.'

The other men made way for David, who slid into the seat next to Alan. The two of them couldn't have been more different in appearance. Alan was tall and slim but muscular. He had a square jawline and stern features, which made him look as though he was always about to have a row with someone. But there was also a look of intelligence behind his eyes, which spoke of his sharp, analytical mind. Although he dressed casually, he had a penchant for designer labels and everything was smart and well laundered.

David, on the other hand, was skinny and unkempt in appearance. Like Alan, he wore designer labels but everything hung loosely on his skinny frame and appeared tatty and unclean. He had weasel-like features, his face pointed and his eyes small and beady, and he often wore a sly grin.

Alan and David went back a long way. They had begun their life of crime together as teenagers and were later joined by Peter, their one-time friend. But things had changed when Alan was put inside for murdering a man during a house break-in with Peter. While Alan served time, Peter started his own gang and was joined by David, until he suspected David of double-crossing him. David still resented the way Peter had punished him before throwing him out of the gang.

David had always maintained his innocence, and although Peter had invited Alan to join his gang after his release from prison, Alan had declined. He had never got over the fact that Peter had run out on him during the house break-in, and Peter's subsequent treatment of his friend, David, had only deepened the divide. Besides, Alan had always been the leader when they were teenagers and he was insulted that Peter had expected things to be different now.

'Right, to start with,' Alan said at the top of his voice. Then he waited until everyone fell silent before he continued. 'I've just found out who's running the Golden Bell while Pete's inside.'

'Glynn Mason, innit?' asked David.

'No, you're wrong. I thought that at first too.'

'It's not that dickhead, Mike Shaftesbury, is it?' David asked again.

'No, wrong again,' said Alan. David noticed the smug grin that lit up his face as he paused for several seconds before putting them all in the picture. 'It's his sister, Adele,' he said. 'Apparently she's been running the show ever since he went inside.'

'You're fuckin' joking!' said David. 'Adele? What the fuck does she know about running a nightclub?'

'Exactly,' said Alan. 'Pete's left himself well fuckin' exposed. Apparently she's looking after his other businesses as well, apart from the security. He's got Glynn Mason looking after that.'

'Well, he's not doing a fuckin' good job,' said David, laughing. 'We've just taken another one of their pubs off them.'

'I know. And we'll be doing a lot more than that,' said Alan.

'Oh, yeah?' said David, raising his eyes inquisitively.

'Yeah, we'll have the fuckin' lot before too long, including the Golden Bell. But for now, I want you to focus on the security side of things. It's time to show them who's the top firm in town.'

Alan looked around the crowd of men occupying the table. 'You're all doing well so keep it up. But be careful. That Glynn and Mike are a ruthless pair of bastards. If they get a chance to get some of their businesses back, they'll fuckin' take it. So you need to watch your backs all the time. You never know when they're gonna strike and I don't wanna lose any of you. Right?'

They all nodded and grunted in agreement and David noticed one or two of them wince when Alan mentioned Glynn and Mike. They all knew what Alan's reference to losing his men could imply: a slow and painful death.

'Why don't we go for the Golden Bell now?' asked David.

'Well, as far as I know there's always either Glynn or Mike doing the rounds in the club and they've got some pretty fuckin' handy blokes on the doors too. But don't worry; I'm keeping an eye on things.'

David smiled; satisfied that Alan had everything under control as usual.

'OK, so let's have your updates,' Alan continued. 'I want to know exactly what's been happening, then we can discuss our strategy.'

The men leant in closer, their heads bowed over the table and their voices lowered as they discussed their plans to take over Peter's protection racket.

Adele was standing at the bar of the Golden Bell chatting with her bar manager, Paula, when she noticed the time.

'It's ten past. Is Cindy due in tonight?' she asked.

'Yeah and it's the second time she's been late this week,' said Paula, rolling her eyes in exasperation.

Adele nodded, saying nothing, but her face showed the anger she felt as she pursed her lips and narrowed her eyes. Cindy's tardiness wasn't the only thing that was bothering her. Ever since Cindy had started seeing Glynn a few weeks ago she had been taking more and more liberties. Adele was fed up with it, as were the bar staff, and she knew it was time to put a stop to Cindy's impudent behaviour.

Another five minutes passed before Cindy drifted in amidst a haze of cheap, cloying perfume. She slowly undid her coat buttons in a tantalising fashion as she entered the bar area.

'Can I have a word?' asked Adele, the lines on her forehead forming a frown.

'In a minute,' said Cindy, unconcerned. 'Let me just put my things in the back first.'

It was a while before Cindy emerged from the staff area behind the bar and Adele could see that her hair was newly teased and her lipstick had been reapplied. She tottered over to the bar on heels that were far too high, her short skirt clinging to her slim but shapely hips.

'Yeah?' she said, eyeing Adele through heavily made-up eyes and casually chewing gum with her mouth open.

Her blasé attitude irritated Adele. 'What time do you call this?' she asked.

Cindy glanced at the clock, seemingly unperturbed, then looked back at Adele. 'It's OK, I cleared it with Glynn,' she said, looking down her nose at Adele before lifting her chin and walking away with her head held high. Paula tutted then looked at Adele for her reaction.

Adele could feel her temper rising at the girl's insolence. 'Hang on a minute!' she shouted. 'Don't walk away when I'm speaking to you.'

Cindy swung round, her expression one of scorn. 'What?' she asked, with attitude.

Adele tried to remain calm as she addressed her, meeting her eyes and keeping her voice slow and even. 'Firstly, I hadn't finished speaking to you and it's bad manners to walk away when you're being addressed.'

'Soz, thought you'd finished,' said Cindy, before flicking the gum to the other side of her mouth with her tongue protruding crudely.

'Secondly,' said Adele, raising her voice slightly, 'I'd appreciate it if you didn't come to work with a mouth full of gum. It doesn't look very professional. Can you remove it, please?'

Cindy tutted then pulled the gum from her mouth and walked to the back of the bar where she dropped it into the bin. 'It's like being at bloody school,' she muttered while her back was to Adele.

Adele waited for her to walk back towards her then continued. 'Thirdly, if you're going to be late you need to clear it with—'

But before she could complete the sentence she felt a presence at her side. It was Glynn, who rudely cut in. 'It's OK, I gave her permission to come in late tonight,' he said.

Adele turned to face him. 'Then why weren't either Paula or myself told about it?' she asked, the question sounding more like an accusation.

'Must have slipped my mind,' he said. 'No worries, it's no biggie.'

Then he walked away without giving Adele a chance to respond, and winked saucily at Cindy, who preened smugly. Adele was livid and for a few moments she stared at Glynn's back then at Cindy, who was wearing a half-smirk. 'In future, you ask either Paula or myself for permission to arrive late, not Glynn,' she said.

Adele didn't hang around to hear Cindy's response; she was too intent on having words with Glynn. She dashed after him as he headed through the back door and towards the upstairs offices.

Catching a glimpse of his heel as he rounded the bend in the stairway, she shouted, 'Oy, I want a word with you.'

She met him on the stair landing. 'What's your problem?' he asked, his face scrunched up in irritation.

'In future, when Cindy asks for permission to arrive late, can you send her to either myself or Paula?' she snapped.

'What's the problem?' he retaliated. 'She was only a few minutes late, for Christ's sake.'

'The problem is that you've undermined me in front of the staff. She shouldn't be led to believe that she can do whatever she pleases; it's not good for the morale of the rest of the team.'

'Have you heard yourself? They're a bunch of fuckin' barmaids, not the board of directors.'

'It doesn't matter what they are,' she vented. 'Discipline is very important for running a tight ship.'

'Yeah, sure,' he muttered, turning away from her as though her argument was insignificant.

'Don't you dare turn your back on me!' she yelled. 'That girl has been getting away with murder since she started seeing you.'

He turned back to face her and grinned. 'Now we're getting to the real problem, aren't we, Adele? Good old-fashioned jealousy. The real reason you're pissed off is because me and Cindy have got something good going on. And you can't stand it.'

'Pfffft,' she hissed. 'Don't flatter yourself. She's bloody welcome to you. I don't give a shit who you're shagging! But what I do care about is when staff think they can take the piss. And you're helping her to do it.

'We can't be seen to be showing favouritism; it isn't fair on the rest of the staff. So from now on I think you need to remember who the boss is around here. You might be running my brother's dodgy protection racket but when it comes to running the Golden Bell, or any of Peter's other businesses, for that matter, you have no authority whatsoever.'

By this time she was shaking with anger, the words spilling from her in a torrent of hatred.

'Jesus, woman, what's wrong with you?' he mocked on noticing her shaking hands. 'Do yourself a favour; go and take a look at the state of yourself in the mirror. Then see if you can pretend you're not jealous.'

Then he barged past her and made his way back down the stairs but as he passed her he hissed, 'Fuckin' sexually frustrated if you ask me.'

Adele stared after him, speechless. Her cheeks reddened with anger and humiliation and for a few moments she stood transfixed. How dare he? Her anger was also directed at herself. Why did she let him get to her? He wasn't worth it.

She marched up to her office, resisting the temptation to down a measure of brandy. Instead she sat at her desk for a good while ruminating about what had just happened.

Adele was fuming and it took her some time to calm down. She was sick to death of Glynn thinking he could walk all over her. It was about time he realised who was the boss. As she sat there raging about her confrontation with Glynn, she decided it was time for her to make a stand. She was going to introduce some changes that would really put him in his place and let him know who was in charge once and for all.

4

Glynn slammed on the brakes of his BMW as he and Mike arrived at the Grey Mare, a rundown urban estate pub clad in pebbledash and sprayed with graffiti. They stepped from the car; Mike's plain features a sharp contrast to Glynn's chiselled good looks, but both equally big and intimidating.

A bunch of streetwise kids hung around the pub doorway shouting insults at the customers. They paused momentarily to watch the two burly men approach. Dressed casually but smartly in expensive designer gear, and oozing authority, Glynn and Mike looked out of place in this run-down area. When Mike shoved viciously past the kids they quickly stepped away from the door.

Glynn and Mike strode confidently up to the bar, which was being manned by Janet, an obese barmaid with grim features who was lethargically wiping the bar top with a manky cloth. It was the sort of pub that employed the barmaids because of their dubious connections rather than for their looks or ability.

Janet knew what they wanted straight away. 'He's upstairs,' she said.

Without speaking Glynn and Mike marched through the pub and up the stairs to the landlord's living quarters and hammered on the door. It didn't take the landlord, Jim, long to answer.

'Oh, it's you,' he said, the apathy evident in his tone of voice as he held the door open for them to pass.

Jim followed them through to the living room then went straight over to a sideboard and opened a drawer. He pulled out an envelope full of cash and stepped towards Glynn.

'Is Ally in?' asked Glynn, referring to the landlord's wife.

'No, she's out shopping. Why?' said Jim.

The landlord narrowed his eyes suspiciously while he waited for Glynn's reply. Jim was a big guy who fancied himself as a bit of a hard man. As landlord of the Grey Mare he had learnt to handle himself. It was a requirement of the job in a pub frequented by aggressive drunks and boisterous gangs of youths. Although he had no problem dealing with the clientele of the Grey Mare, Jim was no match for Glynn and Mike.

'The price has gone up,' said Mike before Jim had the chance to hand them the cash. 'We want an extra hundred quid.'

Jim was quick to retaliate. 'No chance! It's costing me a fuckin' arm and a leg as it is.'

'I hope you're not gonna give us any bother,' said Glynn. 'If you wanna do this the easy way then just hand over the fuckin' cash and we'll be out of here.'

'But you're well out of order. It's a fuckin' joke! No firm charges that much. And what am I getting for it, eh? I sort out all the fuckin' aggro myself.'

'Are you refusing to pay?' Glynn asked, calmly.

Glynn turned his head towards Mike and nodded. Mike was only too willing to respond to the covert signal and he stomped towards Jim, who squared his shoulders and bunched his hands into fists in readiness, letting the envelope full of cash fall to the ground.

'I'll get another firm,' Jim blurted out just as Mike reached him. 'They'll be cheaper than you lot. I bet they'll help me handle any aggro too.'

Mike responded by pulling out a knife and flicking a switch till the keen-edged five-inch blade shot out. Jim stepped back in alarm, and raised his fists while Mike hovered menacingly waiting for Glynn's command.

'This is your last chance,' said Glynn. 'Are you gonna pay up or do we have to make you?'

'You can have that,' said Jim, nodding towards the envelope on the floor, 'but I ain't fucking giving you no more.'

Glynn sighed. This was going to be more difficult than he had anticipated. Without waiting for Jim to respond, he rushed up to him, knowing that Mike would have his back. The two of them charged Jim, Glynn raining punches while Mike sliced the knife repeatedly across Jim's forearms making it difficult for him to defend himself. Within seconds Jim's arms were covered in lacerations, the blood spilling from him like an upturned glass of claret.

But Mike stopped short of plunging the knife. That would have inflicted too much damage. And he didn't want that. He wanted to do just enough to make Jim see sense and pay them what they were asking for. It worked.

'All right, all right, I'll give you your fuckin' money!' yelled Jim, trying to step away from them.

Glynn dropped his fists and grinned triumphantly. Again, Mike followed his lead, lowering the bloodied knife then snatching the envelope from the floor.

'Get the rest,' Glynn ordered while Mike continued to point the knife menacingly at Jim.

Jim walked back to the sideboard, the lacerations on his arms now difficult to discern due to the amount of blood covering them. He whipped a bunch of notes from the drawer, counted them out with trembling hands then crossed the room and handed them to Glynn.

'That's better.' Glynn smiled, pocketing the hundred pounds. He was all charm again now that his objective had been met. 'In future I hope you'll cooperate.'

Then Glynn and Mike left the pub, the streetwise kids staring in shock at their bloodied hands and clothing. Ignoring the children's alarmed mutterings, Glynn stepped inside his BMW, started the engine then drove away with Mike in the passenger seat.

'Awkward bastard, he was,' said Mike.

'Yeah, but I don't think we'll have any trouble in future,' said Glynn. 'We'd best both have our tools at the ready just in case, though. Hopefully he'll find out eventually that it's a waste of time.' He gazed across at Mike. 'Let's get cleaned up before we go back to the club, and swap that envelope for a clean one.'

'OK. You got the rest?' asked Mike.

Glynn knew Mike had seen him pocket the hundred pounds but it was Mike's way of checking that he would get his share. 'Yeah, don't worry. I'll split it as soon as we get back to mine. We'll put the cash in the envelope through the books and the rest is for us. And what Pete doesn't know won't fuckin' hurt him.'

Mike laughed. 'Fat chance of him finding out while he's inside, is there?'

'Yeah, and Adele's fuckin' clueless about the security business so he won't find out through her,' said Glynn. 'I reckon, if we take a mark-up from each job, we'll soon be fuckin' quids in.'

Mike laughed again. 'Yeah, best make sure she doesn't find out, though.'

'Don't worry, she won't. She thinks she's controlling things with all these daft changes she's making; fuckin' bar managers and bookkeepers and all that shit. It makes me laugh! It's her way of letting us know she's the boss but she's well out of her fuckin' depth. Sooner or later she's gonna drop a bollock, and when she does it'll be yours truly who'll be taking control like it should have been in the first fuckin' place.'

5

Adele was sitting in the visiting room of Strangeways prison waiting for her brother to arrive. While she waited she looked around the room at the grim faces of the hardened criminals, whose features softened slightly when they gazed across the table at their hapless partners.

Peter was serving a sentence for GBH after attacking the bouncers in Angels nightclub. Initially he was refused bail because of the seriousness of his crime. But, thanks to a shit-hot solicitor and barrister, Peter was convicted of the lesser GBH offence of wounding without intent and was sentenced to three years' imprisonment. Adele knew that if he behaved himself during his time in prison he might end up only serving half that time.

Peter's barrister had managed to convince the jury that Peter only went to Angels nightclub to persuade Alan's gang to leave his businesses alone. He had then produced a witness who had testified to the beating she had suffered at the hands of Alan's gang when she'd managed one of Peter's sunbed salons.

The barrister had argued that Peter had taken weapons for self-defence knowing about the vicious reputation of Alan's gang. Unfortunately, he had been besieged by the bouncers as soon as he'd entered Angels nightclub and had therefore been forced to defend himself. His barrister had further argued that Peter hadn't gone to the nightclub with the intention of hurting anybody and that he had himself suffered injuries before retaliating.

Eventually Peter strolled into the room. Many of the inmates smiled and nodded as he passed by, interrupting their limited time with their loved ones to grab his attention. It was obvious to Adele that Peter commanded as much respect within these four walls as he did on the outside. Any concerns about how he was coping behind bars dissipated in the few seconds it took him to stride over to the table where Adele was waiting.

'Hiya, sis,' he announced, hugging her tightly before taking his seat at the other side of the table. 'Sorry, I got held up, had a bit of business to attend to.'

'What, inside prison?' she asked.

Peter responded with a wink. 'Gotta keep the wheels of industry moving,' he said before he closed the subject and moved on. 'So, how's things?' he asked.

Adele gave a quick rundown of how much money each of the businesses was taking before telling him about the changes in staffing she had implemented since their last meeting.

'It sounds like you're managing OK,' he said.

She smiled. 'Yeah, things aren't going too bad. What about you? Are things going OK in here?' she asked perfunctorily although she had already guessed the answer.

Peter laughed. 'Yeah, no problems. I mean, I'd rather be on the outside than in here but you just have to manage as best you can and wait for the time to pass, don't you? Anyway, you know me; it's not as if it's my first time inside. The more bird you do, the easier it gets to handle it. You've just gotta know how to play the system to your advantage.'

Adele didn't fully grasp what he was referring to but she chose not to ask, hoping that she would never again find herself serving time. For her it had been amongst the most arduous years of her life and, God knew, she'd had enough of them.

'There is something else I need to chat to you about before I go,' she said.

Peter nodded his head, willing her to continue.

'It's about Glynn,' she said, and as soon as she mentioned his name Peter rolled his eyes.

'What now?' he asked, his expression one of exasperation.

'Don't be like that, Peter,' she said. 'I've got genuine concerns. Him and Mike are up to something. I just know they are but I can't quite put my finger on what it is. They always seem to be huddled together deep in conversation as though they're scheming, and I've noticed Glynn keeps replacing the doormen without consulting me first.'

'And?' asked Peter.

'Well,' said Adele, 'that's about it really. There's definitely something going on though. And, like I've told you before, I think Glynn was behind your arrest. I think we should fire the pair of them before it all blows up in our faces.'

'Hang on a minute,' said Peter. 'You want me to fire two of my main men because you think they're up to something, and all you've got to go on is the fact that they are sometimes deep in conversation and Glynn has replaced a few of the doormen? Come off it, Adele. I need them to run the security business. I can't manage it without them and, like it or not, that business is a high earner.'

'It's more than that,' Adele replied, desperately trying to think of something to validate her suspicions. Unable to think of anything substantial, she said, 'It's how he is with the staff as well. Cindy gets away with murder since she started seeing him and he intimidates a lot of the others.'

Peter gave her a knowing look. 'You sure this isn't just sour grapes over Cindy?'

'No!' Adele cut in a little too sharply. 'It's got nothing to do with that whatsoever. She's bloody welcome to him. I wouldn't touch him with a bargepole now I know what he's like. But, Peter, you've got to listen to me. They're a danger to you and your businesses. I think we need to get rid of them now before it's too late.'

But Peter wouldn't be persuaded. 'I need to weigh up the pros and cons, sis,' he said. 'And right now, as far as I'm concerned, Glynn and Mike have got a fuckin' sight more going for them than against them. But, if you can find out anything to back up what you're saying, let me know.'

'I will,' she said.

For the rest of her visit they chatted amicably about other matters: their mother, her cats and incidents involving the other prisoners. By the time visiting was over, Adele had decided what she would do about Glynn and Mike. She already had changes in mind and if Peter wouldn't do anything about those two then she would put those changes in place. Hopefully that would put a stop to some of Glynn's shady dealings.

Adele didn't tell Peter what she was thinking. She didn't want him to talk her out of it. And, when all was said and done, he had left her managing the nightclub so it was up to her to run it in whichever way she saw fit.

6

'Hi, Margaret,' said Adele when she stepped inside what was once Peter's office. It was 10.30 a.m., a late start for Adele, who had spent the previous evening watching over things in the club and hadn't got to bed till the early hours. 'Is everything OK?' she asked.

Adele took in the scene before her. Margaret was entering some figures onto the computer and appeared to have been hard at work for several hours. An open file was on the desk in front of her with a pen placed across the front sheet on which she had written several notes. To her left lay a stack of files with another smaller pile to her right. There was a half-empty cup of coffee in front of Margaret, the steam no longer visible and the milk congealing on the surface. She must have been so immersed in her work that she had allowed it to go cold.

Not for the first time Adele thought about what a good choice Margaret had been. In the few weeks since she had started work Margaret had eased Adele's burden tremendously. She was a solid, efficient worker who took great pride in everything she did.

'Not too bad,' said Margaret, looking up from her computer screen and smiling at Adele. 'There's a few files there which I need to ask you about,' she added, nodding at the pile of files to her right. 'I've put notes on them so we can see where we're up to.'

'OK,' said Adele. 'Do you want to go through them now?'

'Yes, if that's all right,' said Margaret. 'Oh, and there's one other thing. Mike came in to bank some money late yesterday. I'm afraid I may have upset him. He wanted the keys to the safe but I refused to let him have them. I told him any cash that was banked had to come through me, as you instructed.

'He also wanted to take some petty cash. I asked him what it was for but he wouldn't say so I told him I couldn't release any cash without being able to allocate it to a particular item in the books. He didn't seem very happy. In fact, he was quite irate by the time he walked out of here. I hope I've done the right thing.'

Adele smiled at her. 'Oh, yes. You definitely did the right thing. Thanks for standing your ground and not letting him intimidate you.'

'No problem,' said Margaret, and her shrewd expression told Adele that Margaret was more than capable of handling Mike's tantrums.

Adele pulled up a seat next to Margaret and sat with her for a few minutes while they went through Margaret's queries.

'Oh, by the way,' said Adele when they had finished, 'how did you get on with those phone calls I asked you to make?'

Margaret reached over to the pile of files on the right-hand side of her desk and flicked through them till she found what she was looking for. She pulled out a file with a large note clipped to it. 'Here's a list of the prices and what's included,' she said, detaching the paper clip that held the note in place and passing the list to Adele.

Adele scanned the piece of paper. 'That's great,' she said. 'What about availability?'

'They can all start within the next couple of weeks apart from the one second to the bottom of the list,' said Margaret.

'Ah, yes. I see,' said Adele. Then she picked up a pen and circled three of the names on the list. 'Can you ring these three and arrange for them to meet with me?' she asked. 'I want to find out a bit more about what they can do for us.'

'Certainly,' replied Margaret.

'I'm calling at a couple of the sunbed shops this morning but I'll be back after lunch.'

'OK,' said Margaret. 'I'll let you have the details as soon as you're back.'

'Thank you.'

Adele smiled to herself as she walked the short distance from Margaret's office to her own. Margaret had definitely been a find; there was no doubt about that. Inside her own office, Adele checked that there were no urgent messages on her answer machine before she locked up and set off to visit the first of her sunbed shops.

Adele was looking forward to her return when she would find out about the meetings Margaret had arranged for her. Hopefully one of the firms would be a good fit, as she was eager to employ them as soon as possible. But, most of all, she was eager to let Glynn know that as far as the nightclub was concerned she had things well under control.

It was the following Friday night and the club was heaving. Despite this Cindy had spent the last few minutes chatting with a good-looking male customer. As she watched her from further along the bar, Adele became increasingly annoyed. While Paula and the other bar staff were run off their feet, Cindy had spent the majority of the evening flirting with the customers. It was easy to guess Glynn wasn't in the club; Cindy wouldn't dare flirt with anybody else while he was around.

Adele walked further along the bar, ready to have a word with Cindy. It wasn't the first time she had remonstrated with her about her lazy ways but it didn't seem to make any difference. As Adele drew closer Cindy spotted her out of the corner of her eye.

'All right, I'm going,' said Cindy, stepping away from the customer. 'Mustn't let the boss catch me chatting,' she added, lowering her voice and smiling at the customer. 'She might look as though butter wouldn't melt but she can be a right old nag at times.'

The customer looked at Adele then laughed and walked away.

Adele was seething. 'What did you just call me?' she asked Cindy.

'Oh, it was nothing. Keep your hair on,' said Cindy, leaning across to the next customer along the bar and exposing an eyeful of cleavage. 'What can I get you, love?' she asked, while shuffling a piece of gum with her tongue. Then she reached for a glass and stepped towards the optics at the back of the bar.

'Don't you dare turn your back on me!' yelled Adele, so loud that most of the customers turned to look at her.

Cindy swivelled around. 'What?' she snapped.

'I'll tell you what!' shouted Adele. 'For starters, I want you paying attention to what you should be doing instead of flirting with the customers.'

'I can't help it if they want to chat me up,' said Cindy, cocking her head back and wobbling her breasts.

Adele glared at her for a few seconds, dumbfounded by her audacity. 'If you weren't giving them so much encouragement then perhaps they wouldn't want to take up so much of your time when you should be working.'

Cindy shrugged her shoulders and smirked as she waited for Adele to continue.

'And I don't like your attitude,' said Adele. 'When I'm speaking to you, don't walk away. And wipe that stupid grin off your face!'

'Jesus! So I'm in trouble for smiling now, am I?'

Adele wasn't finished with her. 'I'm not happy with your attitude at all! And what have I told you about chewing gum when you're working?'

'It's hardly a crime, is it? Anyway, Glynn doesn't mind me chewing,' Cindy retorted, playing her trump card.

'Glynn isn't in charge, I am! So, put that gum in the bin and let's have less of your cheek.'

Cindy ignored her and turned back around, heading for the optics again.

'Don't you dare ignore me!' shouted Adele but Cindy carried on walking. Out of the corner of her eye Adele could see that some of the bar staff had stopped what they were doing and were keenly watching and listening to what was happening. The volume around the bar had dropped while customers paused their conversations to listen to the altercation. The pressure of expectation was upon Adele.

'Right, you're fired!' stormed Adele. 'Get your coat and don't bother coming back.'

By now she was consumed with rage and the adrenalin was racing ferociously around her body. How dare the little tart try to belittle her in front of everyone?

Cindy turned towards her again, marched over to the bar and slammed the glass down. 'You can't fire me!' she yelled.

'I just did!' said Adele. 'Now get your coat and go quietly before I have to get one of the bouncers to remove you.'

Cindy stormed off into the staff area behind the bar and emerged a second later carrying her coat and handbag. But she refused to go quietly and hurled a barrage of insults at Adele as she walked out of the club.

'Just what is your fuckin' problem?' she demanded. 'Ever since I've been seeing Glynn you've had it in for me. You're a fuckin' jealous bitch, just because he's finished with you and you're too fuckin' boring and straight-laced to get anyone else.

'If you think you're gonna get away with sacking me, you've got another think coming. Just wait till I tell Glynn. Then you'll be sorry.'

'It won't make any difference,' Adele shouted after her. 'I run this club, not him.'

Once Cindy had marched through the door to the foyer, Adele stopped staring after her. As she looked back at the bar area, she became aware of the number of people watching her. They quickly looked away and continued getting served.

Adele could feel her face flush, suddenly becoming embarrassed that she'd made a show of herself. She walked away, anxious to escape from the crowd, and made her way to the foyer to make sure Cindy had left the building. Barney was manning the doors along with another bouncer.

'Has Cindy left?' she asked.

When Barney nodded she said, 'Good, make sure she doesn't get back in.'

Then she walked to the other side of the foyer without giving Barney a chance to ask why. As she stood there she became conscious of her frantically beating heart and the heat that suffused her face. While she waited to calm down, thoughts sped through her brain.

Yes, she had done the right thing in firing Cindy. The girl had been a problem for some time and she could no longer tolerate her insolence. But although she was relieved to get rid of her, and knew she was perfectly within her rights to do so, she was still worried. The news would soon reach Glynn and, when it did, Adele dreaded how he was going to react.

7

It was the following night. Adele had spent the past hour on the front door of the Golden Bell watching the punters come in while Glynn and Mike were out on business. Having spotted nothing untoward she decided to take a walk around the club. She was circling the periphery and approaching the passageway that led to the toilets when she spotted something suspicious.

A short distance away were two young men standing opposite each other; one of them tall and good-looking with dark hair, the other an average-looking guy with sandy hair. As she passed them she saw the guy with sandy hair grab something and quickly put it into his trouser pocket while passing what looked like money to the taller of the two men. Then he walked away without saying anything.

The taller man glanced around and quickly tucked the money inside his jacket pocket. Adele pretended not to notice and passed him by. But she was curious so she stopped a little further away and watched from a safe distance. The man grabbed a drink from the ledge next to him and for a few seconds he remained where he was. As he stood there he glanced around and tapped his foot in time to the Kylie Minogue track that was playing while nursing the drink in his right hand. Adele assumed he was trying to look inconspicuous.

While Adele was watching the man, Barney came over to her. 'Everything all right?' he asked.

Adele took a deep breath. 'Not sure,' she said. 'I think that guy over there may be dealing drugs. Don't look at him. I don't want him to know we're onto him. Do me a favour, Barney, and wait somewhere out of sight but not too far. I want you to be able to hear me when I shout for help.'

'OK,' said Barney, who then moved away.

Adele continued watching the man, her heart now pounding beneath her ribs. After only a few seconds another man approached and the same thing happened. But this dealer wasn't stupid. He greeted his customer enthusiastically as though he was an old friend, and they exchanged back slaps and handshakes before he placed his drink back on the ledge. The transaction itself was brief; few words were spoken and the money and mystery item exchanged hands simultaneously before the customer walked away.

Adele stared at them, her mouth agape. She was astonished by what had just happened but, at the same time, outraged. How dare he think he could deal drugs in her club.

Without waiting to see any more, she yelled, 'Barney, now!' and raced towards the suspected drug dealer, hoping Barney was close behind.

By the time the man spotted her, she had drawn up close to him. His initial expression was one of alarm, which he quickly disguised by glancing casually in the direction of the dance floor.

Adele grabbed him by the arm. 'Empty your pockets!' she ordered.

'What the fuck?' the man barked, pulling his arm away from her grasp.

Then he rounded on her, his fists raised. Anticipating his next move, Adele quickly dodged a blow from his fist and took up a kickboxing stance ready to intercept his punches. She was so swift and determined that the man hesitated and stood staring at her, weighing up his chances.

'You heard!' shouted Adele. 'Empty your pockets. Now!' Barney soon drew alongside her. 'I'm the manageress of this nightclub and I've seen what you've been up to. I don't take kindly to people dealing drugs on my premises,' she said.

'Drugs? What the fuck you on about?' asked the man.

'Don't try to kid me; I saw you with my own eyes. You've just sold something to two people.'

'Have I fuck! I don't know what you're talking about.'

'Right. Well, if you've nothing to hide, you won't mind my bouncers searching you, will you?' Adele said, letting go of the man's arm while Barney stepped forward.

She nodded at Barney, who searched through the man's pockets and withdrew a wad of cash and a packet full of small pastel-coloured tablets with hearts and stars imprinted onto them. A pallid kaleidoscope of toxic pills.

To Adele they looked like sweets and she thought back to the Love Hearts and Parma Violets she used to eat when she was a kid. These appeared similar, only smaller. In fact, they looked so innocuous that she could imagine what would happen if a child got its hands on them, and the thought appalled her.

'Ecstasy!' Barney confirmed. Then he grabbed the man by the shoulder so that he couldn't run off. 'What do you want me to do with him?'

'I'll take *them*,' said Adele, reaching for the packet of pastel-coloured pills. 'Chuck *him* out!'

Barney tightened his grip on the man, pulling his arms behind him so that he could frogmarch him out of the building. The man, who had stopped denying the facts once the truth was exposed, now began protesting.

'Hang on a minute!' he shouted. 'What the fuck you playing at? You ain't having those. They're mine!'

Adele looked scornfully at the packet of ecstasy pills in her hand. 'I'm getting rid of these so they can't do any more damage,' she said. 'And you can think yourself lucky that we haven't called the police.'

'You wouldn't fuckin' dare!' said the man. 'You'd be frightened of 'em finding out what you're up to. And you can tell Glynn he ain't getting no fuckin' money tonight! I'll need it to cover my losses.'

The man continued to protest and hurled abuse at Adele as Barney marched him through the building. Still perturbed by what had just taken place, Adele strode over to the door marked 'Private', entered the key code then made her way upstairs.

She dashed inside the staff toilets and into a cubicle then locked the door and threw the pills down the pan. She flushed the toilet repeatedly, her anger threatening to erupt at the thought of someone having the audacity to sell ecstasy in her club. As her rage simmered she tugged at the toilet handle again and again; only satisfied when every last trace of those evil pills had been drained away.

Jesus! This could mean the end of the Golden Bell if the police got wind of it. She already knew that the Manchester police force had started taking a hard line against nightclub owners where drug dealing was concerned. So, against her better judgement, she decided not to involve them this time.

Adele still needed to do a bit of damage limitation though. She'd make sure this stayed between her and Barney, and tell him to make sure all the bouncers kept a keen lookout for anyone dealing drugs inside the club. They didn't need to know the full details. The fact that the police had clamped down was reason enough.

But her biggest problem was Glynn. She wondered what exactly the man had meant when he said they'd be frightened of the police finding out what they were up to. And what was the money for Glynn that the man had referred to? She wasn't sure, but she had a good idea and the realisation shook her to the core.

It was bad enough that someone was dealing drugs in the club, but the fact that Glynn might be involved in some way was anathema to her. As she stood over the toilet bowl, seething inside, she was determined to challenge Glynn about it as soon as he returned to the club.

8

Glynn spotted Adele before she saw him and he marched over to her as soon as he arrived back inside the club foyer.

Without any concern about being overheard, he yelled at Adele. 'What the fuck's this about you firing Cindy? She's in bits about it! Can't you stand the fuckin' competition or summat?'

Adele had been seething with anger ever since the drugs incident and, as she had waited for Glynn to enter the club, her anger had intensified.

'Never mind Cindy. She's the least of our problems!' she snapped.

'What you on about?' Glynn asked.

Noticing the number of people who had stopped to listen to their exchange, Adele lowered her voice and spoke between gritted teeth, her jaw clenched tightly. 'Upstairs!' she hissed and she turned on her heel, leaving Glynn to follow behind.

She stomped through the club and entered the door marked 'Private', taking the stairs two at a time. Once inside her office, she plonked herself down in her seat and glared across at Glynn, who remained standing. Not wishing to be at a disadvantage, Adele rose from her seat and leant across the desk as she yelled at him.

'Drug dealers in this fuckin' club! That's what I'm on about. And don't tell me you know nothing about it because I know you're involved. He mentioned you by name.'

'Who did?'

'The bloody drug dealer who we threw out of the club tonight for selling ecstasy! He's been paying you off to turn a blind eye. Hasn't he?'

'I don't know what you're talking about. What does he look like, this so-called drug dealer?'

'Tall, dark hair, good-looking,' she snapped. Then a thought occurred to her. 'Why?' she asked. 'Is there more than one?'

'Is there fuck! I don't know any drug dealers. Someone's trying to set me up. And when I get my fuckin' hands on him, I'll put him straight. Who is he? What did he say?' he demanded.

But Adele wasn't going to be put off so easily. 'Don't give me your bullshit!' she raged. 'I know you're involved. I knew you and Mike were in cahoots about something and now I know what it was.'

'Bollocks! What did he say?'

'That we wouldn't inform the police because we'd be too frightened of them finding out what we're up to. Just what the hell did he mean by that, Glynn?' she screeched.

'I don't fuckin' know, do I? He was probably just having a go cos you threw him out.'

'Then why would he send you a message that you weren't getting your money tonight? Eh? Tell me that! Maybe I should ring the police and let them look into it.'

Glynn shrugged but, even as he did so, she saw a shift in his body language. His shoulders slumped back down and his mouth dropped resignedly. 'No, don't do that,' he said and he pulled up a chair and sat down facing her.

She mimicked his action and glared across the desk at him. 'You'd better fuckin' tell me what's been going on, Glynn, and quick, otherwise I *will* ring the police and you can explain it all to them! And don't even think about wriggling out of it. I've got witnesses that heard what the man said.'

Glynn smirked. 'You really are fuckin' clueless, aren't you? Just look at you sat there as though butter wouldn't fuckin' melt. We're talking about a few little pills that give the punters a good time. It's not the end of the fuckin' world! It happens all the time.'

'Not in my fuckin' club, it doesn't!'

Glynn grinned. 'Well, that's just where you're fuckin' wrong. It happens in every club. And you, on your fuckin' holier than thou mission, aren't gonna stop it.

The way I see it, it's gonna happen whether we like it or not so it's best that we control it rather than letting the dealers do their own thing.'

Adele stared at him, astonished. 'Don't you dare try to excuse what you get up to! You're taking a fuckin' backhander from him, aren't you?'

'I fuckin' earn it!' he yelled back. 'The clubs are full of druggies and dealers. The only reason you've not come across it up to now is because of me. I've been fuckin' protecting you! The dealers know the score. If anything happens they take the rap and we deny all knowledge. But we have to keep them sweet. And you're going about things all arse upwards.'

Adele stared at him, dumbstruck for several seconds. She couldn't believe what she was hearing. Confusion crowded her brain. To think that all this had been going on inside the club and she hadn't even known. She was finding it hard to take in, much less decide what to do about it.

Eventually she found her voice but, unable to articulate what she really felt about the situation, she just stood and yelled, 'Get out! You disgust me.'

Glynn remained seated for several seconds and she could almost visualise the scheming that was going on inside his head. He stood up to go, leaving her with a few parting words. 'Think about this – it's the only way. You start getting the cops involved and I won't be the only one in the firing line.'

His threat sickened her. 'Just fuckin' go!' she shouted until he slowly turned around and breezed out of her office with a smug grin on his face.

Adele sat back down in her chair. Her whole body was shaking with anger. She couldn't believe that Glynn had not only been allowing drug dealers into the club but he'd actually been encouraging them, and making a profit out of it. She was livid.

For a few moments she deliberated over what to do. She was in anguish over whether to tell Peter. But what would she gain by doing so? There wasn't much he could do about it from inside prison. Maybe he would sack Glynn but what if it backfired on her? She knew by now that Glynn was a nasty piece of work and if they got rid of him he would want revenge. And, knowing him as she did, she feared that he would stop at nothing to get it.

She sat toying with a pen on her desk, unable to settle as the thoughts whirled through her head. No, it was best not to involve Peter. Besides, part of her wanted to prove that she could handle any problems herself. After all, Peter had put his trust in her.

As she sat deep in thought she realised that the protection racket was the least of her problems where Glynn was concerned. If he'd been taking a backhander from drug dealers right under her nose, what else did he get up to that she didn't know about?

But she'd already taken the first step in exerting her control. She thought about her meeting with the suave James Merton and her plans to employ his firm. What had happened tonight confirmed to her that she had made the right decision.

9

Adele had managed to avoid Glynn for the past two days. She had needed time to think about how best to tackle him. Then she had rung him on his fancy mobile phone and arranged a meeting. She intended to make it as formal as possible to let him know she was serious, and perhaps unsettle him.

Now, as she waited for him to arrive she tapped her pen nervously on the pad that lay in front of her. She had itemised the matters she wanted to discuss in the order in which she wanted to discuss them. She hoped that taking such a professional approach would give her the edge, and she was determined not to allow him to intimidate or annoy her. But as she sat there looking officious, her outward appearance belied the terror that she felt at the thought of how Glynn would react.

When he walked in she looked up from the numbered list of items on her pad, but she didn't stand. 'Hello,

Glynn, take a seat,' she said, holding out her hand to indicate the seat at the other side of the desk.

Glynn smirked as he pulled out the chair and plonked himself down. 'Funny, I wouldn't have known where the chair was if you hadn't pointed it out,' he said sarcastically.

She forced a wry smile and looked down at the list in front of her then started straight away. 'Since our, erm... discussion... the other day, I've decided to have a meeting with you so that we can address various matters.'

He leant back in his seat, kicked out his feet and folded his arms, his face showing a look of boredom. 'Go on, get on with it,' he said.

Adele glanced briefly at him then back down at her pad, trying to ignore his hostile body language. Although she was trying to stay calm she was quivering inside. 'First, I want to talk about Cindy. The reason I fired her was—'

'She's over it,' he interrupted. 'Don't worry, a good-looking girl like her will soon find another bar job. In fact...' he then made a show of looking at his watch '... it wouldn't surprise me if she hasn't already got one, especially with the glowing reference I gave her on your lovely letter-headed paper.'

'OK,' said Adele, trying to steady the slight tremble in her voice, 'as long as you're aware that she isn't to be allowed in the club again. She's too disruptive.'

Without giving Adele a chance to explain what Cindy had done wrong, he interrupted again. 'Grow up, for fuck's sake. Why are you so bothered? You really are jealous of her, aren't you?'

She rushed to defend herself, realising that he was already starting to get to her. 'This has nothing to do with jealousy,' she snapped. 'It's about running the club efficiently.'

'Yeah, whatever,' he said, waving his hand in front of his wide-open mouth as though stifling a yawn. Then he leant over, peering at her list before saying, 'Next.'

Adele picked up the pad and held it facing towards her so that he couldn't read it, which prompted a brief snigger from him.

'Next, I want to discuss the matter of drug dealing inside the club. From now onwards I don't want any known drug dealers allowed inside the club.' He laughed loudly so she raised her voice. 'Even those employed by you,' she continued. 'And that means an end to you taking backhanders from them.'

'Yeah, good luck with that one,' he said.

She carried on as though he hadn't spoken. 'From now on I'll be making sure the club stays clean, which is why all the doormen are to be made aware of the situation. Anyone caught dealing in drugs, or anyone caught buying them, will be ejected from the premises straight away.'

'You've got no fuckin' chance. Even if I stop them, there's bound to be a few get through.'

'Not if we start searching the customers as they come in.'

'Are you fuckin' serious? You'll be losing customers hand over fist. And I don't think the guys are gonna like doing that, especially with women. You could leave them open to all sorts of accusations.'

'That brings me to item three on my list,' she said, her voice now adopting a stern tone. 'I'm concerned that some of the doormen are willingly letting known drug dealers in the club and it's got to stop.'

Ignoring the antagonistic way he leant forward and glared at her, she carried on speaking, her proposed changes tumbling out of her in a flurry of words as she rushed to get it over with. 'I'm employing a new security firm to man the doors and operate inside the premises.'

As she said this last sentence she saw his face change and could tell he was furious, but she was determined to finish speaking. 'They're starting two weeks on Friday so I want you to get rid of all the existing bouncers by then, with the exception of Barney.

'The new firm are aware of the drug-dealing problems and they've been given strict instructions to stop and search everyone entering the club at least until we've got the problem under control. I'll also be employing a couple of women to support the team and search any females.'

As Adele paused for breath Glynn leant back and puffed out his chest. 'Are you for fuckin' real?' he asked. 'My guys are the best in the business. Who the fuck are this firm and what makes you think they can do a better job than the men we've got working for us now?'

'Well, firstly they've been employed because of their credentials, Glynn, and not because they've been taken on by you and advised to turn a blind eye.' Her voice was now becoming louder, and all thoughts of fear had vanished as she retaliated.

'Who the fuck are they?' he again demanded.

'Merton Security,' she said and she watched the puzzled expression on Glynn's face.

'Where are they from?' he asked.

'Stoke.'

He laughed out loud, pouring scorn on her words. 'Ha, now I know who they are. You must be fuckin' joking! Do you really think an out of town firm can cope with what we're up against in Manchester nowadays? They're fuckin' old school! Those guys still think a bit of brawn, a tux and a dicky bow will go a long way. And they wouldn't know an ecstasy pill if it landed in their fuckin' lap!'

'That's all the more reason why they'll be good for us then because, from what I can gather, your men seem all too familiar with ecstasy and any other poison that your friends might be peddling.'

'All right, all right. Now you listen to me!' he commanded, his booming voice silencing her. 'I know you think you're doing the right thing but, believe me, you're making a fuckin' big mistake. If you get rid of my guys and start this firm of jokers you'll have every fuckin' gang in Manchester trying to take over this place within a week. And, believe me, the people I'm talking about are wearing more than a fuckin' dicky bow. They're armed and very fuckin' dangerous.'

Adele felt a rumble of anxiety deep inside her, on hearing his words. But she quickly quashed it. Why should she believe anything he said? He'd already proved he couldn't be trusted.

'I'm sure Merton Security are more than capable of handling any troublemakers,' she said, managing to sound more confident than she felt.

Now that his aggressive approach had failed, Glynn shook his head and began pleading with her. 'Please, just keep things as they are. It'll be much safer and I'll even give you an in. A mark up on every sale. Name your price and we'll talk about it.'

'Stop it!' she yelled. 'You disgust me. Do you really think I'd want to profit from something that causes damage to so many people?'

Without waiting for his response, she added, 'Merton Security will be starting work two weeks on Friday whether you like it or not so please make sure you let your men know that their services will no longer be required from then onwards.'

'Tell them your fuckin' self!' he raged, getting up from his seat. 'D'you know, Adele, you're fuckin' sick? Ever since we finished, you've tried to get at me in any way you can. First you put a fuckin' bookkeeper in my office and promote Paula to Bar Manager without telling me. Then you sack Cindy. And now this. I'm fucked off with putting up with your shit just cos you're on some kind of fuckin' power trip.'

'It's got nothing to do with that!' she screeched, her temper finally getting the better of her. 'I've had enough of your dirty dealings. From now on I'm going to make sure we run a clean club. You can do what you like with your shady protection racket. I want nothing to do with it! But what happens inside this club is my concern and from now on I'm going to make sure we do things my way.'

'Suit your fuckin' self!' he shouted, backing towards the door. 'But when it all fuckin' blows up in yer face, don't say I didn't warn you.'

'Get out, Glynn. I don't need you trying to destroy everything.'

'Oh, believe me, that's where you're fuckin' wrong,' he said just as he reached the door. 'Don't worry, you'll need me long before I fuckin' need you.'

Then he was gone and Adele heaved a sigh of relief. But her heart was thundering, her hands shaking.

Despite her brave act, his words had got to her. She only hoped that they were all bluff and bluster and that she really was doing the right thing by changing the bouncers.

10

It was just over two weeks later and Adele was standing in the foyer of the Golden Bell with James Merton, head of her new team of bouncers, Merton Security. The man oozed sophistication, unlike Glynn and Mike, who resembled the pair of thugs they were. Adele could see them at the other side of the foyer, deep in conversation, and eyeing the new bouncers with malice in their eyes.

After a great deal of persuasion, Adele had agreed to let Glynn and Mike keep an eye on things in the club just in case the new security firm had any problems. But at the moment everything was going well and Adele doubted whether she needed the sinister presence of Glynn and Mike in the club.

James Merton was unlike anybody she had dealt with on the club scene. Aged in his mid-forties, he had a professional air about him and it was obvious to Adele that he wasn't the sort of man who got involved in any aggravation. He left that to his men to sort out while he concentrated on the business side of things.

Tonight he had agreed to stay with her and make sure his men settled well into the job. He would also be on hand if she needed any help or advice regarding the way he ran things.

As she watched his men operate he pointed out who they were and how long they had been with the firm. Adele was pleased to see that they were all dressed smartly in black tuxedos, white shirts and dicky bows. They also handled the customers well. Any requests to search people were made politely so that the majority of the customers were happy to cooperate. Troublemakers were firmly asked to leave.

Through the crowd Adele noticed the arrival of a friend. With her large physique, dark cropped hair and manly bearing she was unmistakable, and she was currently having a few words with the bouncers. Adele excused herself from James Merton's company while she went to investigate.

'I've told you, she's asked to see me,' she heard the woman saying, but the bouncers refused to let her inside the club.

'It's OK, she's right,' said Adele to the bouncers. 'I am expecting her. Let her through.'

The bouncers looked shocked but nevertheless they obeyed Adele's instructions and let the woman through the doors. Adele exchanged effusive greetings with her and they hugged tightly. 'So glad to have you with us,' she said. 'Come on; let me introduce you to James. He's the head of Merton Security. That's who the bouncers work for.'

They walked over to James Merton. 'James, this is Anna,' said Adele. 'She's one of the two ladies I told you about who are coming to join our team of bouncers. The other lady, Lynn, will be starting work next week.'

James politely held out his hand but Adele could tell by the expression on his face that he was a little put off by Anna's appearance. The pockmarked skin, square jaw line and facial tattoo belied Anna's true personality.

'James will explain how things work and what's expected of you,' said Adele.

Anna smiled at James and shook his hand fervently. 'Pleased to meet you, James,' she said.

Adele smiled at Anna's enthusiasm. She was still the same old Anna; eager to ingratiate herself with those who held power and influence. She'd been just the same when they were inside together. Although they'd got off to a bad start in prison when Anna had made an unwelcome pass at Adele, they'd eventually become firm friends.

Like Adele, Anna had also found it difficult to get work once she was released and Adele knew that this would be just the lifeline she needed. Despite a period without work, however, Anna had adapted well to life on the outside and had stayed out of trouble.

Adele thought fleetingly about the other friends she had left behind in prison, especially Caroline, who had been her best friend inside. Caroline was motherly with a caring nature and had looked after Adele during the time that she was incarcerated. Unfortunately, she was still serving her sentence for the murder of her husband following years of abuse. Adele hoped that she would also be able to adapt to life outside prison once she was released.

Employing Anna was about more than just doing her a favour. Adele knew that Anna's menacing appearance was deceiving. At heart she was a sensitive soul who was also loyal and hardworking. Those were just the qualities Adele needed. Her appearance would be helpful too. The club had had more than its fair share of female troublemakers and perhaps they would think twice if they had Anna to deal with.

As she led Anna out of the foyer and through to the private area of the club she saw the expression on Glynn's face. It was obvious that he wasn't impressed that the club was now employing female bouncers as well as male. But Adele didn't care what he thought. She knew it was the right move and, what was more, she was confident that the other bouncers had been a good choice too.

*

'Just look at the fuckin' state of that,' Glynn said to Mike once Adele and Anna had left the foyer.

'Who is it?' asked Mike.

'It's obviously one of the fuckin' women she's taken on as a bouncer. Well, that's if you can call it a woman. I told her it was a fuckin' daft idea, but she wouldn't listen.'

Mike laughed but Glynn wasn't seeing the funny side of things. 'She makes me laugh with her big ideas, and this new firm of bouncers are a load of fuckin' wimps. She's gonna fall on her arse sooner or later, just you watch.'

But Mike was only half listening as his attention was focused on a young man who was approaching them. 'Hiya, Spinner. You all right?' he asked.

'Yeah,' said Spinner, as he bounced around on his heels. Spinner was jittery as usual, his limbs constantly twitching; a blatant addict who also dealt drugs to feed his habit.

'So much for these efficient new bouncers,' said Glynn, laughing. 'If they're letting Spinner in then they'll let any fucker get past them.'

'Eh, I can look the part when I want to,' said Spinner, pointing to his smart shirt and trousers.

'Aw, look. He's even got proper shoes on,' Mike teased.

When Glynn and Mike had finished laughing, Glynn asked Spinner, 'Seriously, though, how did you manage to get through the search?'

'It was dead fuckin' easy, mate. It's just a quick pat down to make it look as though they're doing summat. But I've got my gear stashed where they won't fuckin' bother looking.'

'Nice one,' said Mike.

'Yeah, but make sure you fuckin' clean it up before you start flogging it,' Glynn chipped in.

'Course I will,' said Spinner, who then asked, 'Am I still good to go, then?'

'Yeah, business as usual,' said Glynn. 'But it's just between us. Make sure none of those bastards catch you at it or you're on your fuckin' own. OK?'

'Yeah, sure. Don't worry, they won't see a fuckin' thing.'

11

Alan was sitting in his favourite room inside the Sportsman's having a meeting with his crew. The number of men attending was growing each week and it was becoming a struggle to contain them all inside the small side room. As usual, he took the corner seat so that he could be seen by his men and, more importantly, so that *he* could see all of *them*.

'Right, listen up,' he said and the chatter around him settled down as his gang listened to what he had to say. 'There's a rave coming up at a warehouse in Blackburn in a couple of weeks' time. The drugs are fuckin' rife at those gigs so I wanna make sure we take advantage of it. We're gonna tax the door and make sure we get a good share of everything they make.

'It means we'll have to go tooled up and we've gotta be prepared to use them. We need to let the bouncers know that we're not pissing about. Is everyone OK with that?'

A murmur of agreement went around the room but some of the men stayed silent. 'If anyone has a problem with that, best fuckin' let me know now,' he said. 'I don't want anyone bottling out at the last minute.'

Nobody spoke. They knew what was expected of them when they joined Alan's gang and anyone who wasn't prepared to do whatever was required knew that they would face repercussions.

When nobody raised any objections, Alan proceeded to outline his plan. Raves were a new line of business for him. Realising that there were rich pickings to be had, he had swooped, using the same strong-arm tactics that he and his men applied to clubs and pubs that fell under their control.

For several minutes he continued talking, addressing any questions or observations made by any of his men.

'Right, so is everyone clear what's needed?' he asked.

This time the men were more vociferous in their agreement, aware that they had to show their enthusiasm. Once Alan had finished, they chatted amongst themselves.

'What about the Golden Bell?' asked David, his voice rising above those of the men present.

'OK, I'm coming to that,' said Alan. A smile lit up his stern features as he said, 'It looks like Pete's sister is making as big a balls-up of running the Golden Bell as I thought she would. She's only gone and replaced the fuckin' bouncers.'

He looked around; satisfied that he had gained the full attention of everyone before he continued. 'With a firm from Stoke. Smart guys, nice suits, very polite, apparently. And fuckin' clueless about what goes down in Manchester.'

Alan allowed his gang a few minutes of laughter following his last comment, then he said, 'That means the Golden Bell is more exposed than ever. Apparently, Glynn Mason and Mike Shaftesbury still hang around the place sometimes but they're out a lot of the time collecting so we need to get our timing right, and make sure they're not around when we hit them.'

'So when are we gonna do it?' asked David, his eyes alight with excitement.

'One thing at a time,' said Alan. 'We've got the rave to concentrate on for now as well as the new businesses we're earning from. But we'll be going for them soon, don't worry about that. And when we do, they won't know what's fuckin' hit 'em.'

Adele was sitting across from her brother, Peter, in the visiting room of Strangeways prison.

'I've changed the security team at the nightclub,' she said. Then she watched as the shock registered on her brother's face.

'You've done what?' Peter asked, raising his voice.

'Shush,' whispered Adele, looking around the prison visiting room to make sure no one was listening before she carried on speaking. 'I've got rid of all the previous bouncers and employed a new team.'

'Why the hell would you do that?'

'Well, remember when I told you Glynn was up to something?'

Peter nodded but, even as he did so, she noticed his lips tighten and his brow furrow.

'I was right about him,' said Adele. 'It seems he's been taking backhanders from a drug dealer.'

'What? Who told you this?'

'I copped the guy dealing and he told me Glynn let him do it.'

'Hang on, are you saying you believe the word of a drug dealer?' he asked, incredulous.

'Glynn's admitted it. The cheeky sod told me that it's best if he controls the drug dealers so they don't run riot. He even offered me part of the money he takes from them.'

Peter screwed up his face and she could tell he was deep in thought. Eventually he asked, 'Why didn't you tell me what was going on?'

'I didn't want to bother you in here. Besides, you gave me carte blanche to run the club.'

'Yeah but...' He let out a gasp of air and didn't finish his sentence. Then he asked, 'Who are this firm anyway?'

'They're called Merton Security and they're from Stoke. They've got very good credentials and the boss, James Merton, seems to run a very tight ship.'

'For Christ's sake!' he said, and she noticed the familiar way he rolled his eyes.

'What?'

'Nothing,' he replied, too quickly. 'It's just... it's a big move to make, that's all. And I would rather you'd run it by me first. I just hope you've done the right thing.'

'What d'you mean?' she asked.

His lack of response unnerved her, and she recalled Glynn's warning that she had left the club vulnerable from gang attacks.

'Peter, please tell me what you mean,' she said.

He sighed. 'There's a lot more to the clubbing game than you think, Adele. I don't want to scare you but there's some bad bastards out there. Are you sure this firm can handle any aggro?'

'Yeah, they've got a lot of experience in the nightclub industry.'

'Where? Stoke?' he asked, and she could detect a note of sarcasm in his voice. 'What about Glynn... and Mike? You haven't got rid of them too, have you?'

'No, I was waiting for the say-so from you. Obviously, after what you said last time, I knew you wanted Glynn running the security business. But, I really think it's time to let him go.'

'No, don't do that!'

Adele recognised an order when she heard one. Her brother's reaction wasn't what she expected. 'Why?' she said.

Peter sighed. 'Look, Adele, I've told you before, Glynn might not be perfect but you never know when he might come in handy. We don't know much about this new firm or whether they can be trusted. Keep Glynn and Mike on for now till we see how it goes.'

'OK,' she said, but she didn't feel OK about things and she was surprised that her brother still seemed to be putting his trust in Glynn after what she had told him.

Again, Glynn's words of warning flashed into her mind. Maybe her brother knew more than he was telling her. As she thought about the possible consequences of changing the bouncers, she felt a sharp pulse of adrenalin course through her body. But she tried not to let her feelings show. After all, her brother had trusted her with the management of his nightclub and it would be reckless of her to let him think she wasn't up to the job.

12

It was Friday night and Adele was feeling happy. As she stood alongside James Merton in the foyer of the Golden Bell she couldn't help but get caught up in the atmosphere. Groups of young women chatted and danced their way through the foyer as the music drew them in while young men eyed up the girls then joined them inside.

It was the time of night when the DJ played a series of well-known soul hits from The Jacksons, Luther Vandross, Aretha Franklin, Marvin Gaye and others. The lively beat usually encouraged people onto the dance floor. In fact, as she listened to 'Never Give Up On A Good Thing' by George Benson and glanced at the darkened interior of the club Adele felt like joining the revellers.

There was a younger crowd in tonight and Adele took this as a good sign. Perhaps they felt safer at the club since the change of bouncers, she thought fleetingly.

'It's busy tonight,' she commented to James.

'Yes, I noticed,' he said, smiling back at her.

As the queue at the entrance died down and the club filled out, Adele decided to go inside and have a wander around. 'I'll see you later,' she said to James as she left his side.

Adele was pleased to see that the place was filling out nicely, the mood friendly and upbeat. She noticed a group of youngsters gathered in a crowd and remembered thinking that it was unusual. The bouncers were generally cautious where large parties were concerned and, as far as she remembered, a lot of the youngsters had entered the club in groups of two or three.

But now there were perhaps twelve or more of them standing in a tight group together. Still, they didn't appear to be doing any harm so she carried on walking. It was only once she had got to the other side of the club that a thought occurred to her: none of them had a drink in his hand. That was so strange in itself that she decided to go back and check everything was OK.

She was too late. By the time the group of youngsters was in her line of vision they had already started creating havoc. She watched in shock as the young men tore through the club, smashing glasses, turning tables over and throwing glasses full of drink at the customers.

Within seconds it was mayhem. The music was now drowned out by the sound of women screaming as the youths barged into them or shoved them viciously out of the way. Adele could see at least three people on the floor who had been pushed over, some of them wounded from the smashed glass.

Adele ran to the aid of two distressed women who were on the floor. While she tended to them she summoned help and the bouncers ran after the youths, trying to grab hold of them. But they were too fast and agile. Adele squirmed as she looked up from the young woman she was tending to and saw the muscle-bound and hefty bouncers lumber towards the youths, who circled them while taunting and shouting obscenities. Instinctively she looked for Glynn but then she remembered that he hadn't been in the club tonight.

'Get them out!' she yelled and then she watched, helpless, while the group rampaged through the Golden Bell.

Panic was starting to take hold amongst the customers, who crowded the exits trying to get out. In the rush for the door, some stepped on those who had fallen. Others fell over them until there was a heaving mass of battered bodies strewn across the floor of the Golden Bell.

Adele rushed up to the DJ's booth. 'Switch the music off!' she ordered. Then she took up the mic. 'Everyone stay calm!' she shouted. 'Security, please remove them.' Then she repeated, 'Everyone stay calm. Stay where you are until Security have removed them from the building.'

Adele wanted to carry on speaking, to offer some assurance to her terrified customers, but she was drowned out by the intense screech of the fire alarm. Somebody had opened the fire escape. She looked over to see the crowd of youths dash outside with a couple of clumsy bouncers giving chase. A lot of customers also sprinted out of the fire exit in their haste to break away from the terrifying scene.

Adele ran out of the DJ's booth and switched off the fire alarm. The DJ responded by playing another track, trying to feign normality. But nobody was dancing. Then James Merton joined Adele at the fire exit and called his men back into the building. Once they were inside he secured the door.

'They're gone,' he said. 'Thank God!'

Adele didn't respond. Instead she looked around her in a daze. It was pandemonium.

The customers were standing in clusters, some in tears, some dishevelled and bloody, and others numb with shock. She could hear their distraught murmurs as a frisson of panic bulldozed its way through the club. A crowd of young men were shouting angrily at the bouncers, and several of them were trying to comfort their hysterical girlfriends.

Eventually she came to her senses, realising she needed to take control of the situation. Ignoring her own shaking limbs, Adele raced up to the DJ's booth again. She left him with instructions to announce an apology to the customers and ask them to be careful while the staff cleared up the smashed glass. Then she rushed to find James again.

'James, have a word with the bouncers, will you? Tell them to reassure everyone, and offer free drinks to anyone who had theirs smashed.'

James was still nodding his assent when Adele rushed off to the bar in search of Paula. She found her busy serving drinks to the customers who were anxious to calm their frayed nerves.

'Paula, I've asked the bouncers to offer free drinks to anyone who lost theirs,' said Adele. 'So, if anyone asks for a free drink, just let them have it. Can you also find someone to clear up the mess? I want them to cordon off the area that got the worst of it then get rid of the smashed glass as it's dangerous.'

'OK, will do,' said Paula.

Then Adele was off again. She wanted to assess just how much damage had been done. By this time everyone was up off the floor but there was still an anxious murmur amongst the customers. Adele spotted a girl bleeding profusely and wet with alcohol. Her hair was no longer secured under the clip that had held it in place and sodden locks were snaking their way down her bloody face.

Adele approached the girls' friends. 'Go to the bar and ask for Paula. Tell her Adele sent you and can she ask one of the barmaids to find the first-aid kit for your friend.'

'But what about her blouse?' asked one of the girls. 'It's been torn.'

'Send a letter to the club with a photo of the blouse asking for compensation and we'll deal with it.'

Some of the crowd, realising that she was someone in authority, began to quiz Adele about what was going on. She quickly offered words of reassurance then continued her inspection of the nightclub.

The worst of the damage seemed to be smashed glasses, although she spotted one area of seating where the upholstery was badly torn. Many chairs had been upended but only one or two of them were broken. As far as Adele could see the major impact had been on the customers themselves, many of whom were in a distressed state. There was no doubt in Adele's mind that many of the people here tonight would think twice about coming to the Golden Bell again.

As she looked around the club Adele could see that it was beginning to empty apart from the bar areas where large queues had formed. She went back to the main bar and asked Paula what was happening.

'They're all here for free drinks,' said a flustered Paula. 'There's no way they could all have had their drinks thrown but how can we keep track of who's who?'

'OK, carry on as you are for now,' said Adele, running from the bar as an idea occurred to her.

She returned a few minutes later with two date stamps and two pads of ink from her upstairs office.

'There,' she said, handing them to Paula. 'Give everyone a free drink but stamp them once they've had it. That way you can make sure they've only had one. I'll get the DJ to announce that all free drinks have to be claimed at this bar and I'll ask a couple of the staff from the other bars to help you out.'

'Thanks,' said Paula, who looked relieved.

The rest of the night passed quickly as Adele dashed about trying to take command of the situation. When Paula and one of the bouncers took the night's takings upstairs to put in the safe Adele went with them. Without counting the takings, Adele could tell that they would be well down for a Friday night.

Once Paula and the bouncer had left, Adele remained in her office. Here it was silent and orderly; a stark contrast to the chaos that had beset the club earlier. Feeling deflated, she sat down at her desk. Her adrenalin was still whizzing furiously around her body even though the initial panic was now over.

A fat tear rolled down her face, taking her by surprise. Then it hit her. Shock. Disappointment. Anger. Helplessness. They all came tumbling out of her in a torrent of tears. She felt like a failure and, for the first time since she had taken on the job of managing the Golden Bell, she also felt completely out of her depth.

For the last couple of hours she had run around the club frantically trying to put right the damage that a group of good-for-nothing wasters had inflicted. And now all she could do was cry.

It was some minutes before the self-pity washed away, and her resilient inner self re-emerged. What would Peter or Glynn have done in her situation? she asked herself. They certainly wouldn't have sat and cried.

She used a tissue to wipe away her tears but her face was still red and puffy when she heard a knock at her office door. 'Come in,' she said, hoping that whoever it was wouldn't notice she had been crying.

It was James. For a few moments he stood observing her, then seemed to deliberate over whether to comment about her blotchy face.

'The staff have gone and I've locked up,' he said, passing her the keys. 'Would you like me to wait until you've gone home?'

'No, it's fine,' she said. 'I'll be OK. We can talk tomorrow.'

'All right,' he said, 'As long as you're sure.'

Adele nodded, thankful when he went. It was obvious he could tell she'd been crying. And she hated that fact. As Adele sat with only her thoughts for company, she admonished herself. She should have been stronger than to let the night's events get the better of her. Instead she needed to get to the bottom of what had happened tonight. So she tried to think logically about it.

It seemed to her that the attack wasn't random. No, it had been organised. But why? She had to find out who was behind it and prevent the same thing from happening again in the future. But she had no idea where to begin. It was obvious who might know something though. Glynn. The world in which he operated was much shadier than hers and, if anyone could help her sort this mess out, it would be Glynn.

But she was wary of relying on him too much. She didn't want him to think she couldn't handle things. Somehow though she knew that Glynn would see tonight's disaster as a weakness on her part and he would waste no time in taking full advantage of the situation.

13

Glynn marched into Adele's office around lunchtime the next day. She cringed as she watched him walk in, knowing that he would see last night's events as proof that she couldn't cope with running the club.

He came straight to the point. 'What the hell went on last night?' he asked. 'I believe it was fuckin' bedlam.'

Adele tried not to let her irritation show. 'We had a few problems with a gang of troublemakers, that's all,' she said. 'Our security team soon had things under control.'

'Under control? Are you fuckin' serious? Furniture ripped and broken, hysterical punters and the bar staff giving everyone free drinks? Is that what you call under control?'

'Things did get a little out of hand until my security team chased the youths off the premises.'

'Really? Only, from what I've been told they were too fuckin' fat and unfit to catch the troublemakers. From what I heard they were less than useless.'

Adele sighed. 'If you've finished, Glynn, I've got work to do.'

'No, I haven't fuckin' finished!' he raged. 'I haven't even started yet. What were your useless doormen doing allowing that many young lads into the club?'

'They didn't allow a big group of lads into the club,' she snapped. 'I was on the door with them; I saw what happened. The lads came in two or three at a time. They must have gathered together once they had all got inside. Anyway, we're taking steps to make sure it doesn't happen in future. Any large gatherings of males will be asked to leave the club and refunded their entrance fee if necessary.'

Glynn laughed. 'And you think that'll sort it?'

'Hopefully, yes. Anyway, it was probably just an isolated incident. It might not happen again.'

'Oh, you think so, do you?' Glynn asked smugly, then he added, 'Well, I wish I felt as fuckin' confident as you.'

His words unnerved her. 'What do you mean?' she asked.

He laughed again. 'This is no isolated incident. It's a fuckin' warning!'

'Rubbish,' she said. 'If it had been a warning, then one of them would have said something. It was just high jinks, that's all.'

'You're still fuckin' clueless, aren't you?' he said. 'You obviously don't know how the gangs operate. This is just the fuckin' start of it.' Adele felt a stab of dread in the pit of her stomach. Her eyes were wide with alarm and were fixed on him as he carried on speaking. 'They'll be back, don't you fuckin' worry!'

Noticing the panic on her face, he didn't let up. 'I told you it was a big mistake to change the security but you wouldn't fuckin' listen, would you?'

His fierce tone told her that this really was something more than high jinks. Forgetting her resolve not to depend on Glynn, she asked, 'What can we do?'

'Fuck all!' he said and he seemed to revel in her fear. 'All we can do now is wait and see, unless you change the doormen. Then at least we'll have a better chance of handling whatever happens.'

'No!' she snapped. 'I'm not having your doormen back. I can't have them letting drug dealers into the club. Trust you to take advantage of the situation.'

'Please your fuckin' self!' he yelled. Then, for a few moments he stood glaring at her, an expression of contempt on his face. When she didn't say anything further, he left her office. He had succeeded in scaring her.

Once he was gone, she tried to brush his words aside, telling herself that he was just being dramatic to frighten her. But then the thought occurred to her that when she had asked him what they should do about the situation even he didn't seem that confident. And Glynn wasn't the type to scare easily. That could mean only one thing. They really did have a major problem.

Early on Saturday afternoon a young man walked into the Sportsman's searching for Alan. Aged only seventeen, Todd was tall for his age and stringy. He had a craggy, washed-out complexion caused by smoking from a young age and a difficult upbringing. This disguised his youth so he could pass for someone in his twenties.

He lived on a run-down council estate in Longsight, a couple of miles from the city centre. It was near to the demolished Fort Ardwick, which had consisted of several concrete blocks of flats linked by walkways. They had been given the name because they had collectively resembled a fortress, although in effect they had represented nothing more than a beleaguered collection of failed slum replacements.

Like a lot of his friends Todd was bored and out of work, and he spent most evenings hanging about the littered, graffiti-ridden streets with the other estate kids, taunting and harassing passers-by. He was always on the lookout for a way to earn some ready money, which could help to ease the boredom. Alan had provided him with such an opportunity and now he had come to collect.

Alan spotted him as soon as he walked into the side room where Alan was sitting with David and a few others. Todd strutted across the room and stood looking around at the gang members as though he was unsure how much to divulge in front of them.

Alan sensed his unease and opened up the conversation. 'How did it go?' he asked.

'Fuckin' brilliant,' said Todd. 'We did everything you wanted; fuckin' smashed the place up good and proper.'

Alan already knew what had happened in the Golden Bell the previous night but he was enjoying Todd's eagerness to fill him in on the details. Wanting to be sure that Todd and his friends had carried out his instructions, he had sent one of his men, Jacko, to keep watch while remaining incognito. It was important for Alan to find out exactly how things had gone. If Todd and his friends proved themselves then Alan decided he might want to recruit them for other jobs or even enrol them as fully fledged gang members.

'Good job,' said Alan, reaching into his trouser pocket and pulling out a wad of cash. 'Share this with your mates. You've done well. Come and see me in a few days; I might have some more work for you.'

Todd's eyes lit up and he quickly snatched the cash out of Alan's hand. 'Cheers, mate. See you soon,' he said, practically skipping out of the pub in his rush to spend his share of the spoils.

Alan turned to David, who was sitting by his side. 'Good kid,' he said, smiling. 'We could definitely use him again. He's got a lot of bottle from what Jacko told me.'

David grinned at him. 'What was the damage?' he asked.

'Broken chairs, slashed furniture and smashed glasses. And, according to Jacko, the customers were in a right fuckin' panic, falling over each other trying to get out of the fire exits and demanding free drinks cos Todd and his mates had chucked a load of booze all over the place.'

'Nice one. I bet that put the frighteners on Pete's sister,' said David. 'What was Jacko doing there anyway?'

'I sent him to watch. I wanted to fuckin' make sure Todd did a good job, didn't I?'

David grinned. 'You're not fuckin' daft, are you?'

Alan grinned back but said nothing.

David sniffed. 'So what's next?' he asked.

'Well,' said Alan. 'That was just a little taster to let them see what damage we can do. So how are you fixed to pay them a little visit later on today?'

'Sound,' David gushed.

'OK. Let's see if Adele's scared enough yet to cooperate,' said Alan.

'And if she isn't?'

'Then it will be time to up our game. She'll be fuckin' begging us for protection before much longer.'

David sniggered. 'Nice one,' he said. 'I can't wait to see the look on that stuck-up bitch's face.'

14

Despite the fact that it was early Saturday evening, Adele was in her office going over some figures. Although Margaret did a good job of the bookkeeping, Adele still liked to keep her eye on things. The ringing of the phone made her jump. Perhaps the incident the previous night had made her more on edge than she realised. She quickly picked up the receiver; it was one of the barmaids, who told her there were two men downstairs wanting to see her.

'Who are they?' she asked.

Adele felt a tremor of fear when she heard the names. 'Alan Palmer and David Scott.'

'OK, is Glynn about?' she asked instinctively, knowing that she would feel safer if he was around, and hating herself for feeling that way.

'No, he went out with Mike earlier,' said the barmaid.

Adele felt a moment's panic. The thought of Alan and David visiting her office made her feel vulnerable and exposed. Although she had her kickboxing skills to fall back on and could put up a good fight if necessary, she wondered whether that would be enough against those two. But she didn't want to meet Alan and David downstairs either; she couldn't risk panicking the staff if they overheard what Alan and David had to say. She had a feeling it wouldn't be good.

'OK, can you get Barney and another of the bouncers to bring them up to my office, please?' she asked, knowing that sending them away wasn't an option. If she was right about the reason for their visit then she couldn't allow them to think she was running scared.

Adele put down the phone and waited for her unwelcome visitors. A rush of thoughts crowded her brain and her heart pounded in her chest. Recollections of a childhood in torment. Street bullies; taunting and intimidating. Nasty names, evil looks. The omnipresent worry and the pain of humiliation.

As a child Adele had suffered at the hands of Alan, David and their friends. She had never forgotten the look of glee on David's wicked face as she'd stepped closer to him and his mates, dreading what they might do. Then she had passed them only to hear the frightening sound of advancing footsteps behind her. She flinched as she relived the sharp blow to her back that had almost felled her, and the terror of what might follow.

During her troubled childhood Adele had fought to make a better life for herself. Studying hard to pass her exams, she'd had no time to hang about the streets like a lot of the youngsters. Because of that she hadn't fitted in. And where had all her studying got her? Like all the other bad things in her life, the torment from the bullies never went away. It seemed that, no matter what she did, she could never escape her harrowing childhood.

And now the bullies were back. Thoughts of Glynn's warning were uppermost in her mind. What if they had been behind the trouble in the club the previous night? She took a deep breath and tried to steady her trembling limbs as she awaited their arrival. When she heard footsteps in the corridor, she steeled herself for what was to come.

Barney's head peered around the door while the other bouncer waited outside with Alan and David. 'I've got your visitors,' he said.

Adele noticed the cynical way he emphasised the word *visitors*, and she wondered whether Barney knew of them.

'OK, bring them in,' said Adele. 'But would you both wait outside the door, please?' She noticed Barney raise his eyebrows inquisitively, and she added, 'So you can show them back downstairs when we're finished. This shouldn't take a minute.'

In spite of her trepidation, Adele decided to play it down. It wouldn't do to alert the staff; she didn't want a mass panic on her hands.

'OK,' said Barney and, before she knew it, her childhood tormentors were facing her across her office.

Adele didn't offer them a seat; she didn't want them to stay. Instead she sat and scrutinised them while she waited for them to speak. She hadn't seen Alan for many years due to the amount of time he'd spent inside. As he'd transitioned from a boy into a man he had grown in stature too. Although slim, he was also muscular. His features were even sterner than she recalled; his facial muscles seeming as taut as those on his body.

Her memory of David was more recent. His own particular brand of body odour triggered a flashback to the last time she had seen him only a few months ago. He and another man had attacked her in her own front garden and threatened reprisals against Peter's gang. The attack had left her badly shaken and worried about the future.

Adele looked at David, skinny and bedraggled, his clothes creased and hanging loosely on him. She took in his weasel features, his broken front tooth and the rest of his crooked and discoloured teeth. Then she saw the aggressive way he was standing. His arms were tensed and slightly back from his body, his chin jutted forward and his brow was scrunched. As she noticed his hard stare a chill went through her.

Alan was the first to speak. 'I believe you had a bit of trouble last night,' he announced casually.

'Nothing we couldn't handle,' she said, her jaw stiff as she tried to stay in control.

'Looks like Glynn and Mike might be losing their touch since your brother got sent down,' he continued.

The fact that he knew their names unnerved her. 'They weren't here last night,' she replied automatically. Then, realising her mistake, she added, 'Anyway, my security team had things very much under control.'

'That's not what I heard,' he said. 'In fact, I've just taken a look downstairs and you can still see the damage. They did a bit of a fuckin' job on the upholstery, didn't they?'

'That's OK, we can soon have it re-covered,' she said, trying to sound unperturbed.

'It sounds to me like you could do with an extra hand with the security. Someone who can fuckin' handle things. My firm are the big boys in town now, no matter what—'

'That won't be necessary,' she cut in, more sharply than she had intended as she didn't want to aggravate them. Then, to smooth over her harsh words, she added, 'But thanks for the offer.'

'Well,' said Alan. 'I just hope for your sake that things don't get much fuckin' worse... and they could do. There are a lot of clubs being hit at the moment and some people are getting very badly hurt.'

Adele noticed David's slight grin on hearing the veiled threat and, rather than instil more fear into her, it annoyed her.

'I said no!' she said. This time the strident tone of her voice was deliberate.

'OK,' said Alan. He stepped forward and Adele recoiled. She was just about to summon Barney and the other bouncer when Alan tore a slip of paper from the pad on her desk and used one of her pens with which to scrawl a phone number. 'If you change your mind... or should I say, *when* you change your mind, just give us a ring. The offer will still be there. Then we can discuss terms.'

'Don't worry, I won't change my mind,' she said, 'and I'd appreciate it if you didn't call again.' Before they had chance to respond she shouted for Barney, who rushed through the door. 'These gentlemen have said what they had to say, Barney. Please could you show them out?'

'Sure,' said Barney. Then, looking at Alan and David, he said, 'Follow me.'

Adele waited until she heard them reach the end of the corridor and go through the internal door, then she picked up the phone and rang the main bar of the club. 'Put Paula on,' she said, noticing that her mouth had gone dry and her sweaty palms made the phone feel clammy under her tight grip. 'Paula, will you let me know as soon as Glynn gets back?' she asked, thanking Paula as soon as she heard her reply then quickly putting down the receiver.

The incident had shaken her and she was no longer able to concentrate on work as she thought about the consequences of Alan's visit. There was no doubt in her mind that things had taken a very nasty turn. She was petrified, the blood pulsating fiercely around her body as she thought about Alan's threat.

The very thing that she hadn't wanted to happen had now happened. Adele didn't want to get involved in the security side of things but it seemed that she was being dragged into it, willingly or not. She didn't know how to handle this. The world of protection rackets was both alien and terrifying to her.

Glynn would know how to deal with Alan's gang. It irked her having to turn to Glynn for help after arguing that she could manage without him, but she couldn't think what else to do. If Alan was to follow through with his threat then she and all the rest of the staff would be in grave danger. And when it came to protecting them all, she knew that she would have to put her pride aside and do whatever was necessary.

15

Glynn came straight up to her office once he was back inside the club. 'What's the matter?' he asked, pulling up a chair opposite her.

'We've had a visit,' she said, noticing her lips tremble slightly as she spoke.

'Oh, yeah? Who?'

'Alan Palmer and David Scott.'

Adele watched his expression change as he heard their names; his eyes narrowed and his lips tightened. 'What the fuck did that pair of bastards want?' he asked.

'They were threatening me, not in so many words, of course, but it was a threat all the same.'

Adele felt a quiver of emotion, which she tried to suppress. It was fed by her sense of inadequacy in having to call on Glynn for help. But she didn't have a choice. Who else could she turn to? She couldn't call the police. It wasn't as if she had any evidence of Alan's threat; it would be easy for him to just deny it. And, anyway, it wasn't the done thing in their world. Any reports to the police would only be met by more reprisals.

But as she sat there looking across the desk at him, she felt like a failure. What was it Glynn had said? *You'll need me long before I need you.* And now she was playing right into his hands.

'What the fuck did they say exactly?' he asked, bristling with anger.

'They started by mentioning last night. Then they said it could have been a lot worse and that people are getting very badly hurt nowadays.' She tried to disguise the tremble in her voice as she continued. 'Then Alan offered his services, which I turned down, of course.

'Before I got Barney to show them out Alan said that the offer would still be open when things got worse... Oh, and apparently, you and Mike have lost your touch since Peter went inside and they're the top firm in town now.'

'Really? That's what they fuckin' think!'

Before he got too carried away in his condemnation, she butted in, 'What can we do, Glynn?'

'I'll tell you what you can do: you can get my fuckin' men back on the doors for starters. I'll make sure we're ready for the bastards if they start anything.'

'I can't do that, Glynn.'

'Well, why the fuck are you asking for my advice if you won't do what I fuckin' tell you? If you hadn't changed the bouncers this wouldn't have happened in the first fuckin' place!'

Adele tried to stay calm as she responded. 'You don't know that, Glynn. They might still have tried it on.'

'Would they fuck! I told you, last night's attack was a warning. But they were testing the fuckin' water as well. And now they've seen what a docile bunch of pricks you've got working for you, there'll be no fuckin' stopping them!'

'I'm not changing the bouncers!' she snapped. 'There must be something else we can do.'

'Forget it,' he said, rising from his chair. 'If you won't take my advice then why should I waste any more of my fuckin' time? You're on your own with this one.'

'No!' she retaliated. 'Sit down. Let's talk it through.'

He sat back down, eyeing her warily as he waited to see what she had to say.

'Can't you and Mike stay around the club on the weekends until all this dies down, and get someone else to do the collections?'

'Why? Why should we, Adele? We'd be like sitting fuckin' ducks, waiting for them to hit.'

'Because you know how these people operate. They might not try it on if they know you're here.' Glynn didn't look convinced so she quickly added, 'We can't afford to let them in, Glynn. If they take over, they'll take most of the profits, and where will that leave the rest of us?'

Adele gauged his reaction. She didn't mention the profits he personally took from drugs but she knew that was what he was thinking. It was best not to mention the drug dealing outright because that might make him think she condoned it. She didn't but, deep down, she knew he was still finding a way to get drugs inside the club. She wasn't daft.

That was a problem for another day though. Right now, she had more pressing concerns and she needed Glynn to help her.

Finally, after she had let him think about the threat to his profits for a moment, he relented and decided to help out. 'OK,' he sighed. 'For now me and Mike will stay in the club at weekends. But I'll need a couple of handy men on the doors with us.'

'You've got James's men on the doors. They'll help you out.'

'Huh!' he scoffed. 'I mean real men who aren't too fuckin' scared to get stuck in if they need to.'

'No, Glynn. I've already said: I want James's men on the doors.'

'OK, inside the club, then? They can even come in incognito if you like.'

'All right, do it,' she said, aware that they might not reach agreement otherwise.

'Right, that's that sorted, then. We'll keep an eye on things for a few weeks and see how it goes. Oh, and my men will want paying, the usual rate.'

'All right,' she said. 'Let me have their details once you start them and I'll put it through the books.'

'Sure,' he said.

Adele hadn't wanted to tell the staff about any imminent trouble as she couldn't risk frightening them off over something that might not even happen. But Glynn insisted that they needed to be prepared and he had attached this condition to his agreement to help out.

Because of the way in which James's company operated, none of his staff carried weapons. But, unknown to Adele, Glynn and Mike would make sure they and their two hired hands were tooled up when Alan's gang made their attack. Under the circumstances, Adele had done the best she could to protect Peter's nightclub. Now all she could do was wait and hope that things wouldn't turn out as bad as she feared.

16

After she had finished her meeting with Glynn, Adele decided to go down to the club to keep an eye on things herself. She also needed to warn James. In the end Adele asked James to make his staff aware of potential trouble but she played it down. As far as he was concerned, there were a group of troublemakers doing the rounds of Manchester's nightclubs, and there might be a recurrence of the previous night's events.

It was only a couple of hours previously that Alan and David had left the club, having issued their warning, so she doubted that they would have time to plan an attack tonight. Nevertheless, she wasn't taking any chances.

James responded to her understated warning with his usual finesse. 'Not a problem,' he said politely. 'I'll let my employees know. Don't you worry about it; I'm sure we'll soon have things under control now we're aware of a possible attack.'

He smiled confidently and Adele managed a weak smile in return. She only wished she felt as confident as James seemed to feel.

Once she had spoken to James, Adele walked into the foyer. There she saw Anna and her other female bouncer, Lynn, at the front door together with some of James's staff. Adele studied them from the other side of the foyer. Despite her worries about what had been happening, Adele felt a warm glow as she watched Anna operate.

Since she'd started working at the Golden Bell Anna had been an absolute treasure. She had relished the opportunity to have honest employment and had thrown herself into the job wholeheartedly. Combining a menacing exterior, which warned customers not to push their luck, with a friendly manner, she had proved popular with both staff and customers.

Adele had grown fond of Anna during their time inside. It was an unlikely friendship and one that Adele wouldn't have fostered otherwise. But, nevertheless, Anna had proved to be a loyal and trustworthy friend. Because of her positive approach towards her work, Adele had become even fonder of her.

While she stood at the other side of the foyer, Adele also watched her other female bouncer, Lynn. She was doing a good job as well although she wasn't quite as keen as Anna. Lynn was different from Anna in appearance; plain but with a feminine manner, and slim but quite tall. She was currently searching the handbag of one of the female customers and chatting to her reassuringly while she carried out this task.

The thought occurred to Adele that it perhaps wasn't a good idea to have both women on the door at the moment. After all, she needed big, strong men who could handle themselves if there was an attack. A brief glance at Glynn and Mike told her that they were exactly what was needed.

Adele walked over and asked Lynn if she could work indoors instead. She deliberated over whether to remove Anna from the door too but decided that it was best if she had at least one female member of staff to handle any rowdy women. Then Adele returned to her observation point at the other side of the foyer.

The club had a strange feel about it tonight, or was it perhaps just her imagination? The music was the same; a heady mix of eighties' hits, old soul and popular classics pulsating from the speakers. Like every other club night, the revellers eagerly crowded inside. The events of the previous night didn't seem to have quelled their enthusiasm; if anything there seemed to be more people than usual. Perhaps they were curious to view the scene of last night's incident. The drink was flowing, the dancing lively and the lights bright and colourful. But something was different.

Then Adele realised what it was. Each of the door staff was cloaked in ominous anticipation. They wore it like a coat of armour; hard and stiff. She could see it in their clenched muscles, their raised shoulders and the harsh expressions on their faces. And she could feel it inside herself too.

Now that she had acknowledged its existence she noticed how tetchy she was feeling. Tonight the music seemed a little too loud, the lights a little too bright and the customers a little too lively. Adele could feel her heart fluttering and a persistent growl in her stomach. She tried to relax, telling herself that there was little chance of an attack and desperately hoping that she was right.

'So, I believe you had a bit of trouble last Friday night,' said Peter when Adele went to visit him a few days later. He noticed her surprised expression.

'Who told you?' she asked. Then a look of realisation flashed across her face. 'Oh, as if I need to ask. Glynn?'

'He did right,' said Peter, eager to get straight to the point. 'What the hell's going on, Adele?'

He already knew the details but he wanted to get things from his sister's point of view.

'We just had some idiots in the club last Friday, that's all,' she said resignedly.

'And?'

'And I think Alan and David might be behind it.' She sighed. 'They came to see me the next day offering their services. But we don't need them. Our new firm are doing fine.'

Peter guessed that she was trying to play things down. He could see the worry lines etched across her forehead and, so far, her story didn't quite match what Glynn had already told him.

'Look, Adele, I'm gonna come straight to the point. I think it's time you got rid of that firm of fuckin' amateurs. They're well out of their depth.'

'According to who?' she snapped. 'Bloody Glynn? I've already told you they're doing OK. We need to give them a chance. Glynn's bound to have a downer on them; he just wants to take control again.'

'Adele, I don't need Glynn to tell me what to do. I know what's going on myself. Don't forget, I've been running security for a few years now. I know it like the back of my hand.'

'There isn't time to change the team anyway,' she said, her words coming out in a flurry. 'It's almost the weekend now. Glynn could never put a team of men together that quickly. We'll have to go with what we've got.'

It was Peter's turn to sigh. 'OK, point taken, but I want Glynn's men back on the doors as soon as possible. I don't care what he gets up to! At the moment, protecting the club is more important.'

'I am protecting the club!' she argued. 'And as soon as we've sorted this problem, I'm going to find out exactly what he's up to. Can't you see, Peter? If he carries on encouraging drug dealing in the club, we'll get shut down anyway.'

'Shush,' warned Peter, looking around him. 'First things first. Let's get the doors secure then we can look at the other problems.'

'OK,' she muttered but he could tell her reply was half-hearted.

When the prison officers announced that it was the end of visiting time, Peter gave Adele a hug then made his way back to his cell. Before he went through the door he took a last look at his sister, who was at the back of the queue for the exit. He could tell by the way she trudged dejectedly towards the door that she didn't really believe the new bouncers had things under control. He realised she was worried sick.

They both knew Alan and David of old, and were also aware of how ruthless they could be. Not for the first time Peter wished he were on the outside. It was obvious that his sister didn't have things under control and it frustrated the hell out of him. If only there were something he could do.

But there wasn't; he was behind bars. And being behind bars made it even harder to accept that the club was at risk and there wasn't a damn thing he could do about it. Not only was he worried about attacks from rival gangs but he was also concerned that Glynn's shady deals could backfire on them.

Although Adele was trying her best, Peter knew that the firm she had employed weren't the only ones who were out of their depth. She was too. It left him with no choice. He would have to rely on Glynn to put up a fight when Alan's gang came calling and pray to God that things didn't get any worse.

17

It was Friday night. There hadn't been any further incidents in the club since the previous Friday. But tonight was the night when Alan's gang were going to hit them. Glynn had had a tip-off from one of his sources. He wouldn't reveal to Adele who the source was but he was glad of the tip-off. It meant that he was ready.

As he and Mike stood at the entrance to the Golden Bell, Glynn looked at the doormen who were amongst them. Bunch of tossers! They didn't have a fuckin' clue. And as for that butch bird, what fuckin' use would a woman be when it all kicked off? Adele had asked James to warn his men about a possible attack but she had played it down again. She didn't want to worry everyone and have the doormen not showing up for work.

Glynn had taken his own precautions. Apart from him and Mike, he had another two men inside the club, working incognito. Despite Adele's protestations, he would have enrolled even more but it was too short notice and most of the handy blokes he knew were working elsewhere tonight.

While he waited for Alan's men to strike he could feel the buzz of adrenalin pulsing around his body. It made him sharper and ready to hit back. His eyes roamed the street outside looking for any early signs. His ears picked out sounds from the crowd, analysing any aggressive tones or misplaced words. And his muscles were taut, primed for the attack.

As his gloved fingers grasped the head of the claw hammer concealed up his jacket sleeve, he wished they would hurry up and get it over with. His bladder was full and for a few moments he deliberated over whether he would have enough time to visit the toilet. In the end he couldn't wait any longer and he rushed off, telling Mike he would be back as soon as possible.

Adele watched nervously from the other side of the foyer. All around her the club-goers and bouncers carried on as normal, most of them oblivious to the havoc that was about to take place. She felt clammy, her limbs twitchy, as she waited for Alan's men to strike.

Looking over at the door, she could see Glynn and Mike as well as some of the other bouncers. She'd made sure there were plenty of them manning the door tonight. She was struck by Glynn and Mike's body language. Unlike her, they seemed as though they were looking forward to the challenge, bouncing around excitedly while they kept a tight check on everyone entering the club.

Then she noticed Anna. Blissfully ignorant, she was currently sharing a joke with one of the customers. Anna loved the banter with the customers and other bouncers. Adele had decided not to tell her anything other than what she already knew about last Friday's events and the possibility that the youths might return to cause more disruption. Knowing Anna, if she knew the full scale of the threat she'd work herself up so much that she'd probably end up walking off the job.

Adele was just about to cross the foyer and head towards the front door when Glynn came charging towards her. 'Where do you think you're going?' he demanded.

She stared at him, nonplussed. 'What do you mean, where am I going? I'm going to the door to check on things.'

'Oh, no, you're fuckin' not!' he blasted. Then he lowered his voice. 'When it kicks off it's gonna be nasty, and it'll be no place for a woman.'

'Listen, if I want to keep an eye on things, I will do!' she retaliated. 'I am managing this place when all's said and done.'

'It's not about who's fuckin' managing things,' he bit back. 'I'm telling you, it's gonna get fuckin' ugly!'

'I can handle myself, remember?'

Glynn closed in on her and hissed into her ear. 'What use are a few fuckin' kicks against knives and firearms?'

His words chilled her and she pulled back, staring at him, the horror of his words written on her face. When he had given her a chance to take in his warning, he said, 'Right, I've got to go to the gents but I'll be back as quick as I can.'

Adele watched him dash across the nightclub, towards the gents. As he rushed, a man tried to grab his attention but he shunned him and carried on moving. His words had alarmed her; so had the fact that he wanted to get back as soon as he could. Adele hovered for a moment but then decided to take Glynn's advice on board. She moved away from the foyer and back into the relative safety of the Golden Bell's interior.

She had completed a circuit of the nightclub when a thought came to her with startling clarity. If Glynn had warned her away from the door because she was a woman then why was Anna still there?

In a way she was flattered that Glynn was so concerned about her well-being but she was also annoyed that he had overlooked Anna. In his bigoted world he probably didn't even view Anna in the same way as he viewed other women. Adele was just about to go and bring

Anna inside when a crowd of terrified nightclubbers raced towards her, screeching and yelling.

It was pandemonium! For a few moments Adele stood slack-jawed as she tried to take in what was happening. Several men were tearing through the club wielding machetes, baseball bats and other deadly weapons. At high speed they were attacking anyone in their path, leaving a trail of devastation.

As the men bashed and sliced into the crowd, a large body of punters ran screaming; a frenzied mass of tangled limbs tripping over each other in their haste to escape. High heels were discarded and drinks spilt as they rushed away from their attackers.

The noise was deafening, a cacophony of panic. Bloodied customers were screaming and yelling friends' names, trying to reach them in the swollen crowd, their eyes wide with terror. One or two drunken have-a-go heroes were trying to put up a fight but soon they lay battered and bleeding in defeat. The pulsating music and vivid lights added to the general mayhem, as the strobes illuminated bodies gushing blood.

Where were the bouncers?

Before Adele could think properly, the throng of hysteria caught up with her. The might of the panicked crowd rammed into Adele, pushing her off her feet and sending her hurtling into the plastic barrier that surrounded the dance floor. She landed with a heavy thud, her head crashing into the barrier. Then she lay dazed and vaguely aware of what was going on around her.

For a few minutes she was unable to get up. There were too many people pushing against her, and her head was swimming. She watched horrified as the men brutalised her customers leaving them damaged and bloody. A throbbing horde of vermilion-streaked bodies, terrified and weeping, was frantically trying to escape. But the men continued their wicked assault, their faces fierce and menacing.

Eventually the carnage stopped as the men ran out of the club leaving droves of traumatised punters behind. As Adele came to, she began to worry about the staff on the doors: Anna, James's employees, even Glynn, she thought, to her consternation. She desperately hoped they were all right. Struggling to her feet, she tried to ignore the chaos around her as she made her way unsteadily to the foyer.

Glynn had only just returned from the gents when Anna noticed a disturbance at the entrance to the Golden Bell. She was standing to one side of the door, carrying out bag searches and directing customers to the pay desk. At first she thought it was another rowdy crowd of troublemakers but then things turned really nasty.

Anna watched dumbstruck as a bunch of men surged through the door of the club armed with an assortment of weapons. She stepped back automatically then stood still, staring in shock as the scene unfolded. Around her, the nightclubbers screamed and dashed, terrorised, out of the club and into the street. Others darted through the foyer and into the club, trying to get away.

Several of the bouncers were trying to fight the men off. Anna saw Glynn and Mike charge at the men, carrying their own weapons. She noticed the hammer in Glynn's hand and was puzzled for a moment as she hadn't noticed it earlier. Lifting it above his head, he repeatedly bashed it into the gang of men.

Anna's flight response kicked in when the men broke through the group of bouncers and hurried into the club's foyer. As the adrenalin pulsed around her body, she instinctively turned around and started to run. But before she could break away Anna felt a sharp blow on the back of her head, which felled her to the ground. Then everything went black.

18

As soon as Glynn returned from the gents, he had taken up his position at the nightclub doors again. He hadn't been back long when he saw the men arrive. He knew it was them straight away. Their grave expressions, rigid posture, and the weapons they carried set them apart from the rest of the crowd.

The men dashed across the pavement in a tight group. Letting out an angry roar that sounded to Glynn like a war cry, they shoved aside anyone who got in their path. The crowd of punters outside the Golden Bell backed away, their faces a mix of confusion and alarm.

Glynn nodded across to Mike. Then he forced his way in front of the other bouncers and slid the hammer out of his sleeve.

The first man to arrive at the club's doorway felt the full force of the hammer as Glynn brought it down sharply onto his head. As the man stood dazed from the fierce blow, Glynn brought the hammer down again.

This time he struck another of the attackers on his shoulder. The man yelped in pain.

Glynn continued to hack away at the group of men. With Mike alongside him, they did their best to hold them back. He could see some of the bouncers close by but they were fighting a losing battle. Their fists and feet were no match against the men's deadly weapons. As the enemy sliced at them with their machetes and baseball bats the bouncers fell away, bruised and defeated.

Despite Glynn and Mike's efforts, there were too many of Alan's men. Glynn wished he had the help of his other two men but they were inside the club and it had all happened too quickly for him to summon them. Soon the enemy had fought their way through the bouncers. Sprinting into the club, they brandished their weapons as they charged at the hysterical customers.

'Don't just stand there looking fuckin' gormless!' Glynn shouted at the bouncers. 'Get after the bastards.'

But too few of the bouncers were still standing. Many of them lay on the ground, groaning in pain. A handful of bouncers tried valiantly to pursue the men. Mike started to race after them too till Glynn stopped him. 'No! You stay here with me,' he ordered.

When Mike walked back and stared at him, puzzled, Glynn said, 'Hear that?'

On hearing a siren in the distance, Mike nodded. Glynn quickly scanned the foyer noticing the injured bouncers lying on the floor. A few steps away he could see James Merton, crumpled on the ground, his smart suit spattered with blood.

Glynn leant into Mike. 'We need to be ready,' he whispered, urgently. 'And I wanna make sure there aren't any more of the bastards.'

As he nodded towards the interior of the club, he knew Mike understood. Glynn didn't want to risk going after the men inside when more of Alan's men might arrive. They also needed to be ready for the imminent arrival of the police, so he slipped the hammer back up his sleeve.

For a few minutes Glynn and Mike stood at the door barking orders at the crowd. 'Get back!' Glynn shouted, forcing them out onto the street. 'Clear the way. The police will be here any minute.'

He dropped back into the foyer just in time to see Alan's men running from the club. He pulled out the hammer again, trying to inflict as much damage as he could on the retreating enemy. When the last of the men had escaped from the Golden Bell, Glynn turned to Mike as the sound of the sirens grew louder and more insistent.

'Get rid!' he said, passing him the hammer. 'And yours too,' he added, looking at the baseball bat that Mike was gripping in his right hand. 'Don't worry; I'll handle things with the police.'

As Mike pulled the hammer out of Glynn's hand and raced across the foyer, Glynn spotted one of the wounded bouncers keenly watching them. 'Not a fuckin' word!' he spat. 'After all, we were saving your fuckin' arses.'

He turned his head and peered out into the street where a police van had just pulled up, followed by two police cars. Then he tore off the white cotton gloves he had been wearing and stuffed them inside his pocket. At least if the police found the hammer, it wouldn't have his fingerprints on it.

For a few seconds he watched the action in the street as the police chased after Alan's men. They succeeded in bundling a few of them inside the van but the others fled. Then Glynn saw one of the officers striding across the road and making his way to the club.

The way the officer walked with a sense of purpose and his upright bearing told Glynn that this was a senior officer. As he drew nearer, this was verified by the pips on his epaulettes, and Glynn recognised straight away that he was an inspector.

Glynn stepped outside to meet him. 'Good to see you, officer,' he said, feigning sincerity. 'We've taken a bit of a bashing, I'm afraid,' he added as they both walked inside the club and he nodded towards the couple of bouncers who were still sprawled on the floor of the foyer.

The police inspector barked an order to one of his officers on the street, calling for ambulance backup before he turned back to Glynn. 'Stay here for now. I'll need you to make a statement,' he said before he walked further into the club, assessing the damage and giving commands to the officers who followed him inside.

Just as the inspector left Glynn, Mike appeared by his side. 'Jesus, it's bedlam in there,' he said. 'Thank God the police are here!'

Glynn supressed a wicked grin, happy that Mike was eager to play along with the role of innocent victims. Then they waited while the police carried out their duties.

Adele stumbled through the club, heading for the foyer. All around her people were damaged and bleeding. Their panicked cries had replaced the lively music from earlier, and piercing shrieks now polluted the air. Others chattered, their tones nervous yet animated, sending an eerie drone throughout the club.

The people huddled in clusters, clutching at each other, their knuckles white with strain as they attempted to comfort their friends. Their faces bore a combination of alarm and distress. Others appeared numb with shock as they stood around, some barefoot and weeping silent tears. Adele had never seen anything like it.

There was furniture overturned and Adele saw a meat cleaver embedded into a table, its blade coloured crimson. A flash of anger zipped through her as she took in the devastation.

As she made her way through the club Adele noticed a young girl standing alone, her face bearing a pained expression as tears gushed down her face, diluting the blood that ran freely from a head wound.

Adele wanted to help, to comfort the girl and tell her everything was going to be all right. But she couldn't. She needed to get to the door and check on her staff. Adele wondered desperately whether they were all right. Anna? James? Barney? Glynn? She hoped to God they were!

As Adele approached the foyer she saw the police arrive and try to restore order amongst the crowd of traumatised club-goers. While they busied themselves, she slipped through the door and into the foyer.

Straight away she could see that there were two bouncers on the floor and others standing around nursing injuries. Her eyes flitted about as she tried to pick out faces from the sea of damaged bodies. When she spotted Glynn standing near the door with Mike, she let out an automatic sigh of relief.

Then her eyes quickly switched to the two bouncers on the floor. One of them she recognised as one of James's men but the other had the rounded curves of a woman. Anna!

Adele raced over, calling Anna's name, but she was stopped by a policeman. 'Don't touch her!' he ordered. 'We've put her in the recovery position while we wait for the ambulance.' Then he took out a notepad and pen before asking, 'What's her name?'

'Anna. Anna Tomlinson,' said Adele before her voice cracked as she asked, 'Is she OK?'

'She's unconscious,' said the policeman, whose colleague had joined him, helping to hold Adele back. 'We'll have to wait till the ambulance crews assess her.'

'No!' wailed Adele as she strained against the policemen, trying to get to Anna.

'Stand back!' ordered one of the policemen but Adele continued to struggle.

She needed to get to her. She wanted to know if Anna was all right. But the policemen held her firmly back.

Then Glynn was by her side. 'Come on, Adele,' he said. His voice was so uncharacteristically gentle that she allowed him to lead her away. 'The ambulance crews will be here soon, then we'll find out.'

He drew her to one side of the foyer where he remained holding her. Leaning into him, she drew comfort from his embrace as she waited.

'You're bleeding,' he said.

Examining her head wound with his fingers, he then pulled his hand away and looked at the scarlet streaks on his fingers. 'You need to get that checked out.'

'I'm OK,' she snapped. 'I need to know if Anna's all right.'

She could see the concern on his face as he examined her wound. Looking at his expression, it was obvious that he still cared but she tried to dismiss such thoughts while she peered anxiously over his shoulder to see what was happening with Anna.

It wasn't long before the ambulance crews arrived. As the police officers directed one ambulance crew to attend Anna, Adele rushed over to her again. She was aware of Glynn at her side once more, holding her back while they awaited the outcome.

'We need to get this one to hospital,' said an ambulance man. He and his colleague then hauled Anna onto a stretcher and dashed towards the door.

'Wait, I want to come with her. She's my friend,' shouted Adele as she chased after the stretcher.

'It's OK, you go,' Glynn shouted after her. 'I'll take care of things here.'

But Adele was oblivious to everything else that was going on. Her main concern was Anna and making sure she was all right. She tried to rush after the ambulance crew but a policeman stopped her.

'You can't go out there!' he said. 'We'll need you to make a statement.'

'But I'm her friend,' she said to the policeman, who eyed her warily.

'Are you staff?' he asked.

'Yes, I'm the manager.'

'In that case you'll definitely need to make a statement,' he said, taking hold of her hand and guiding her back inside the club.

Once the policeman was out of reach Adele dashed through the club. Trying to ignore the havoc that was going on around her, she made her way to the fire escape. A distressed customer, who recognised Adele as the manager, tried to stop her, but she shrugged her off and carried on running through the club.

Once Adele had reached the fire escape she pushed the lever marked 'emergency' and rushed out into the chilly night air. Ignoring a harried shout from someone trying to stop her, she sprinted along the side road and round to the front of the club. There she saw three ambulances in the street and two ambulance men carrying a stretcher towards one of them.

She recognised the person on the stretcher as Anna and raced across the street. But Adele failed to reach the ambulance as the driver shut the back doors and ran round to the front of the vehicle.

'Wait!' she shouted but the ambulance driver ignored her frantic cries.

Adele pushed through the crowd in her haste to reach the ambulance. She drew close just as it set off down the street. Unperturbed, she raced after it. But it was no use. As the ambulance sped away, Adele became aware of the growing gap and the futility of her efforts. Eventually, when her lungs screamed out in pain she stopped running and stared in despair at the vehicle that had carried her friend away.

19

Back inside the club Adele was intending to order a taxi that would take her to the hospital to see Anna, but she was inundated by people wanting her attention. An ambulance man walked over and examined her head injury.

'You'll need to get that seen to at the hospital,' he said.

'I will. Later,' said Adele, shrugging him off.

Then Glynn rushed over with a police officer. 'I thought you'd gone with Anna,' he said.

'No, they wouldn't let me,' Adele replied, her voice shaky.

'They want a statement,' said Glynn, nodding at the police officer.

'OK.'

'Are you sure you're up to it?' asked the officer, eyeing her head wound.

'Yes, it's OK. I'll get it seen to later,' she said.

Adele allowed herself to be led away by the policeman, who took her to a table in a quieter area of the club. She sighed resignedly as he withdrew a notepad and pen. By the time he had finished there was a queue of staff and customers waiting to see her, each too taken up with their own concerns to pay any regard to her injuries.

She managed to snatch a few words with Glynn while they were tending to the aftermath of the attack.

'How many were injured?' she asked.

'A few of James's men,' he replied. 'James has been taken to the hospital as well as another of his men who seemed pretty badly cut up. One or two of the customers were in a bad way too. James had a blow to the head but I think he'll be all right. At least he was lucid when they took him out.'

His words made Adele think of Anna and she shuddered as she recalled her friend lying injured and unconscious on the floor. 'What happened with Anna?' she asked.

'Don't know. I was a bit busy at the time.'

Adele looked him up and down, irritated at his flippant response. 'How come you and Mike are OK if you were at the front door?' she asked.

Adele thought she detected a slight smirk as he replied. 'Because no one fucks with me if they know what's good for them.'

She wasn't in the mood for his bravado. Her thoughts were with Anna. Eventually they managed to restore some degree of order inside the club and once the emergency services had left she shut the club early.

Now she could make the journey to the hospital and find out how Anna was. She'd get her own injury looked at while she was there but she wasn't too concerned for her own welfare. After all, it hadn't stopped her for the last hour or two. No, Adele's concern was for her friend.

By the time Adele arrived at Manchester Royal Infirmary it was the early hours of Saturday morning. She jumped out of the cab outside the A & E department and raced up to the desk to enquire about Anna. Unfortunately there was a queue and Adele fidgeted impatiently as she waited to be seen.

While she stood there, Adele glanced around the waiting room. She hadn't been in an A & E department in the early hours on a weekend before, and what she saw shocked her.

The place was packed with sick and injured people, many of whom were sitting on the floor as all the seats were taken. An assortment of casualties vied for medical attention: parents nursing wailing infants, distressed elderly people, blood-spattered youths and girls in skimpy clothing. One man lay there battered, his clothes resembling those of a vagrant, his hair matted and streaked red, and his head lolling to the side as though he had drunk far too much cheap wine.

In the corner a heated argument was taking place between a group of young men and women. A nurse was trying to keep things calm as the disagreement threatened to escalate. As Adele eyed the people involved, many of them covered in blood and some with torn clothing, she guessed that they must have already been in a fight.

Looking around at the number of young people dressed in smart but dishevelled clubbing gear, she wondered how many of them had come from the Golden Bell. If so, they had waited a long time to be attended to by the medical staff.

After a few minutes Adele reached the head of the queue at the reception desk, and she enquired after Anna. A harassed receptionist consulted her records for admissions. Then she looked up at Adele and asked, 'Are you a relative?'

'I'm a very good friend and also her manager.' When the receptionist stared at her, nonplussed, Adele added, 'She works for me at the Golden Bell. That's where she got her injury.'

'Oh, I see,' said the receptionist, nodding gravely. Then, after a brief pause, she added, 'Yes. She was brought in earlier. If you take a seat in the waiting room I'll send someone out to take you through.'

Adele smiled, sardonically. It was obvious that the receptionist was on autopilot. A quick glance around the room would have told her that there were no seats available. Nevertheless, Adele walked through to the seating area and leant uncomfortably against the wall while she waited to be called through.

Adele was surprised when only a few minutes later a nurse called out her name and took her to the A & E assessment area. Adele saw that there were a number of booths with people lying on beds surrounded by their loved ones. Around one of the booths the curtains were drawn and Adele could hear someone, who she presumed to be a doctor, talking to someone else. She wondered if Anna was on the other side of that curtain.

'Could you wait here a minute while I find out where she's been taken?' asked the nurse, nodding at a single free seat, which had been placed outside the booths.

Then she went away, through another door, leaving Adele waiting again. It hadn't escaped Adele's attention that she had been called through very quickly in view of the number of people in the waiting room. She hoped that wasn't a bad sign and tried to dismiss it from her mind. There was no point in getting worked up till she knew exactly how badly hurt Anna was.

While Adele sat there she also became aware of the pain in her head where she had banged it. This was the first time she'd noticed it as things had been so hectic inside the club. She hadn't even thought to have it checked when she arrived; her mind was too preoccupied about Anna. Maybe she'd have it seen to later once she found out how Anna was.

After several more minutes the nurse reappeared. As she approached she didn't make eye contact with Adele, staring at the ground instead. When she finally drew level, her eyes met Adele's fleetingly before gazing about her as she spoke.

'She's still in surgery, I'm afraid.'

'Surgery? Why?' asked Adele.

The nurse paused before speaking slowly and deliberately, her eyes still flitting from Adele, down the corridor, then back again. 'I'm afraid there's swelling on the brain and some bleeding. We're having to operate to relieve some of the pressure.'

'W-w-w...' Adele uttered, flummoxed. 'Will that sort things out? How bad is it?'

'At the moment I'm afraid we still don't know. We're hoping we'll be able to alleviate some of the pressure but only time will tell.'

'Oh,' muttered Adele.

She was dumbfounded and couldn't think what else to say. The nurse put her hand on her shoulder then finally made eye contact as she said, 'I know it's a bit of a shock but try not to worry. We're doing everything we can. Why don't you go and get yourself something to drink, then perhaps you should get your own injury looked at?'

Adele put her hand up to the cut on her head then nodded, her eyes staring blankly ahead. Then the nurse was gone.

For a few moments Adele remained there in stunned silence. The news had shaken her badly and she was finding it difficult to take in. Her mind drifted back to only a few hours prior when Anna was sharing a joke with the customers, full of her usual enthusiasm and loving the job. And now this!

Eventually Adele went back to reception, the shock of Anna's news prompting her to get her own head injury looked at. After several hours' waiting around and a series of tests and questions from a junior doctor the conclusion was reached that Adele had mild concussion. He told her to go home and rest, and to come back if she started to suffer from certain symptoms such as loss of balance, blurred vision or vomiting.

As dawn began to break, Adele tumbled into bed, exhausted. She fell into a tearful and troubled sleep as her mind festered over whether Anna would ever fully recover from her injuries. It was as the nurse had said: only time would tell.

20

Adele awoke with a sense of dread. For a few moments she hovered in a state of semi-alertness before she came fully to, and the events of the previous day came back to her. She looked at the clock then sprang out of bed in a panic. Twenty past twelve! How had she managed to sleep that long?

Then she remembered how she hadn't got into bed until the early hours of the morning. She must have been exhausted from all the stress and angst. Adele dashed into the shower then quickly got ready. Within half an hour she was out of her flat without having eaten. She was too preoccupied to eat. She had to get to the hospital as soon as possible and check on Anna.

Once Adele reached the Manchester Royal Infirmary she quickly rushed inside to enquire after Anna. A receptionist directed her to a ward and for several minutes she wandered around the large building trying to locate it. Then she saw a sign for the ward and sped up again.

Adele walked down the corridor leading to the ward then stopped outside a room. The door was slightly ajar and she could see a few nurses inside chatting. She tapped on the door until one of them came out.

'I'm here to see Anna Tomlinson,' said Adele.

'Aah, yes. We've put her in a side ward,' said the nurse. 'It's down there on the left.'

Adele thanked the nurse then continued to make her way down the corridor, stopping to peek into the side wards. The first two patients were clearly not Anna but then Adele looked into the third side ward. It was the size of the patient that first drew her attention and made her think it might be Anna. But she looked different somehow. Curious, Adele inched open the door and crept inside to take a better look.

No! It couldn't be.

But it was. Adele stared in horror at her friend. The familiar features were there but were somehow shrunken inside a swollen head that looked almost twice its normal size. As the shock hit her she heard someone let out an anguished shriek, which pierced through the air like a siren. It was only when the nurse dashed into the room that Adele realised the sound was coming from her own mouth.

'Shush,' whispered the nurse, taking Adele by the arm. 'We mustn't disturb the patients.'

Adele allowed the nurse to lead her out of the side ward and into the visitors' waiting room.

'Take a seat,' said the nurse. 'I'll get you a cup of tea for the shock.'

But Adele just stared back at her without speaking. She was numb.

'Are you a relative?' asked the nurse.

Adele snapped to. 'N-no, but I'm a close friend and she works for me. She doesn't have any family in Manchester as far as I know.'

The nurse nodded sympathetically and left the room. For a few moments Adele sat there rigid, trying to take it all in. Despite what she had been told the previous night, seeing it for herself was completely different. It made her realise just how badly injured Anna was. And that realisation had just hit Adele like a ten-tonne truck.

When the nurse returned she had a doctor with her. He was middle-aged and looked friendly but efficient in his white overalls and squeaky clean shoes as he plonked himself down beside Adele while the nurse remained standing. The nurse held out a cup of tea, which Adele grasped with shaking hands. Then she spoke to Adele.

'I'm sorry, I should have warned you,' she said. 'It can be a bit disturbing when you see a brain-injury patient for the first time. But the swelling will go down eventually.'

'H-how bad is she?' asked Adele as she gazed intently at the nurse to gauge her reaction.

It was the doctor who responded to her question in a calm, businesslike manner. 'Hello, I'm Dr Grey,' he said, holding out his hand for Adele to shake. 'I'm afraid Anna has been very badly hurt,' he continued. 'She's currently in a coma and we're waiting to see whether she'll wake up.'

'A coma?' snapped Adele. She could feel her heart pounding. 'Oh, my God! I can't believe it's that bad.'

The nurse sat to the other side of Adele and placed her hand on top of Adele's. 'We're doing everything we can,' she said and Adele felt herself bristle at the stock response. 'Try not to be too alarmed. It can sometimes be the body's way of healing itself.'

'How long will it be till she comes round?' Adele dared to ask.

The doctor spoke again. 'We don't know. At the moment we just have to take things one day at a time.'

'What are you saying?' asked Adele, who felt as if a heavy weight had lodged in the pit of her stomach. 'Are you saying she might not pull through?'

'We just don't know at the moment but the operation was a moderate success. We managed to alleviate some of the pressure from her brain so now we just have to wait and see.' Then he paused before saying, 'I'll leave you alone for a few minutes.'

When he had finished speaking the doctor left the waiting room but the nurse remained for a short while longer. 'Take your time for things to sink in,' she said.

'I know you've had a bit of a shock. Feel free to go and visit your friend again once you're ready.' Then she patted Adele's hand one last time before leaving her alone.

Adele gulped back the cup of tea, hoping it might calm her down, but it didn't. An inner instinct drove her to go and see her friend again. She had to satisfy herself that it really was Anna inside the room. And part of her wanted to view things afresh in the hope that the sight of Anna wouldn't seem so bad the second time around.

She followed her instinct but as she stood staring at Anna, swollen and barely recognisable, she felt a tremendous sense of guilt. It seemed perverse to be standing watching Anna in that state, as though she were some sort of sick ghoul. She also felt desperately sad as she contrasted the person lying helpless in that bed with the recent vivid memory of Anna, happy and enjoying life.

Unable to stand it any longer, Adele rushed from the room on the verge of tears. There in the corridor was James with a bandage wrapped around his head. Adele almost crashed into him in her haste to get away.

'Hey, steady,' he uttered kindly, grabbing hold of her by the arms.

As Adele gazed at his familiar face she couldn't hold back her tears any longer and she collapsed, sobbing, into his arms.

'Hey, it's OK,' he said, stroking back her hair and comforting her till her tears lessened.

'A-are you here to see Anna?' she asked once she had calmed down.

'Yes. I've just been given the all clear to go home but I heard Anna had been taken in and I thought I'd nip in to see her before I go home. I've already checked on Billy,' he said, referring to a member of his staff who had also been taken to hospital. 'He's quite badly beaten and cut. I think he should heal OK physically, apart from the scarring to his arms, but the mental effects might take a while longer.'

'It's good of you to drop by and see her,' said Adele. 'Why don't we go into the waiting room and chat for a short while?'

She wanted to prepare him before he went in to see Anna. 'What about yourself?' she asked as they walked into the waiting room and each took a seat.

'I'm fine,' he said. 'They kept me in for observation overnight but I'm OK. What about you?'

'Slight concussion but I'll be OK... Anna's in a bad way, I'm afraid, so I wanted to warn you before you go in to see her. Her head's very swollen... it doesn't look like her at all,' she said, choking back another sob.

'Oh, I'm sorry to hear that. How bad?'

'She's in a coma,' said Adele, her voice shaking. 'We've just got to wait and see if she comes out of it.'

'Oh, I am sorry,' said James.

'Has anyone else been to see her?' asked Adele.

'Not as far as I know.'

Adele felt a stab of irritation as she thought about Glynn and Mike with hardly a scratch on them. The least they could have done would be to come and visit the injured staff in hospital.

For a few moments she sat silently with her troubled thoughts, almost forgetting James was there. Then she felt him touch her lightly on the shoulder. 'You've been through a lot yourself, you know,' he said. 'And, if you don't mind me saying so, you're looking a little peaky. Why don't you go home and get some rest?'

'Thanks, James. I will,' she said. 'I'll nip in to see Billy on the way out.'

'All right,' James replied. 'I'll pop in to see Anna then I must dash. My wife's downstairs getting the car ready. She can't wait to get me home and smother me with fuss and attention.'

Adele managed a weak smile. She knew that James would probably relish all the attention from his wife. He'd spoken fondly about her so many times that Adele recognised the affection in his offhand comment. She wondered fleetingly whether she'd be like James and his wife in another twenty years' time; happily settled with someone she could rely on in times of trouble.

She left James on his way to visit Anna. Then she made her way out of the ward and headed to see Billy before leaving the hospital. On the journey home she thought about what a nice thoughtful man James was, almost too nice to be in the job he was in. Then she thought about the sharp difference between him and Glynn, and she became annoyed once more.

It was because of people like Glynn that Anna was in that state. Him and his stupid battle for control of Manchester's nightclubs! Was it worth it? But she knew that people like Glynn wouldn't stop till they got what they wanted.

As she thought about Glynn, Mike, Alan, David and all the countless others like them, who traded in violence and other people's misfortune, she doubted whether there would be any end to the trouble. In fact, if none of them would back down then she worried that things were bound to get even worse.

21

When Adele arrived home, she was feeling tired and emotional. It was hard to believe that her friend was lying in a hospital bed barely alive when she had been so animated just the day before. The doctor's words kept spinning around in Adele's brain, like a record on repeat. *The operation was a moderate success... We're waiting to see whether she'll wake up... We just have to take things one day at a time.*

She tried to shake the thoughts from her head but it was difficult. They were all-consuming. Eventually, when her mind had overplayed the same heart-rending lines, it drifted to thoughts of Anna's family. Adele wasn't sure if Anna had any family; it was something she had never mentioned during their time inside. Adele hoped that the police would be able to find out, because if Anna did have family then surely they would want to know what had happened to her.

It seemed sad that only Adele and James had bothered visiting Anna up to now. Again Adele thought of Glynn and was angry at his apparent lack of interest. While she was thinking of Glynn she decided to give him a call and let him know that she wouldn't be going in to work that evening. After her upset of these past two days, the Golden Bell was the last place she wanted to be. All the rushing around and emotional trauma on top of having an injury was finally taking its toll and Adele knew she needed to rest.

Glynn answered her call after only two rings. Adele felt her heart flutter at the sound of his voice and she despised herself for it. For her Glynn still sparked a powerful roller coaster of emotions.

'I'm just ringing to let you know I won't be in today,' said Adele.

'Are you OK?' he asked.

'Yeah, I'm all right. I've got slight concussion, that's all.'

'Shit! You need to take it easy, then. Have a few days off if you like. Don't worry about things here; I'll take care of them. Do you want me to pass any instructions on to the staff? What about Margaret? Does she know what needs doing?'

I bet you'll take care of things, thought Adele sardonically. She was also irritated by the fact that he assumed she wouldn't be in by Monday when her assistant, Margaret, was due back at work. But she didn't voice her thoughts. Instead she said, 'Yes, don't worry about Margaret. She knows what needs to be done. I'll probably be back in the office by then anyway. Paula will be fine with running the bar too. You'll need to make sure there are enough men on the doors though. Some of James's staff won't be fit for work.'

'Oh, yeah. How were things at the hospital? Did you see any of the staff?'

'I thought you'd never ask,' she said sarcastically before giving him a rundown of her hospital visit.

'Bad news about Anna,' he said, but his voice lacked emotion. Then she heard him sniff before adding, 'Anyway, take care. Like I say, don't rush back. I'll sort things out here.'

He soon put the phone down and Adele felt as though he couldn't get her off the line quickly enough. He was obviously pleased to have the run of the Golden Bell. Despite feeling shattered and overwrought, she vowed to herself that she would return to work as soon as possible. She didn't want to give Glynn the chance to think he was in charge.

Adele returned to the hospital the following day to visit Anna. She didn't relish the thought of seeing her in that state again but she cared about her and wanted to see how she was. Maybe she had come out of the coma by now, Adele hoped.

When Adele headed up the corridor towards the side ward where Anna was she was surprised to hear the sound of voices coming from the room. She pushed open the door tentatively, wary of intruding on Anna's visitors. Straight away the room fell silent and two pairs of eyes shot towards Adele, making her feel very self-conscious. They were a middle-aged couple, smartly dressed and with a sophisticated air about them.

'Hello, I'm Adele,' she said, walking towards the man, who stepped forward and formally held out his hand.

While the man briskly shook Adele's hand, the woman stared down her nose at her.

'We're Anna's parents,' said the man. 'I presume you're a friend of Anna's, are you?' he asked. His voice was cultured, its tone haughty.

'I… yes. She works for me too,' said Adele.

Neither of the couple spoke but the man raised his eyebrows inquisitively.

'She tends the doors in the nightclub I manage,' said Adele in response to his unspoken question.

'Good Lord!' said the woman. 'I thought Anna had come by her injuries while out at a nightclub. That would have been bad enough. I can't abide the damn places, full of drunken debauchery if you ask me. But I didn't think for one minute that she'd be working in one!'

Her manner was snooty, her words combative, and Adele was tempted to retaliate. But it wasn't the right time or place for an argument.

'She enjoyed her work,' said Adele. 'And she was very good at her job too.' Adele's voice shook as she spoke and the couple stared boldly at her, waiting to hear what else she had to say for herself, but she couldn't continue. 'I'm sorry,' she said. 'I'll go and sit in the waiting room, give you some time alone with your daughter.'

'That won't be necessary,' said the man. 'We were just about to go anyway, weren't we, Noreen?'

'Yes, we've got a long journey to make,' said the woman. Then she fumbled inside her handbag and withdrew a piece of paper and a pen. 'Perhaps you would be good enough to let us know if she comes out of the coma,' she said, scribbling down her phone number. 'Then we can make appropriate arrangements for her care.'

Adele was shocked by the woman's impassivity. Her daughter lay tragically injured and in a coma, and she was acting as though she were carrying out a business transaction.

'Yes, I will do,' said Adele as she took the paper from Anna's mother, avoiding eye contact with her and placing it inside her own handbag. She wondered why they weren't leaving their phone number with the nursing staff, but perhaps that would have meant having to explain why they wouldn't be visiting Anna in the interim.

Within no time the couple had made their way to the door. The man swung around just as he was pulling the door open. 'Do let her know that we came to see her, won't you?' he asked and Adele thought she detected a slight hint of warmth in his voice.

'Yes,' said Adele. 'I'll let her know.'

She didn't say anything more as she watched the couple walk through the door. It didn't seem appropriate under the circumstances to tell them she was pleased to have met them or to make a similarly banal comment.

Apart from Anna's condition, meeting her parents had been anything but a pleasure. It was obvious to Adele that the couple had a strained relationship with Anna and were visiting her out of a sense of duty rather than for any other reason.

Anna's parents were entirely different from what Adele would have expected. Where Anna had a guttural Mancunian accent, their accents were far more formal. By the way they dressed and conducted themselves, Adele guessed that they were well-to-do, and she had no doubt that Anna wouldn't have fitted in with their social circles.

As Adele thought about the frosty encounter, she wondered at what point in the past Anna's parents had turned their backs on her: when she became a convicted criminal or when they discovered she was gay.

Trying not to think about Anna's unfriendly parents, Adele slowly made her way towards the bed where her injured friend lay. Just like yesterday, Anna lay there silently, her facial features dwarfed by her engorged, damaged head, and Adele recoiled once more. She looked on for a few minutes, switching her eyes from Anna to the machines that monitored her then back again.

After a short while she had to walk away. The situation was too much for her to handle. She had a quick word with the nursing staff only to find out there had been no change. Then, with a feeling of deep sadness, she made her way out of the hospital, desperately praying that her friend's acute condition would soon get better.

22

It was Sunday evening. As a crowd of bored youths hung about outside the Grey Mare, a couple of miles from the city centre, a BMW screeched to a halt a few yards away. Inside the car sat Glynn and Mike, hidden behind tinted windows, with Glynn at the wheel and Mike in the front passenger seat. The tinted windows had been a good investment; his flash motor was already attracting a lot of interest from the estate kids and he didn't want to feel like a goldfish in a bowl.

Mike looked out of the window. 'Fuckin' shit heap,' he muttered.

Glynn leant across Mike and looked through the passenger window at the Grey Mare. Like a lot of estate pubs, it was a soulless place, built in the seventies from drab beige bricks, which were showing decline through the cracks and the mouldy patches that clung to them.

The only sign of character lay in the bold graffiti that daubed the pub walls.

Outside was a patch of untended, weed-strewn grass with a well-used dirt path dissecting it en route to the pub. The edges of the green were also worn where the gangs of youths surrounding the pub doorway spilt onto the grass, treading it down till it was no more than compacted soil.

Glynn did a quick check of the youths that were there. 'He's not with that lot,' he commented. 'Must be inside. We'll wait.'

While they waited Glynn continued to gaze out of the car window. Mike was right: it was a shit heap. The infamous Fort Ardwick had now been demolished but there was still an estate, which had been built in the seventies. The houses already resembled slums, their bricks chipped and discoloured and a few of their windows boarded up. Many of the gardens were overgrown and filled with an assortment of unwanted items from broken bikes to dilapidated sofas.

Wild dogs, abandoned by their neglectful owners, roamed the streets depositing their faeces on the jaded pavements. Meanwhile, unwitting children played amongst the apathy and rubble.

It reminded Glynn of the area where he'd grown up. Not for the first time, he was glad he'd found a way to escape from that life. And he earnt plenty now, which would ensure that he never returned, even if he did have to resort to illegal means to earn his cash. Honest work had never been an option for him; not when there were much easier ways to make big money.

The sound of Mike's voice interrupted his thoughts. 'You sure he's in there?' he asked.

'That's what I was told,' said Glynn. 'We'll give it a bit longer, see if he comes out.'

'Why don't we just go in and haul the little shit out of there?'

'Because, Mike, the less that people know about this, the better,' said Glynn, impatiently.

After a few more minutes, they were rewarded by the sight of Todd emerging from the pub doorway. 'Here he is now,' said Glynn, an amused grin lighting up his face as he watched Todd swagger confidently from the pub, exchanging banter and high fives with the youths who were hanging about. It was obvious that he was well respected by the younger kids in the area.

Glynn continued watching as Todd walked away from the pub and disappeared down an alleyway. 'Right, I'll go round to the other side of that alleyway then you can go after him on foot,' said Glynn. 'But don't let any bastard see you!'

He started the engine and they raced around to the avenue where Todd was heading. Glynn spotted him ahead of them and quickly drew level before slamming on the brakes.

'Grab him quick while there's no one around!' he ordered Mike. 'I'll keep the engine running.'

Within no time Mike had jumped from the car then thrust Todd onto the back seat before jumping back into the front passenger seat. Glynn locked the doors as soon as Todd was inside.

'What the fuck? Let me out!' yelled Todd, the cockiness still evident in his demeanour and his aggressive tone.

But Glynn ignored Todd's shouts as he put the car back into gear and shot off down the road. Mike turned around and leant over to Todd. Then he thrust his hand at Todd's throat, pinning him to the back seat.

'You'll shut the fuck up if you know what's good for you!' he warned.

As Todd stared back in terror, Mike tightened his grip. Just as Todd's eyes began to bulge in his head and his lips turned blue, Mike released his hand.

'Right, now are you gonna shut your fuckin' squealing or do I have to go even fuckin' harder on you?' Mike threatened.

'OK!' Todd snapped. His bottom lip then jutted out and his shoulders slumped, forming the image of a sulky teenager. 'What's all this about anyway?' he asked, taking care to keep his voice low.

'You'll find out soon enough,' said Mike, who then turned back around before repeating his warning, 'Now keep your fuckin' trap shut!'

During the journey Glynn kept catching glimpses of Todd in his rear-view mirror. He could see his body language and facial expression transition from aggrieved teenager to terrified child. Todd was obviously beginning to realise that he was in deep shit.

Glynn pulled up outside an abandoned warehouse in Ancoats, on the fringes of the city centre. The place was familiar to him and Mike; they had made use of it before. With no other property within sight or hearing distance it was the perfect place in which to exact revenge on the enemy. And nobody but them would be able to hear the boy's screams.

By the time they pulled him out of the car and headed towards the warehouse, Todd's cockiness had disappeared and he looked terrified. As Mike dragged him across the beaten tarmac that led to the entrance, Todd squealed pitifully.

Mike clamped his hand over Todd's mouth. In his haste to escape, Todd bit down hard into the palm of Mike's hand then continued screaming and trying to wriggle free from Mike's clutches.

'You little bastard! You'll fuckin' pay for that,' yelled Mike, swiping Todd's face with the back of his hand before clamping his hands around the boy's throat once more. Glynn rushed forward to help Mike push him inside the warehouse.

The rope was already waiting for them, on the floor next to a tarnished metal pillar. They quickly strapped

Todd to the pillar then stood back, laughing while he screamed and cursed at them. When Mike took out the meat cleaver, Todd's screams became more shrill and urgent, and his pupils dilated as the terror consumed him. He struggled against the rope, trying desperately to break free. But it was no use.

Glynn felt a moment's pity for someone so young to have to go through this. But he quickly shrugged it off. If their sole intention had been to frighten the boy then they could have left it at that. But they didn't just want to frighten him; they wanted to send a message loud and clear to Alan's gang that they weren't going to be fucked with. And the best way to send that message would be visually.

'Right, you little shit!' said Glynn. 'I believe you're working for Alan's mob now.'

'No, no. I'm not in his gang!' pleaded the boy. 'I just do little jobs for him now and again, that's all.'

'Yeah, little jobs like tear-arsing through the Golden Bell with your shitty little mates and wrecking the fuckin' place!' yelled Glynn.

Todd visibly flinched and an expression of guilt was soon replaced by one of fear. 'I didn't mean any harm,' said Todd, an obsequious edge to his voice. 'Alan paid me to do it. I needed the money for me mam.'

'Well, I think it's about time we sent a fuckin' message back to Alan,' said Glynn.

Then he gave Mike the nod, and Mike moved towards the boy with the meat cleaver held tight. As Mike hacked away at the boy's fingers, Todd's agonised screams filled the air. Glynn looked on dispassionately. His only concern was in making sure they did enough damage to make Alan back off from their territory.

When Mike had finished they wrapped Todd's bleeding hand in a filthy rag. Glynn didn't want to risk any of the blood spilling inside his car.

Then they drove Todd into the city centre and dropped him outside the Sportsman's, Glynn's message ringing inside his head as the acute pain from his fingers threatened to overwhelm him:

This is what happens to people who fuck with us.

Alan was holding court in his regular corner of a side room inside the Sportsman's. Their raid on the Golden Bell had been cause for a weekend of celebration. He felt confident that it was only a matter of time before Adele gave in to their demands to run the doors.

As he leant towards David to listen to one of his witty remarks, he became aware of a nervous muttering around his group of men. He looked up to see Todd stumbling into the room, clutching a blood-soaked rag, which had been tied around one of his hands.

'What the fuck?' he exclaimed as Todd approached his table.

The boy was sobbing uncontrollably, all thoughts of bravado now lost as the aftershock of his recent trauma combined with the torturous pain left him distraught.

'Get him a fuckin' chair!' Alan yelled, getting up and walking towards Todd. 'Who the fuck did this to you?' he demanded, but the boy struggled to get his words out as he sobbed hysterically, his body shuddering with uncontrolled spasms.

Alan gave him a sharp slap to his face and for a few moments the boy stared at him, stunned, his sobs now replaced by a continuous whimper.

'Was it that fuckin' Glynn's lot?' Alan continued.

The boy nodded solemnly.

'Who was with him?' asked Alan, but the boy remained whimpering, his speech lost to the trauma. 'Was it that twat, Mike Shaftesbury?' Alan asked and the boy nodded again.

'Fuckin' pair of cunts!' Alan cursed, pacing around the room.

As he tried to register the enormity of what had happened, he heard his men echoing his own thoughts, the angry din growing progressively louder. He paced for several minutes, intermittently barking out orders. 'Get him a brandy to calm him down!' 'Take that shitty fuckin' rag off his hand and get something clean to wrap it in!'

The thoughts rushed around his head. Bastards! How could they do that to a kid? He needed to get the boy help. But he couldn't risk having the police sticking their noses in. As he paced around his attention was drawn to one of his men who was shouting his name.

'Alan. We need to get his fuckin' hand seen to,' said Jacko, one of the older gang members who often managed to stay calm when everyone else was in a panic. 'I know someone who's a medic. I can trust him to keep schtum.'

'You sure?' asked Alan.

'Yeah, sure,' said Jacko. 'He knows what would fuckin' happen if he blabbed.'

'OK, take him,' said Alan, glad to get rid of the distressed boy.

Once the boy had gone Alan eventually felt calm enough to address his men. 'Right, lads, you know what this means, don't you? We ain't gonna fuckin' take this lying down!'

A roar of assent came from the rest of his men. 'What you gonna do?' asked David.

Alan sighed. 'Not sure yet but let's just bide our time. I don't wanna act in anger and get it wrong. Let me sleep on it then we'll meet here tomorrow night and we can plan things. I wanna make sure the bastards are punished for this. Doing that to a kid is fuckin' sick. But don't worry; they won't fuckin' get away with it!'

23

It was Monday morning and Adele had just walked into her office at the Golden Bell. As she took her seat behind the desk she tried to ignore the persistent headache that she'd had since the incident in the club the previous Friday. She was also feeling tired and upset about her friend, Anna. But, despite all this, she had come back to work. She couldn't afford to let Glynn think he was in control now.

Adele had sneaked past Margaret's office as she wanted to have a few moments to herself before discussing business. She sat sipping coffee, hoping it would help her shake off the tiredness that had dogged her since Friday.

When Adele heard footsteps in the corridor, she had a sinking feeling. She didn't feel up to dealing with anyone over work matters yet, and she regretted coming in. Maybe she should have stayed at home and rested, as the doctor had suggested. Adele looked up to see Glynn walk through the doorway, and that sinking feeling grew stronger.

'Morning, didn't expect to see you back so soon,' he said. 'How are you?'

'Fine,' she responded perfunctorily.

Without waiting for an invitation he pulled out the seat facing her. 'You didn't need to return so soon, y'know. You must be feeling like shit if you're suffering from concussion,' he said.

Adele forced a tight smile. 'I told you, I'm fine.'

'OK, well, now you're here, I'm glad in a way because we need to talk.'

This was just what Adele didn't need right now but she couldn't think of a good enough excuse to put off their inevitable discussion. 'What about?' she asked even though she already had a good idea what it was.

'We need to get my men back on the doors,' he said. 'As soon as possible.'

Adele shook her head, then wished she hadn't as the dull ache intensified, reminding her that it wasn't going away. She winced as she said, 'No, Glynn, that's not going to happen.'

'Are you for real?' he asked. 'Merton's guys fucked up big time and you know it. We need blokes who can handle themselves.'

'What, like you and Mike, do you mean? I don't think so.'

'Look, Adele. You can pretend to play things by the book as much as you want but it doesn't fuckin' cut it in the real world. Do you think Alan's gang play things by the book?'

'Just because they carry on like that doesn't mean we have to,' she said. 'There are other ways of handling this situation.'

'Go on, then, enlighten me,' he responded, sarcastically.

As the throbbing in her head refused to subside, she wished he would just go away and leave her alone. Despite her rising temper, she tried to hold herself in check, knowing that the stress would only make her feel worse.

'Well, I'll need to speak to the police,' she said. 'See if they can keep a closer eye on the club. We'll also make sure there are more men on the front doors so the gangs can't break in so easily.' But even as she spoke she knew her proposals sounded feeble.

'Don't make me fuckin' laugh!' he barked. 'It doesn't matter how many of Merton's men you put on the doors. They can't fuckin' cut it, and that's that.'

For a few moments she stared at him across the desk, willing him to go away and leave her alone. But Glynn was determined to have his say. Homing in on her vulnerability after all that had happened, he tried another tack.

'Do you think Anna would have been injured like that if Merton's men had had the balls to protect her? I told you the door was no place for a woman but you wouldn't fuckin' listen!'

'Don't you dare!' she snapped and she could feel her eyes cloud with tears as sorrow and guilt over her friend gnawed away at her.

For a few moments Adele remained silent, trying to fight back her tears and frightened that her trembling voice would expose how she was feeling. But Glynn had spotted it. Within no time he had walked around the desk and flung his arms around her shoulders, cradling her head in his big hands.

'It's OK,' he said. 'We can sort it. We won't let them get away with this, don't you worry. We'll fuckin' have 'em!'

His words felt as if he had just taken a claw hammer to her pounding head. She couldn't believe his insensitivity! Her friend was lying in a coma and all he could think about was retaliation. In a fit of temper she pulled her head away, raised her hands to his chest and shoved hard till he stumbled backwards.

'Get out!' she yelled. 'Have you got no fuckin' understanding? Do you honestly think that revenge will help Anna? You're nothing but a fuckin' thug!'

'Hey, hang on a minute,' he said, stepping back towards her.

Adele yelled at him at the top of her voice, her mouth opened wide and the tendons on her neck stretched to their limit as her head jutted forward in a fit of rage. 'I said get out!'

Before Glynn could say anything further, Margaret rushed through the door.

'What on earth's the matter?' she asked.

'Get him out of my sight!' yelled Adele.

In her usual no-nonsense manner Margaret rushed around to Adele's side of the desk and took hold of Glynn by the hand. 'Come on,' she said. 'This isn't good for her. She's been through enough.'

Adele marvelled at how soon Margaret had heard about the weekend's events, especially since the bar staff weren't in on a Monday morning. Maybe somebody had phoned her over the weekend. Margaret's calm, authoritative approach must have plucked at Glynn's conscience because he drew back and edged past her till he stood at the other side of the desk.

'I'll come back when you're feeling better,' he said to Adele. 'We need to talk about this whether you like it or not.'

'Can you go now, please?' said Margaret, raising her voice and staring at Glynn till he left the office.

Then she turned to Adele. 'Dearie me, this can't be doing you any good at all. What on earth are you doing in work? I didn't realise you were here. You should be at home resting.'

Margaret had a certain way about her that made you forget who was boss. As she took matters firmly in hand, in her usual confident manner, Adele found herself responding.

'I wanted to make sure everything was all right,' she said, although she didn't let Margaret know the real reason she was there: to keep an eye on Glynn.

'Yes, everything's absolutely fine,' said Margaret. 'Now calm yourself down and then get yourself home. You need to rest with concussion, not be arguing with the likes of him.'

Adele noticed the derogatory way Margaret referred to Glynn, and she guessed that Margaret was wise enough to have him figured out.

'It's OK. Leave me for a few minutes. I'll be all right,' said Adele.

'All right but don't forget, I have everything under control so there's no need for you to worry. And if I have any questions I can always give you a quick call.'

'Thanks, Margaret,' said Adele as Margaret turned to leave her office.

She was thankful that Margaret hadn't probed her about Anna as she couldn't handle that at the moment. Maybe the staff had already told her the facts or maybe Margaret was perceptive enough to know when to keep schtum. But Adele was curious.

'Margaret,' she called just as she was on her way out of the door. Margaret stopped and turned around. 'Who told you what had happened?' asked Adele.

'Glynn,' said Margaret. 'Who else?' Then she left Adele's office.

Damn him! thought Adele. He was already acting as though he were running things. He'd probably told Margaret to get her onside in the hope that she'd pressure Adele to take some time off.

As soon as Margaret was gone Adele noticed that the throbbing inside her head had become much worse. And she felt so tired. Maybe Margaret was right. She should go home and come back when she was feeling a bit better and more rested. Even though she wanted to stay she knew that she could trust Margaret to take care of the admin and accounts while she was away.

Eventually Adele left for home, stopping to have a few quick words with Margaret before she left things under her control. As she left the building she hoped that she was doing the right thing by taking some time off. But although Margaret could be trusted with the accounts, elsewhere in the business things were anything but under control.

Adele was completely unaware that Glynn and Mike had already taken the first steps in exacting revenge on Alan and his gang. And now that Alan knew about the callous way in which they had punished Todd, he was just waiting for his chance to hit back.

24

It was the following weekend. Despite the events of the previous week the club was back in operation, the need for profits overriding any other concerns. But Adele wasn't there; she was still at home finally heeding her doctor's advice to rest. She had reluctantly left Glynn in charge of the club but also had James keeping an eye on things now that he was making a good recovery from his cuts and bruises.

Since her row with Glynn she had resisted his advice to put his men back on the doors and he and Mike were currently watching the doormen from the other side of the foyer.

'Fuckin' tossers!' cursed Mike. 'Isn't it about time you got rid of that lot? I can't believe you're letting a fuckin' woman make all the decisions.'

'No fuckin' choice, mate. Pete left her in charge. Remember?'

'Yeah, well. It was a fuckin' stupid idea if you ask me. As if it's not bad enough that Alan's men walked all over us, our fuckin' profits are down as well. Have you seen any of our lads in tonight?'

'Not as many as usual, I must admit,' said Glynn.

They were referring to the drug dealers they allowed into the club and the profits they took from them. Since James Merton's men had been on the doors there had been a reduction in the number of dealers operating inside, although one or two still managed to get through the security checks.

'Anyway,' said Glynn, 'I've not fuckin' given up hope yet. I spoke to Pete today. He was fuckin' clueless about what happened last Friday.'

'You're joking! I can't believe she hasn't told him,' said Mike.

'Yeah, well, she's frightened he'll find out that she can't fuckin' cut it,' Glynn replied. 'But don't worry, I've put him straight. And he agrees with me. He wants our men back on the doors. So, we've just got to sit tight now till he puts big sister in her place, then we can let in as many fuckin' dealers as we want.'

Glynn looked across at Mike. Noticing the smug grin that lit up Mike's face, Glynn smiled back. Then they carried on watching the front doors.

*

Peter was ready for Adele when she walked into the visitors' room of Strangeways prison a few days later.

'You all right?' he asked after she had sat down.

'Yeah,' she said. 'Considering everything that's happened.'

'Go on,' he said.

He noticed how she took a deep breath before speaking. 'We had a bit of trouble at the club the Friday before last. We think it was Alan's gang. I got pushed into the barriers and got concussion. Anna was injured as well. She's in a really bad way, Peter.'

Peter watched his sister's body language as she told him her version of events, and heard the way her voice dropped when she mentioned Anna. It was obvious from her screwed-up facial features and scrunched-up shoulders that she was finding things difficult.

'Yeah, I know,' he said. 'Glynn's already told me. I'm sorry about Anna.' Then he paused briefly before asking, 'Why didn't you tell me before now, Adele? And why didn't you put Glynn's men back on the doors like I told you to?'

'I've been suffering from concussion, I told you. And you know why I don't want Glynn's men on the doors.'

But Peter wasn't satisfied with her response. 'Why do I have to rely on Glynn to tell me what's been going on, Adele? This isn't the first time you've kept me in the dark. I put you in charge because I thought I could rely on you.'

'You *can* rely on me!' she snapped, sticking her chin forward and her shoulders back. 'It's typical of Glynn to take advantage while I'm recovering. I bet he couldn't wait to get on the phone to you, could he? I suppose he's been telling you that I can't cope with running the club, hasn't he?'

'Why? Can't you?'

'Are you fuckin' serious, Peter? You don't honestly believe him, do you? Nobody would have been able to stop the club from being attacked. They had weapons.'

'You've got to treat them the same way, Adele. I fuckin' knew they'd be armed if it was Alan's mob. Why do you think I wanted Glynn's men back on the doors?'

He watched her face contort as she tried to think of something to back up her point but he didn't give her the chance to reply before he stepped up his argument. 'I want Glynn's men back on the doors, Adele. We need to be ready for Alan's lot when they come back. And they will come back. They won't give up till they get what they want, and you know what that is, don't you? They're after controlling the doors at the Golden Bell. Do you really fuckin' think I'm gonna let that happen?'

'No, Peter! You left me in charge and I'm not having Glynn's men on the doors. I've already told you about them letting drug dealers in. They can't be trusted.'

'We've got no fuckin' choice, Adele! You can't stick bouncers on the doors that can't defend themselves.

What the hell was a woman doing on the doors anyway? Don't you realise how fuckin' dangerous it is?'

'Of course I realise. But I didn't think they'd be armed, did I?'

Peter realised the discussion was starting to draw interest from neighbouring tables. He didn't want the guards to overhear them so he kept quiet for a moment while the heat died down. When he spoke his voice was much calmer, but his question was nonetheless pointed.

'Are you sure you're up to all this, Adele? You can always go back to running the office, y'know.'

'Yeah, course I am,' she said. 'I don't need to be in the office all the time. Margaret can handle the office work.'

Again they sat in silence, unable to agree. The mood between them had become awkward and it wasn't long before Adele made her excuses and left before visiting time had finished.

As they said their goodbyes Peter made one last attempt to convince her. 'Don't forget what I said, Adele. It's dangerous on the doors. I still think you should get Glynn's men back.'

'I've got to rush,' she said before dashing away.

When she had gone Peter hammered his fist on the table, his frustration finally getting to him. This attracted the attention of a prison guard, who rushed over to the table. 'Robinson, get back to your cell!' he yelled.

Peter kicked out his chair and traipsed back to his cell with his shoulders slumped. He felt angry and frustrated at his lack of control. It was impossible to run things properly from behind the prison walls. And he was having serious doubts about whether Adele could handle it all.

Adele hadn't said anything to put his mind at ease either. Her argument for keeping Glynn's men off the doors was weak and he thought it was more about getting at Glynn than doing what was right for the business. It annoyed him that she wouldn't do what he was telling her even though the Golden Bell was still his business.

It wasn't as if he could fully trust Glynn either. He knew that; he wasn't stupid. But he wasn't going to tell Adele that he had doubts about him. It would only strengthen her argument against Glynn, and Peter needed him.

Glynn was a good guy to have on your side when things went down. Apart from being a sharp operator, Glynn wasn't frightened of doing whatever was needed to scare the enemy off. In this line of work you had to have men with balls, and Glynn was one of the hardest in Manchester.

Peter had thought he was doing the right thing by leaving Adele in charge of the businesses but now he wasn't so sure. If she carried on being so intractable he wouldn't have any businesses left by the time he was released. And he would have no choice but to fester in prison while everything turned to shit.

25

It was nearly two weeks since Anna had been admitted to hospital and over a week since Adele had been to see her. She felt terrible for neglecting her friend, but the truth was she found it heartbreaking to see her in that condition. So she'd avoided visiting, telling herself that she needed time to recuperate from her own injuries and that Anna wouldn't know whether she was there or not.

But the nurses knew. Adele recognised the nurse that walked into the side ward and began bustling around Anna's bed. It was the same nurse that had been there the first time Adele saw Anna after the accident. She was short, slightly rounded and middle-aged with a sensible haircut and a practical approach.

'Hi, I'm Val. There hasn't been much change, I'm afraid,' she said, 'although the swelling has gone down a little.'

Adele gazed more intently at her friend. Since the swelling had reduced, Anna was now more recognisable but she still didn't look like the Anna Adele knew. She lay there motionless in her unflattering hospital gown, her hair in a mess and wires protruding from her mouth and arms. The sound of machinery filled the side ward, drawing Adele's attention to the omnipresent monitor with its brightly coloured lines zigzagging across the screen.

'I think you're the first visitor in a week,' said the nurse, matter-of-factly.

'Have her parents not been?' asked Adele.

'No, but I believe they had to travel a long way to come and see her.'

Adele nodded but said nothing.

'I know it's not easy when they're in this condition,' the nurse continued. 'But it sometimes helps to talk to them.'

Adele stared at the nurse, bemused till she elucidated. 'Sometimes they can hear and it can be good for them to hear a familiar voice or perhaps a favourite piece of music. Do you know what type of music she likes?'

A smile graced Adele's lips as she thought about Anna's obsession with Chrissie Hynde when they were inside. 'The Pretenders,' she said. 'Anna likes The Pretenders. I'll bring some in for her.'

Once the nurse had gone Adele took up her suggestion and tried to talk to Anna. But she felt self-conscious and didn't know what to say. So she talked about their time inside. It wasn't an easy topic of conversation; after all, Anna hadn't had it easy in prison. And as she racked her brains for something else to talk about Adele realised that she didn't really know Anna at all.

Suddenly she felt an overwhelming sense of sadness. Poor Anna, to be reduced to this state with not even a single visitor in a week. The feeling of sadness transitioned into guilt as it always did with Adele. If only she hadn't given Anna the job at the Golden Bell then this wouldn't have happened. If only she'd pulled her off the doors earlier and let her work inside the club along with the other female bouncer, Lynn.

If only.

It wasn't the first time she'd blamed herself for things she should have done differently. She had carried a feeling of guilt all her life. It started when she was a child and had to suffer the criticisms and scornful looks of the local gossips because she had the misfortune of belonging to *that* family. Then her guilt complex intensified into later life when she beat her father to death in a violent rage.

The anger had been with Adele most of her life too. Anger at her father's maltreatment of her and her brother and his abuse of their mother. It had festered within her and grown throughout the ensuing years.

Eventually Adele couldn't bear to look at Anna in that sorry state any longer and she bid goodbye to her unhearing friend, vowing to herself that she would return soon. All the way home she was downcast, her brother's words replaying in her mind. *What the hell was a woman doing on the doors?*

Peter was right; she shouldn't have put women on the doors. And, as loath as she was to admit it, even to herself, Glynn had probably been right too. She should never have changed the doormen, then perhaps none of this would have happened.

As soon as she arrived home, crestfallen, Adele made straight for the phone. She dialled Glynn's number and braced herself as his familiar voice sounded on the other end of the line.

'OK, have it your way,' she said. 'But I hope you're right. Put your men back on the doors.'

'What?' asked Glynn.

'You heard. Put your men back on the doors.'

She could hear the surprised tone in his voice as he asked, 'What? The Golden Bell, do you mean?'

She sighed. 'Yes, that's right. The Golden Bell.'

'OK. What's prompted this? You were dead against it before.'

But Adele didn't want to discuss it any further with him. 'Just do it!' she said before terminating the call.

She hoped to God that she had done the right thing. A brief recollection flashed through her mind but she tried to quash it. The memory was of how roughly Glynn's men had handled the customers. To have to give in to their bullying ways didn't sit well with her at all. But she didn't feel as though she had a choice.

As Peter had said, they had to treat Alan's men the same way they had treated them. She just hoped she was doing the right thing and that by standing up to Alan's men she could finally see an end to this senseless war for control of the nightclub doors.

26

The following week Adele went to visit her mother, Shirley. She was still feeling downcast and, had she thought about it beforehand, she would have realised that a visit to her mother was more likely to make her feel worse rather than cheer her up. Adele hadn't visited her for such a long time and was driven by a sense of duty.

There was also a part of her that was seeking comfort. She felt overburdened by her troubles and was desperate to confide in somebody close. As she'd lost most of her old friends after serving time in prison, that left only her mother. But she was a poor choice. How Adele wished her grandma were still alive. She had been the true mother figure in Adele's life and would have offered her comfort and reassurance at a time when she desperately needed it.

Adele's mother had always been weak-willed and, although she had improved in recent years, she would never be the strong support that Adele would have liked. Shirley still had difficulties dealing with the routine of day-to-day life and was so wrapped up in her own little world that she was often insensitive to other people's troubles. But she was the only mother Adele had.

'Yer not looking too bright, love,' Shirley commented routinely as Adele stepped into the hall. Then Shirley walked through to the kitchen and busied herself making some drinks without waiting for Adele's response.

Adele waited patiently until her mother had switched the kettle on and pulled two cups out of a kitchen cupboard before spooning coffee into them. 'Come on, let's go and sit down while we're waiting for the kettle to boil,' she said to her mother, leading the way out of the kitchen and into the living room.

Her mother began rambling as soon as they sat down. 'Well, it's nice to see you, love. I've had a right bloody couple of weeks, I can tell yer. One of the cats has gone missing. It's been over a week now and he's still not home. My arthritis is playing up as well. Then, to top it all, the handle broke on the big shopping bag yesterday and all my bloody food spilt out into the road. Talk about being embarrassed. I was—'

'Mam!' Adele interrupted.

'What?' asked Shirley, appearing put out that her monologue had been interrupted.

'I just… nothing.'

'Is summat the matter?' asked Shirley, making eye contact with Adele for the first time since she had arrived.

'Yes,' said Adele. 'My friend, Anna, has been badly injured. She's in a coma.'

'Oh. I'm sorry to hear that, love. Who's Anna anyway? I've never heard you mention her before.'

'I met her inside,' Adele said reluctantly.

As soon as she mentioned her time inside, Adele could sense a shift in her mother's manner and for Adele it brought to mind the reason she hadn't mentioned Anna to her before. Because it was a reminder of Adele's time in prison and, more to the point, why she had been in prison.

Despite everything Adele had done for her mother throughout the years, and particularly since her release from prison, the fact that she had killed her father would always stand between them. Not for the first time, Adele marvelled at her mother's sense of misguided loyalty towards her abusive husband.

'How did it happen?' asked Shirley, quickly diverting their attention from Adele's mention of her time inside.

'There was a bit of trouble at the club,' said Adele. 'It was attacked by a gang of troublemakers and, unfortunately, Anna got caught up in it.'

Adele didn't give her mother any other details, knowing that she would be unable to cope with the full enormity of Adele's troubles.

'Oh, that's a shame,' Shirley said. 'I hope she'll be OK. Did you get caught up in it?'

'I banged my head but it was only minor. I'm fine.'

'Ooh, you should have told me,' said Shirley.

Adele left it at that. What would have been the point of telling her mother earlier? She'd never been the doting type. It wasn't so much that she didn't care; it was more because she was too overwhelmed by the burden of life to cope with any additional problems.

'Eh, did I tell you about her up the road?' asked her mother, suddenly becoming animated. 'Her son's gone to live in Australia. Tommy. Do you remember him? A couple of years older than our Peter, he is.'

For the next half-hour Adele listened while her mother gossiped non-stop about her neighbours and their lives. Eventually, feeling irritated with her mother's ceaseless chat about trivia, she told her she needed to go.

'So soon?' asked Shirley. 'You've not been here five minutes.'

'I need to keep an eye on things at the club,' said Adele. 'Friday nights are always busy.'

'Eh, you be careful. You don't wanna get hurt again if there's any trouble. Let the men handle things and you stay out of it.'

'I will,' said Adele before leaving her mother with a promise to visit again soon.

Her job managing the club had provided the perfect excuse for her to break away from her mother before her annoyance threatened to erupt. She didn't really need to go to the club. After all, she was the manager; she could please herself. But, as with her mother, Adele felt duty-bound to go to the Golden Bell and keep an eye on things. It seemed that lately a sense of duty was the only thing that was driving her. What she wanted or what made her happy didn't seem to count any more.

Glynn and Mike were on the doors of the Golden Bell when Adele arrived. Glynn nodded as she walked inside and took up a position at the back of the foyer. An ominous feeling was hanging over the bouncers as they stood at the doors. Glynn had been expecting Alan's crew to hit back ever since they'd punished Todd. But all had been eerily quiet up to now. He wondered whether Alan had given up in his battle to take control of the Golden Bell, having seen the damage he and Mike could inflict. But, somehow, he doubted it; Alan wasn't the type to let that go.

Glynn could feel Adele's eyes on him as he dealt with the customers. 'I wish she'd fuck off,' he whispered to Mike. 'Just because she's let that bunch of tossers go, she's frightened to death of losing control.'

'I know, mate,' said Mike. 'Don't worry about it. At least we know we'll be all right if it kicks off, now we've got some handy blokes on the doors.'

The sound of Glynn's mobile phone rang out. Taking it out of his pocket, he said to Mike, 'I've just got to take this, mate.' Then he moved a little further from the door so he could hear the caller.

'You're fuckin' joking!' he hollered down the phone when he heard what the caller had to say.

Glynn cut the call, and was just about to put his phone back into his pocket when it rang again and he quickly answered it. 'Fuck's sake!' he shouted, just as upset by this call as the previous one. Again he cut the call then called Mike over. 'Mike, we're gonna have to go, mate. Some fucker's attacking our businesses. They've just hit the George and Dragon and now they've broken into one of the fuckin' sunbed shops in Heaton Moor.'

'What, the same people?'

'Dunno. They're not in the same area, are they? But it might be the same gang who are sending different men to different places.'

'What the fuck?' asked Mike, checking his pocket to make sure his weapon was still hidden there before preparing to leave the Golden Bell with Glynn.

It was the first night that Glynn's men had been back on the doors. Adele was standing at the other side of the foyer, facing the front of the club. The entrance was comprised of two large glass doors with metal handles and glass window panels at either side from floor to ceiling. The windows were encased in metal frames, the glass tinted to a smoky grey. A string of flickering neon blue lights danced around the outside perimeter, creating a spectacular border.

Adele had been sad to say goodbye to James and his team, and now, as she watched Glynn and Mike operate, she felt James's absence even more. The approach by Glynn's men was completely different from that of James's team. Gone was the polite conduct and friendly chat with the customers. Instead, Glynn's men were ordering people around and reacting aggressively to any groups of young men that they didn't want inside the club.

The faces of the revellers were as bright as the lights; their enthusiasm for a night out making them unperturbed by the brusqueness of the bouncers. Adele tried to reassure herself that she had done the right thing in changing the bouncers but she couldn't help becoming irritated as she observed their activity. She was also missing the friendly face of Anna.

A series of troubled thoughts occupied Adele's mind as she stood and watched. Her focus switched from irritation at Glynn to concerns about drug dealing in the club. Now that Glynn was back in control of the doors, the problems were bound to get worse. She vowed to herself that she would do something about it but at the moment she had other concerns such as imminent attacks from rival firms.

And as Adele's worries played out in her mind, like a disjointed disaster movie, the vision of Anna in her helpless state was always there, hovering in the background.

Adele watched Glynn step away from the doors and take his phone out of his pocket. He answered two calls in quick succession and Adele could see his features become clouded by fury. Then he walked back to the doors, said something to Mike and walked outside.

Adele was just about to go and ask where they were going when she heard a loud bang. It was coming from the front of the club. Adele stared in the direction the noise had come from. Then she heard another bang and the whole of the club's frontage vibrated. A sense of dread quashed all her other thoughts as she realised that Alan's gang were back.

27

Adele watched, awestruck, as the large glass frontage of the Golden Bell shuddered repeatedly. Through the tinted window panes, she could see the outline of numerous bodies pounding against the reinforced glass. The noise was ear-piercing; the shrill screams of frightened club-goers accompanying the resounding clatter of glass and metal. Many of the revellers raced around frantically, trying to escape the threat. Others stood around, their mouths agape, as they took in what was happening.

The bouncers sped outside, and soon Adele could see a tussle played out in the form of frantic silhouettes against the tinted window panes. But the banging continued. Adele breathed in sharply as she felt a shock wave reverberating throughout the foyer. She dreaded the whole thing shattering and spraying customers with shards of glass and steel.

Without thinking about her own welfare, she raced towards the front of the nightclub and began shepherding customers away from the windows. Cries of, 'It's going to smash,' rang out from the panicked crowd, who trampled over each other in their sudden haste to escape.

While Adele was directing people away from the windows, she heard an even louder crash. On the other side of the window, only a few feet away from her, she saw a large crowd bashing bricks and other items against the glass. She winced as a huge crack snaked its way along one of the panes.

In a state of trepidation, Adele continued to usher people away from the glass, which threatened to break at any minute. She directed them inside the club, regardless of whether they had paid their entrance fee. Before she could get everyone away from the windows, the bouncers ran back inside and those attacking the club began to back away. She dashed to the doors to see what was happening, just in time to see Mike secrete a knife inside his pocket as he strutted brashly across the foyer. Adele ran outside.

She heard the police sirens at the same time as she spotted their presence. Several cars had pulled up and were now parked haphazardly on the road, their lights flashing. A few policemen were bundling people inside a police van as their colleagues pursued others.

Adele was alarmed at the sight of the troublemakers. Many of them were bloody and two of them lay injured on the ground. She had no doubt that their injuries were down to Glynn and his men. A mix of emotions surged through her: relief that the troublemakers were being apprehended and abhorrence at the brutality of it all.

Looking back towards the club, she saw Glynn standing alongside Mike, the two of them deep in conversation. She wondered whether the phone calls that had driven them out of the club were in any way connected to tonight's attack.

Her attention was drawn away from them as a police sergeant began to direct the crowd. 'Come on, stand back,' he ordered.

'But it's my club,' said Adele.

'OK, go back inside,' he instructed. 'My inspector will need to have a word with you.'

As she walked through the door Glynn spoke to her. 'I knew the bastards would be back,' he said. 'It's a fuckin' good job we were here to sort them out.'

She ignored his barbed comment and made her way back inside, where she helped the police to restore order while she mentally prepared herself for another long night of police questioning.

It was coming towards the end of the night, and the police and customers had left the club. After hours of police questioning and trying to put everything back in order, Adele was shattered. She was currently inside instructing the staff as they cleared away glasses and tidied up the mess. Out of the corner of her eye she saw Glynn approaching.

'Thank fuck that's over with,' he said as he drew level.

'Was it Alan's lot?' she asked, keeping her voice low so none of the staff could overhear.

'Course it fuckin' was.'

'How do you know?'

'I recognised a couple of them outside.'

'Thank God none of the customers were hurt,' said Adele. 'It's gonna cost a fortune to replace the glass though.'

'I hope you're not gonna fuckin' shut the club while you're waiting for it to be fixed. It might take ages.'

'No, it's OK. We'll cordon it off; make sure nobody gets too close just in case it does go altogether.'

'Nah.' He sniffed. 'It'll be OK. It's only a crack.'

'We still need to put the barrier up to be on the safe side though, Glynn.'

'Sure, go for it... Anyway, it's not the only damage they've done tonight.'

'What do you mean?' asked Adele.

'The club isn't the only place they've hit,' said Glynn. 'They've been attacking some of the pubs we look after and have even smashed the windows at one of the fuckin' sunbed shops. Me and Mike were on our way over there when they turned up here.'

'Oh, my God! I hope nobody's been hurt.'

'No, just property this time.'

'Thank God for that,' she said. 'How bad is the damage?'

'Dunno, like I say, me and Mike were on our way over to the sunbed shop when we saw that bunch of tossers outside. Anyway, it's a good job us lot were here. The bunch of bastards got more than they bargained for. They still managed a bit of damage though. But don't you worry; we're not gonna fuckin' take this lying down. Some bastard will pay for it,' he growled.

His menacing tone drew her gaze to him and she noticed how his features were contorted with rage. And as Adele took in the fierce expression on Glynn's face and the blood spatter on his shirt a feeling of dread consumed her. It reminded her of how dangerous Glynn was to have as an enemy, and she wondered just how far he would go to get revenge.

28

It was a few weeks later and Glynn was visiting Peter in prison and giving him an update on how things were going.

'Nah, we've not had any trouble at the club from Alan's lot, not since we saw them off a few weeks ago,' Glynn said, smugly. 'I think those tossers have finally got the message that our men are back on the doors and aren't gonna be fucked with. And that's more than I can say for that bunch of ponces that Adele employed. That lot couldn't fight their way out of a fuckin' paper bag. Honestly, what the fuck was she thinking?'

Peter screwed up his face as he listened to Glynn criticising his sister, but he didn't say anything; he knew Glynn had a point. It didn't stop him feeling irritated with Glynn though. He had noticed a change come over him recently. Since Adele had put his men back on the doors of the Golden Bell he was becoming cockier. It made Peter nervous; he didn't want Glynn to lose sight of who was really in charge.

'Those bastards are still having a go at our other businesses though,' Glynn continued, in reference to Alan's gang.

'Have they taken over any?'

'Nah, they get away with it for a couple of days till we go round. Then we let the owners know who's in charge. We've had to step in once or twice and make sure we were there when Alan's men came calling. We copped a gang of kids trying to collect at the Grey Mare last week; bastards shit themselves when they saw us. I don't think they'd have had much luck with the landlord anyway; Jim's no mug.

'The trouble with that bunch of tossers that work for your mate, Alan, is that they keep changing their collection days. One of the owners was frightened of saying no to them so he's ended up paying two lots of protection.'

'Let's get one thing straight,' said Peter, allowing his annoyance to show. 'Alan is not my fuckin' mate!'

'OK, easy mistake,' said Glynn, holding up his hands in mock surrender and grinning. 'You were mates once, weren't you?'

'That was a fuckin' long time ago,' snapped Peter, gauging Glynn's reaction. When the smirk had left Glynn's face, Peter continued speaking. 'Which business is paying double?' he asked.

'The Lord Nelson.'

'We can't afford to let that happen,' said Peter. 'We've got a fuckin' reputation to protect.'

'Don't worry. I've got guys there every fuckin' day of the week. As soon as Alan's lot turn up again, they'll kick the shit out of them. The bastards will get the message sooner or later.'

As Glynn spoke, Peter scrutinised him. There was no doubt in Peter's mind that Glynn was in his element. He loved the power of getting one over on the enemy. It was written all over him; in his hurried speech and excited hand gestures. And Peter was becoming more and more unsettled by it all.

While he watched Glynn all of Adele's warnings came back to him. Maybe it was more than a personal grudge on her part; maybe she was right. Peter knew Glynn had his bad points but he had hoped they wouldn't backfire on him. Now he wasn't so sure.

'You all right, mate? You seem miles away,' said Glynn.

Peter snapped to, hoping Glynn couldn't tell what was on his mind. It wouldn't pay to give anything away now, not while he was still locked up behind bars. The situation felt so hopeless.

'Sure, I'm fine,' Peter said, but he felt anything but fine. He couldn't wait till his sentence was finally over. Then he could get back control of his businesses and make sure that neither Glynn nor anyone else could stand in his way.

Adele was standing at the bar of the Golden Bell chatting to Paula. It was early evening so the club was still quiet. Adele noticed that the staff seemed more relaxed since the attacks on the Golden Bell had stopped. They weren't the only ones; she was relieved that, for the time being at least, she didn't have that to worry about.

Adele wasn't quite sure why the attacks had stopped. Was it because Alan's men had got more than they bargained for last time, as Glynn had said, or were they deterred by the fact that Glynn's men were back on the doors? She didn't know and she suspected there was a lot happening outside the Golden Bell which Glynn wasn't telling her about. All she knew was that things were a lot better since the attacks had stopped.

But aside from the Golden Bell, Adele was having a traumatic time over her friend, Anna. She had visited her several times but it was always the same. Anna just lay there, not speaking or moving, and surrounded by wires and machinery. Although Adele found it upsetting to visit Anna, it was her guilt over Anna's injuries that made her keep returning; that, and the fact that Anna had been a good friend.

As Adele stood at the bar chatting, she heard the phone ring and Paula went over to the back of the bar to answer it. Adele could feel Paula's eyes on her as soon as she picked up the receiver, and Adele continued watching her, curious.

'It's for you,' said Paula, her face full of concern as she put the receiver down to rest.

Adele went to the end of the bar and lifted the hatch to gain access. Then she walked over to the phone. Before she had a chance to answer, Paula looked at her and mouthed, *It's the hospital.*

Adele knew who the phone call was about even before she lifted the receiver. She had given the hospital the number of the Golden Bell so that they could contact her in case of any change in Anna's condition. It was with a mixture of trepidation and eager anticipation that she put the phone to her ear. She recognised the voice of the nurse called Val who had been helping to look after Anna.

'Hello, Miss Robinson,' said Val. 'I'm calling to let you know that your friend, Anna, woke up this afternoon.'

'Oh, my God!' yelled Adele, her joy getting the better of her. 'When can I come and see her?'

'Normal visiting times but—'

Adele missed Val's next words as she shouted across to Paula, 'Anna's come out of the coma!'

Paula let out an excited whoop and other members of staff dashed over to Adele. 'Anna's out of the coma,' she shouted again, putting the phone receiver down on the counter top. 'She can have visitors.'

For several minutes the staff made a fuss, hugging her and asking for more details. In her excitement Adele forgot that she still had Val on the other end of the phone. By the time she realised, the line had gone dead. But she'd already made up her mind that she would go to see Anna straight away.

She dashed out of the club with a smile on her face while the staff wished her good luck, and sent their best wishes to Anna. This was the moment she had been waiting for all these weeks. She couldn't wait to see her friend and tell her how much she had missed her.

29

When Adele walked into the side ward a nurse was already at Anna's bedside, checking her chart. Adele didn't recognise her from previous visits and guessed that she must be new to the ward. Adele smiled at the nurse and said hello, then her glance shifted to Anna, who was sitting up in bed.

'Hi, Anna, how are you?' she asked as she approached the bed, leaning over till she was in Anna's line of vision.

There was no response so Adele pulled up a seat and sat down next to the bed. She looked at Anna again but was disconcerted to notice that Anna didn't look back. Instead she continued to look straight ahead, her eyes unfocused as though she was staring into space.

'Anna?' Adele said again but Anna still didn't respond.

A feeling of disquiet stirred in Adele's stomach and began to gnaw at her insides.

'Chat to her,' said the nurse. 'Let her know who you are and tell her about your day.'

Adele felt a bit awkward as she spoke. 'Hi, Anna,' she said again. 'It's me, Adele.'

She continued to stare at Anna, who still didn't react. Adele tried to ignore the feeling of unease as she continued. 'I've just come from work. Everyone was excited to hear about you and they all send their good wishes. Paula says she'll be coming to see you soon.'

Adele knew she was waffling but she was desperate to catch Anna's attention.

'I'll play her some music,' she said to the nurse and she pressed the play button on the CD player. The sound of Chrissie Hynde filled the room and Adele glanced across at Anna again. But still there was nothing.

The nurse seemed to sense Adele's unease and she stepped forward, taking a glass of water from the tray at Anna's bedside.

'Anna, would you like a drink?' she asked.

Anna still didn't speak but her hand shot out randomly, knocking the glass from the nurse's hand. As the glass toppled onto the bed, spilling its contents, Anna let out a distressed whine and her eyes seemed to focus momentarily on the glass.

'Oh dear,' said the nurse, quickly picking up the glass and then wiping the bed covers with some paper towel.

Then she topped up the glass again. 'Here, let me help you,' she said, holding the glass up to Anna's lips and waiting while she took a sip.

'Do you want to try?' she asked Adele.

But Adele was struggling. Seeing Anna like this brought tears to her eyes. Her expectations had been so high on the way to the hospital. And now she felt deflated. Anna still wasn't herself, that was clear, and Adele was finding it difficult to handle.

'I j-just need a minute,' she stammered, fleeing from the room.

Adele went to sit in the visitors' waiting room while the tears flowed. Once she had calmed down she felt ashamed for reacting like that but it had been such a shock. She didn't really know what she had expected Anna to do when she walked into the room. But, whatever it was, she had thought that Anna would at least be able to acknowledge her.

After a few minutes the nurse stepped inside the waiting room. 'I'm sorry if it was a bit of a shock for you,' she said. 'It can be alarming for friends and family when someone first comes out of a coma.'

'Sorry, but I didn't think she'd be like that,' said Adele.

'It's OK, I understand. It's difficult to know what to expect and it's different for each patient but it will take time.'

'How long will it take?' asked Adele.

The nurse covered Adele's hand with her own. 'Why don't I go and fetch the doctor? He should be able to tell you more.'

'OK,' said Adele.

Just as the nurse was about to leave the waiting room, she turned back and said, 'It's probably best if the doctor speaks to you in here. Anna will be able to hear what you're saying and we don't want to upset her.'

Then she was gone and Adele waited patiently for the doctor to arrive. She was upset and confused. She had no previous experience of brain damage and she couldn't understand it. If Anna could hear what she was saying then why didn't she respond? And what could be so bad that the nurse didn't want Anna to overhear it?

After a few minutes Dr Grey stepped through the door of the visitors' waiting room. He crossed the room and took the seat next to Adele, sitting at an angle so that he could look at her.

Then he held out his hand, smiling. 'Dr Grey, we've met before,' he said.

'Y-yes,' stammered Adele.

'Well,' he said. 'It's good to see that Anna has woken up.'

'Yes, but, she's…' Adele struggled to find the right words to convey what she was thinking. Finally she settled on, 'She didn't seem to recognise me.'

'Yes, that's quite natural after such a lengthy period in a coma,' he said. 'Hopefully she will do so in time.'

He continued to look at Adele for several seconds before adding, 'I'm afraid it's nothing like you see on television. Patients who have suffered a severe brain injury usually have to learn to do everything all over again. That includes even the most basic things like coordinating their hand and eye movements so that they can eat and drink unaided, for example. It can be quite a slow recovery. But the fact that Anna has woken up is a huge step forward.'

'So, how long will it be before she's back to normal?' Adele asked.

'It depends what you consider to be normal,' said the doctor.

Adele felt a pang of guilt as she noticed the emphasis he placed on the word *normal*.

'If you mean compared to how she was before the accident,' he said, 'then it all depends. Recovery time varies from patient to patient and some take longer than others, I'm afraid.'

'But she will get better, won't she?'

'At the moment we don't know fully which functions Anna will recover. I'm afraid it's a matter of waiting. But you need to prepare yourself. In many cases patients don't fully recover, especially after a lengthy period in a coma.'

Adele gulped. His words had stunned her and she couldn't think of anything else to say so she settled for, 'OK, thank you.'

Then the doctor left the room and she was alone once more. After being on such a high on the way to the hospital, it was difficult to take in. What if Anna never recovered?

She tried to tell herself to keep positive. The doctor had been quite blunt but she supposed it was his way of preparing her for the worst. But he'd also said that the fact Anna had woken up was a good sign. Maybe it was best to give it time and see what happened. After all, Anna had only just come out of the coma.

Adele decided to go back in to see her friend before leaving the hospital. This time she was prepared and she took a deep breath and squared her shoulders before she eased open the door to the side ward.

The nurse was no longer in the room. Adele took up the seat next to the bed and stared into her friend's eyes. But Anna was still staring into space. Feeling less self-conscious now that the nurse had gone, Adele began talking to Anna. She told her all about work and what the various staff had been up to. As she did so, she looked at Anna for a reaction. But there was nothing.

Feeling the tears sting her eyes once more, Adele took hold of Anna's hand and continued talking. About work, their time in prison, her mother. Anything. She knew she was waffling but she was desperate for a reaction.

Then she felt it. A squeeze of her hand. She was sure of it. But it was so weak that she began to doubt herself and wonder whether it was just her imagination. Before she could brush it aside it happened again. This time it was stronger, a definite squeeze, and Adele looked from their clasped hands up to Anna's face. Her expression was still unreadable, her eyes unfocused. But she had communicated, even if only through a tiny squeeze of the hand.

All of a sudden Adele became overcome with emotion and when she couldn't bear it any longer she gave Anna a quick pat on the shoulder, bade her goodbye and dashed from the room. Outside the ward she cried all the way back home.

During the journey she replayed the doctor's words in her mind, desperately clinging onto the little hope he had given her. But the thought that Anna wasn't likely to make a full recovery, and that she was responsible, didn't escape her.

No matter how much Adele tried to convince herself that Anna's accident wasn't her fault, her conscience told her otherwise. Maybe Glynn had been right: if she hadn't put Anna on the doors of the Golden Bell in the first place then none of this would have happened.

But Adele knew that it was about more than just that. Anna had become another victim of the pointless war for control of the doors of Manchester's nightclubs. And as Adele thought about Anna's injuries and all the other bad things that had happened since she came to work for her brother, she couldn't help wondering where it was all going to end.

30

It was a few months later. Adele had continued to visit Anna, who had now been moved from hospital into a rehabilitation centre. During that time she had seen some improvement, but progress had been slow. Although Anna could now hold a conversation, Adele wondered whether Anna really knew who she was talking to and how much of their conversation she understood. And did Anna know who the people were that Adele referred to when she mentioned their work colleagues at the Golden Bell? Adele wasn't sure.

Sometimes she would meet her eyes as they talked, and a look of recognition seemed to flash across her face. But at other times she seemed disconnected and often stared into space.

Anna was still finding it difficult to feed herself too. Her hand–eye coordination had improved but it wasn't 100 per cent. One particular day Anna was holding a cup of water, and Adele was helping to guide Anna's hand towards her lips, when Anna's parents arrived. It was only the second time she had seen them.

'Oh, hello,' announced the father in a loud, confident manner. 'I do believe we've met before.'

'Yes, I'm Adele,' she said, putting the cup down on top of the side cupboard while she got up from her seat and went to shake hands with them.

As she did so, Anna's mother, Noreen, seemed to stare through Adele, then she quickly walked past her and plonked herself in the seat that Adele had vacated.

'Hello, Anna, love,' she said, picking up the cup. 'Were you having a drink?'

While Noreen picked up the cup and put it to Anna's mouth, Adele and Mr Tomlinson gazed awkwardly at each other.

'Have a seat,' Adele offered, breaking the tension. Then she pulled up a chair alongside the one where Mrs Tomlinson was sitting, and beckoned to Mr Tomlinson to sit down.

For several minutes Anna's parents focused their attention on Anna and acted as though Adele weren't there. As the two chairs in the room were now taken, Adele stood watching them uncomfortably from the end of the bed.

Eventually Adele decided to leave them to share their time with Anna. She could always return when they weren't around.

She tried to interrupt them. 'Ahem,' she said and they both turned around at once. Anna looked vaguely in Adele's direction. 'I need to go now,' said Adele. 'It was nice meeting you both again.' Then she switched her attention to Anna. 'Bye, Anna. I'll come and see you again in a couple of days.'

'Goodbye,' Anna's parents chorused and while Adele picked up her coat from where she had left it on the end of Anna's bed, Noreen Tomlinson carried on tending to Anna and ignoring Adele.

But Mr Tomlinson continued to stare at Adele. It was as though he was going to tell her something but didn't quite know how to start.

'Erm, I'm afraid Anna won't be here next time you come,' he said.

Adele stared back at him in alarm. 'Why?' she asked.

'We've found her another rehabilitation centre close to home. We're taking her back with us today. She'll be well looked after and won't want for anything.'

'Oh,' said Adele, lost for words for several seconds. Then she asked, 'Will I be able to come and see her?'

Mrs Tomlinson looked up at her with eyes full of venom. 'I don't think that would be a good idea,' she snapped.

Mr Tomlinson looked embarrassed by his wife's frosty manner. 'It's quite a way to travel,' he quickly interjected. 'We live in Hertfordshire, you see. It's too far for a day trip, I think. And there aren't many hotels near to our village.'

Hertfordshire? thought Adele. How could it be good for Anna moving her away from Manchester and all she knew? She'd grown up here; that was obvious from her accent. But her parents spoke differently from Anna; a slight hint of Mancunian but with aspirational overtones. She guessed they must have moved down south in search of a better life.

'Oh,' said Adele again, noticing that there was no offer to put her up if she went there to visit Anna. She wasn't convinced by Mr Tomlinson's claim that there weren't many hotels either. 'Perhaps I could take your phone number so that I can ring to see how Anna's getting on,' she said, taking out a pen and paper from her handbag and offering it to Mr Tomlinson.

He quickly scribbled a few numbers down while Noreen looked on haughtily. Adele sensed that the number had been given reluctantly and that Noreen would probably admonish him for letting Adele have the number, once she was out of earshot.

Adele muttered a last sad farewell to Anna, while Anna stared back, her face devoid of emotion, and Anna's reluctant parents made a show of tending to her. Adele felt rejected and at the moment she just wanted to get out of there. She didn't stop to dwell on her unhappiness at saying a final goodbye to her friend. But that would come later when she was alone once more and became engulfed in the sheer sorrow of it all.

Glynn was inside the Golden Bell watching out for any signs of trouble, when Mike arrived.

'Can you believe it?' said Mike. 'Those cheeky bastards had a go at the Grey Mare again.'

'What, Alan's lot?' asked Glynn.

'Yeah.'

'You're joking!' said Glynn. 'What the fuck happened?'

'They were trying to collect again when we got there so me and the lads gave them a good kicking.'

'I can't believe the fuckin' nerve of 'em. No matter how much we sort them out, they still keep coming back for more. Just keep doing what you're good at, Mike. Hopefully they'll get the message eventually.'

'Will do but it's taking up a lot of our fuckin' manpower having to keep checking on all our businesses.'

'I know that,' said Glynn. 'But there isn't any other fuckin' alternative at the moment. Anyway, at least takings are up here. I've got a few dealers onside now.'

'Yeah, I noticed. It's working out well.'

'Dead right. But make the most of it while it fuckin' lasts.'

'Why?' asked Mike, a look of concern plastered across his face.

'Because there's about to be some fuckin' big changes in the club in a couple of weeks' time. That's why.'

Mike stared at Glynn, wide-eyed with curiosity. Then he listened intently while Glynn explained what was about to happen.

31

'Paula, could you send someone to the men's toilets, please? There's a load of graffiti on one of the cubicle doors. I need it removed,' said Adele.

Then she turned to walk away, too occupied to chat today. As she busied herself around the club, trying to get everything just right, her stress was evident from the creases on her brow and her abrupt tone with the staff.

'Sure,' said Paula, summoning one of the barmen.

Just as she was about to walk away, Adele noticed something else and turned back to address Paula again.

'Jesus! Just look at the state of those chairs; they're all over the place. Could you ask someone to straighten them up, please, Paula?'

Paula flashed an amused smile at Adele.

'What?' Adele asked.

'Chill,' said Paula. 'Trust me; nobody will be looking at how the chairs are arranged.'

'Oh, you never know,' said Adele. 'And I just want everything to be right.'

'Everything's fine,' Paula continued. 'You've been doing a great job. You've got nothing to worry about.'

But Adele wasn't so sure. She crossed the club and went through the back door that led to the offices, checking her watch to see how much time she had left. Glynn had been gone over an hour and was probably due back any minute. Adele rushed up the stairs hoping she would be able to make one last check before Glynn returned with their special visitor.

As Adele tidied around the offices, her mind wandered. She wasn't sure why she was so worried. Paula was right; she had done a good job. Well, as good as could be expected under the circumstances. Then a memory came to mind of Anna lying injured in the club foyer while the entire club was in mayhem, and she quickly switched her attention to straightening the files on the shelf.

Maybe it was Glynn's constant criticisms that had shaken her confidence; that and the nagging thought that she was a failure as a club manager.

It didn't take long to sort the offices out; she had Margaret to thank for that. The woman was a godsend and Adele didn't know how she would have coped without her. She just hoped that Margaret would be OK with the changes that were about to take place.

Once Adele was happy that the offices were in good order, she dashed down the stairs and pushed open the door to the club. She was just in time to see the arrival of their special visitor. It was her brother, Peter, who was waltzing across the club and greeting the staff effusively. As he caught her eye, she dashed over to him.

'Peter, it's so lovely to have you back,' she enthused, flinging her arms around him.

'Good to be back too, sis. I see you've been keeping everything in good order,' he said, breaking from her embrace as he looked around the club at the tidily arranged tables and chairs, and the walls and woodwork, which had been given a fresh coat of paint since he'd been inside. 'I like the colours,' he said. 'They suit the place.'

Adele smiled, pleased that Peter was happy with that at least. As she looked at him she caught sight of Glynn hovering in the background. He'd returned with Peter after collecting him from Strangeways on his release. Peter had now served his sentence for GBH following the raid on Angels nightclub. Glynn's face bore a strange expression. While Peter enthused at being back in the club, Glynn smiled, but the smile looked forced, as though it was hiding his true feelings.

Seeing the expression on Glynn's face made Adele think about the implications of her brother's return to the Golden Bell. There was no doubt that Peter was delighted to be back, but did he fully comprehend what exactly was waiting for him?

Since Peter had been inside things had changed a lot. And the problems in the club were far from over because Glynn and his men were now allowing drug dealers back inside.

Then there was the dodgy protection racket; God alone knew what Glynn got up to in connection with that. But Adele was willing to bet that it probably involved a whole heap of other troubles, which were awaiting Peter's intervention.

Aside from all that, Glynn was becoming increasingly cocksure of himself. This had particularly been the case since she'd had to capitulate and allow his men back on the doors of the Golden Bell. While Adele had been running the club, Glynn had thought he could take advantage although she'd fought against it at every stage. Now Adele wondered how Glynn would cope with having Peter back in charge.

But one thing she hadn't given much thought to was how she herself would handle having to relinquish control over the day-to-day operations of the club. Apart from having to put Glynn in his place from time to time, she'd grown used to being in charge and making most of the big decisions in relation to the Golden Bell.

But now all that was about to change.

Peter had a different way of doing things from her, and his methods often operated on the fringes of

VENDETTA

the law. Could she stand back and say nothing if she fundamentally disagreed with what he was doing? Or would their joint interest in the Golden Bell perhaps bring them even closer?

Ever since they'd been children Adele and Peter had stood up for each other. They hadn't always seen eye to eye but their childhood bond had ultimately held them together.

But what if they couldn't see eye to eye in relation to the club?

What if they should become immersed in a battle for control of the Golden Bell, which would inevitably become their final undoing?

PART TWO

1992–1993

32

Peter had only been out of prison two days when there was an incident in the club. It was a Saturday night. Sitting at the bar, celebrating his release in the company of an attractive redhead, Peter was oblivious to what was happening. But Adele wasn't.

Seeing a crowd of people tightly gathered usually indicated that something was afoot. Now, as she caught sight of the number of people packed into an area of the club, Adele sensed that whatever was going on, it wasn't good. She rushed over to the crowd, which formed a circle. There was a buzz of excitement tinged with panic as the crowd watched something taking place. Adele overheard several comments from anxious onlookers, which cut through the sound of the music. *Oh my God! Is he OK? Has anyone rung an ambulance?*

Adele fought her way through the throng of people with the help of two bouncers, who pushed the crowd aside. Right in the centre of the mass of people was a young man who couldn't have been more than twenty. He was collapsed on the ground; his two friends bent over him, looking distressed but unsure what to do. The blue strobe lights of the Golden Bell flashed intermittently on the three youths, as if highlighting the desperate scene.

As Adele and the bouncers approached, one of the friends looked anxiously at them. 'He just collapsed,' the youth said, his voice cracking. 'One minute he was all right then the next minute he was on the floor.'

'Out of the way,' ordered one of the bouncers while Adele knelt down and felt for a pulse.

'He's alive,' she said to the youth's friends. When one of them cried tears of relief she decided not to tell him how weak his friend's pulse was. 'Barney, ring for an ambulance,' she said. 'We need to get him seen to as soon as possible.'

Adele felt a hurried thud as the other bouncer knelt down next to her. 'We need to put him in the recovery position till they arrive,' he said.

Adele nodded, glad of his help. Then they waited for the ambulance to arrive. It was only a few minutes but it seemed to last forever. While they waited, Peter walked over after finally realising what had happened. Adele watched in dismay as he stumbled drunkenly towards them.

'What the fuck's happened?' he demanded, and Adele quickly brought him up to speed.

While Adele and the bouncer kept watch over the unconscious youth, Peter spoke to the crowd, trying to keep them at bay. His drunkenness made his speech sound harried and aggressive, and the crowd were eager to comply. Eventually the ambulance arrived. As the ambulance crew rushed towards them, Adele was disturbed to notice that they were accompanied by the police. A feeling of trepidation descended on her.

The police flitted about, asking questions, but she tried to put them out of her mind for now; her first priority was to get the young man seen to. Under her instructions, the bouncers held the crowd back so the ambulance crew could make their way through.

The ambulance crew assessed the young man and asked his friends what had happened. A tearful youth reluctantly admitted that the young man had taken a series of drugs prior to his collapse. Adele flinched as she saw the reaction of a policeman who had overheard the confession. He quickly zoomed in on the friend.

'We'll need to ask you a few more questions,' he said, grabbing the youth by the arm and leading him away.

Once the ambulance had taken the unconscious youth away, Adele looked around her. She could see Peter in conversation with a police officer, and she rushed to join them, worried that Peter's drunken state might not give a good impression.

Adele cringed when she heard her brother say, 'No, I don't know fuck all about it, officer.' He'd obviously had even more to drink than she realised.

She quickly cut in, 'I'm Adele Robinson. I've been looking after the club while my brother has been away. I can help you with any questions you may have.'

'Fair enough,' said the policeman. 'We'll start with you first. Then we'll come back to you,' he said, addressing Peter and glaring at him. Peter shrugged his shoulders and staggered towards the bar to join his attractive companion.

The police stayed in the club long after the ambulance crew had left. They conducted a series of interviews with anyone who might have more information about what had taken place. Meanwhile, Adele tried to restore some kind of order. To her consternation, her brother had disappeared, and when she asked the bar staff where he was, she was told that he had left the club with the redhead.

It was almost two hours since Adele had been questioned when she noticed the officer who had interviewed her. She was alarmed to see him standing next to an older officer and pointing in her direction and she waited anxiously while the older officer approached.

He looked to be in his mid-forties, tall and with a commanding presence; he held out his hand as soon as he reached her. 'Miss Robinson, I'm Inspector Williams. Is there somewhere quiet we could talk, please?'

The serious expression on his face and his severe tone unsettled Adele and as she led him through the club and into her upstairs office, her feeling of anxiety morphed into utter dread.

Once inside the office, Inspector Williams came straight to the point. 'I'm afraid the young man who was taken to hospital, Craig Moss, was dead on arrival. We expect the hospital to conduct a full post-mortem but from the information we have received up to now, we believe that Craig had taken various drugs prior to his death.'

Adele's hand shot up to her mouth and a ripple of fear scurried through her. 'I'm so sorry,' she said before the inspector quickly interrupted.

'We will be carrying out a full investigation,' he said. 'This is a very serious matter and we intend to find out who sold Craig the drugs that killed him.'

'Yes, of course,' said Adele, unsure what else to say in the face of such a tragedy.

'That will be all for now,' he said, heading towards the office door. 'But we'll be sending more officers tomorrow. Can you please make sure you are available for questioning?'

'Yes,' she said, rushing to get the door for him and leading him out of the office.

'And we'll need to see your brother tomorrow as well,' added the inspector, his tone even more stern. 'He might not have been out of prison long but he's still the owner of this establishment and is therefore responsible for what goes on inside it.'

Adele nodded and bowed her head in shame at the way in which her brother had fled the scene. No words were spoken between her and the inspector as she led him down the corridor and out of the club. By the time the police left, Glynn had returned after being out on business earlier in the evening. Straight away, he demanded to know what had gone on.

'And where the hell was Pete while all this was happening?' he asked, after Adele had recounted the evening's tragic events.

It was difficult to explain, much less justify Peter's actions given the circumstances. 'He didn't know the boy had died,' she proffered. Then, realising that her explanation was too feeble, she added, 'And he was a bit the worse for wear.'

Glynn tutted, and eyed her with distaste.

'He's not been out long, Glynn. Give him a chance. He's still celebrating his release.'

Glynn didn't reply and as he stormed off she sensed that, like her, he thought that her brother's behaviour had been insensitive and irresponsible no matter what Peter's reasons were for leaving the club at such a critical time. Even though Adele had tried to defend Peter to

Glynn, she was livid at the way in which her brother had behaved. Not only was his behaviour insensitive, it wasn't fair to her. He had left her to handle the police as well as trying to restore some sort of order inside the club and trying to justify his actions to a dissatisfied Glynn.

Adele hoped that when Peter sobered up he would feel remorseful and ashamed. She also hoped that his behaviour would improve with time but a niggling doubt took root in her mind. What if prison had changed him? Would he be able to settle back into his role as owner of the Golden Bell?

While she appreciated that he wanted to celebrate, there was a point at which he would need to knuckle down and get back to business. As she looked around her brother's club, still put out by the way in which Glynn had treated her, she was determined to tackle Peter the next day. She was so concerned about Peter fitting in that the thought didn't occur to her as to how *she* would fit in now that he was back.

33

As Adele was winding things up for the night, her feelings of anger and despair were replaced by weariness. The evening's events had taken their toll and she was eager to finish work and go home to bed. Having sent Barney to lock the front doors, she was surprised to see him approach a couple of minutes later.

'There's a lady at the door who wants to see you,' he said.

'Can't you get rid of her?' Adele asked, knowing that if it was the police who had returned they would have produced ID. 'Tell her we're closed.'

'I've tried to but she won't take no for an answer,' said Barney. 'She seems to know you. She mentioned you by name.'

A feeling of disquiet gripped Adele as a thought occurred to her – the damn press had got hold of the story already!

'All right,' she said, 'I'll handle it.'

She marched to the front doors determined to challenge this unwelcome visitor. But as she stomped across the foyer and saw the outline of a woman through the smoky glass of the door panels, she thought she recognised her. Adele drew nearer, noting the fair hair, soft feminine lines and familiar form of the woman on the other side of the door. No, it couldn't be!

But it was.

Adele rushed to open the door. Then she flung her arms around her visitor, overjoyed. 'Caroline!' she greeted. 'I can't believe it's you. What are you doing here at this time of night? How are you?'

Caroline smiled at her effusiveness and returned her greeting. 'I'm good,' she said. 'How are you?'

'Not bad although I've had better nights. Come inside out of the cold, for God's sake,' Adele said, holding one of the doors wide open.

Caroline stepped inside the foyer and Adele shut and bolted the doors then turned around, noticing that Caroline's eyes were taking in the club's interior. Adele spotted Glynn across the foyer watching them. She didn't want him to know anything about Caroline. As far as she was concerned it was her business.

'Come on,' said Adele. 'I'll take you up to my office where we can talk in private.'

Then she left instructions for Glynn to secure the building once all the staff had left, telling him she would be a while and would make sure she locked up again before she left for home. All thoughts of tiredness had now escaped her as she was so delighted at seeing her best friend for the first time since they had been in prison together.

Adele had got along with Caroline almost as soon as she had met her even though she was around ten years her senior. She had a motherly, caring nature and had always stood up for Adele during her time inside.

Caroline was a former schoolteacher, smart and sensible, a woman who had always stayed on the right side of the law until her husband had pushed her too far one day. After years of abuse she had finally flipped and killed him in the most callous way, stabbing him repeatedly with a kitchen knife then cutting off and setting fire to his genitalia.

But to look at her you would never have thought she was capable of such a heinous crime. Adele had accepted her at face value. After all, she had committed a similar crime herself and knew what it felt like to be pushed beyond all reason.

Despite her crime, Caroline was the most loyal and trustworthy friend Adele had ever had, and Adele knew that, unlike some of her previous friends, Caroline would never hold her crime against her.

Once inside her office, Adele offered Caroline a chair then plonked herself in the seat opposite. 'I think this deserves a celebration,' she said, pulling a bottle of brandy from her desk drawer and pouring a good measure into two mugs. 'How on earth did you know where to find me, and what made you come at this time of night?' she asked.

'Well, finding you wasn't difficult. You'd mentioned the Golden Bell often enough while we were inside together so I thought I'd check whether your brother could tell me where to find you. I rang the club a few days ago and asked for Peter but they said he was away. When I asked who was running the club in his absence they gave me your name and offered to put you on the phone.

'But I wanted to surprise you so I decided to pay the club a visit when it was open. Unfortunately I got waylaid on my way here tonight, so I arrived much later than I intended. I'm glad I caught you though.

'I must admit, I was a bit surprised to find out you were the manager. Well done! You must be very proud of yourself.'

'I'm not any more,' said Adele, her voice subdued. 'Peter's just been released from prison. He's back in charge now.'

'Oh, good God! What's he been up to?'

'It's a long story, Caroline. Trust me, you don't wanna know.'

Caroline smiled wryly but didn't press Adele for information. Instead she said, 'You don't sound too thrilled about him being back in charge.'

Adele shrugged. 'It's early days yet. We'll see how things go. What about you anyway? What are you up to these days?'

'Well, I've not been out long myself but I've been given the opportunity to work with victims of domestic violence. It's voluntary at first but I'm hoping it will lead to paid work. I'm also going to start campaigning on behalf of domestic abuse victims.'

Adele smiled. That sounded like just the sort of thing Caroline would do with her caring nature, and she wasn't the sort to let her prison record stand in the way of doing something worthwhile. 'That sounds great,' Adele said. 'I hope it all works out for you.'

There was a few moments' silence before Caroline switched the conversation. 'How have you found life outside prison?' she asked.

Caroline's words stabbed at Adele's heart. It was like pouring antiseptic on an open wound. She spoke with kindness but, nevertheless, it got to Adele. Suddenly a tear sprang to her eye as all that had happened over the past few months came flooding back to her. Maybe this was what she had needed: someone sensitive and level-headed in whom she could confide.

'Anna came to work for me,' she said. 'It was great at first. I gave her a job on the doors and she seemed to relish the opportunity. I'd never seen her so happy. But then we had a bit of trouble and... and...'

As Adele tried to tell Caroline all that had happened she felt overcome with emotion and unable to continue. Caroline covered Adele's hand with her own. 'It's OK,' she said. 'Take your time.'

Adele took a deep breath and tried to compose herself. Then she told Caroline all that had happened since her time inside. She was so relieved to see a friendly, supportive face that once she started speaking, she found that all her troubles came tumbling out of her, including tonight's incident.

'I did hear a rumour about Anna,' said Caroline. 'Although I didn't know the exact circumstances and I haven't seen her yet. Please don't blame yourself for what happened, Adele. It isn't your fault. It sounds like you gave Anna a chance that she wouldn't otherwise have had. If things had worked out differently I'm sure the job at the Golden Bell would have kept Anna on the straight and narrow. But, unfortunately, things don't always work out the way we plan, do they?'

'I know,' said Adele. 'I'm sorry to put on you like this but sometimes it all gets a bit much and now, with this latest business, I'm worried sick. The police will be conducting an investigation and, the way Peter is since his release, it feels like he doesn't give a damn.

'But part of me feels like I've let him down too. He left me to look after the place and since he's been inside it's all gone to pot.'

'Stop taking the blame for everything, Adele. It sounds to me like there were a lot of problems even before you took control. These things would probably have happened anyway. It's just unfortunate for you that they've happened under your management.

'And as for Peter; give him time. Like you said, he's only just been released. It takes time to adjust to life on the outside, we both know that.' Caroline smiled sympathetically. 'It is a bit of a baptism of fire for him, isn't it?'

'I suppose so,' said Adele.

'Well, while you're waiting for your brother to get his act together, there's nothing to stop you taking matters into your own hands.'

'What do you mean?' asked Adele, hoping that her friend would provide the answer to her predicament. As an ex-con and a very intelligent woman, Caroline was probably the best person to help her.

'Be open with the police. Tell them you don't condone drug dealing in the club and you have an anti-drugs policy. Let them know that you want to stamp out the problem as much as they do. You've just told me you used to search customers' bags at the door. Why not reinstate the bag searches? And take whatever other action you can think of that might show the police you're doing your bit.'

A smile of relief appeared on Adele's face. 'Thank you,' she said. 'I'll do that.'

Adele was surprised that she hadn't thought of that herself. She had let the stress of recent events get to her so that she was plagued by panic instead of thinking rationally.

By the time Caroline left the club Adele was feeling a lot better, although her worries hadn't disappeared altogether. She still wasn't looking forward to the police visit tomorrow but at least she now knew how she would handle them.

As Adele got into bed that night her troubled thoughts whirled around inside her head. The police weren't Adele's only concern. She still had Peter to deal with, and the more she thought about his behaviour tonight, the angrier she became. Despite his recent release from prison, as far as Adele was concerned there was no excuse for leaving the scene of an overdose in the club that was owned by him. As she drifted off to sleep she was determined that she would confront him the next day.

34

Adele didn't wait for Peter to put in an appearance at the club the following day. After a restless night she awoke early, unable to get back off to sleep. It was nine o'clock in the morning when she arrived at Peter's apartment. She rang the bell insistently but it was still several minutes before someone answered the door.

Adele stared in disgust at the redhead who was standing in the doorway of her brother's apartment wearing Peter's shirt and last night's make-up, her hair strewn haphazardly around her shoulders. 'Is Peter in?' Adele asked curtly, although the woman's appearance told her all she needed to know.

The woman didn't speak as she stood to one side allowing Adele to enter. Adele barged past her and marched straight to the bedroom and rapped on the door. 'Peter, are you up?' she demanded.

She could hear some muttering before Peter grumbled his response. 'Give me a minute.'

Adele then stormed off into the lounge where the woman was already sitting drinking a cup of something hot. She gazed across at Adele, who plonked herself on another seat. 'You want one?' asked the woman.

'No! I won't be stopping long,' said Adele.

It was a few seconds later when Peter appeared, his appearance just as dishevelled as the woman's. He had buttoned his shirt lopsidedly and it hung unevenly outside his jeans. His hair was also messy.

'We need to talk,' said Adele, eyeing the woman scornfully.

'Tammy, can you go?' he asked.

'I haven't finished my coffee,' she complained.

'Well, take the fuckin' thing with you while you get dressed,' he said, his patience soon wearing thin when he spotted the steely look on Adele's face.

But Tammy was feistier than most of his conquests. 'That's a fine way to talk to me,' she said. 'Got what you want now, have you?' she challenged.

'For fuck's sake!' he muttered, running his hands through his hair.

Adele could see that the woman wasn't about to go willingly so she stepped in. 'Yes, he has, love. And if it's any consolation, you're just one in a long line. But your services are no longer required so get your things and fuck off!'

'Who the hell do you think you are?' demanded Tammy.

Adele stepped up to her and grabbed hold of the shirt she was wearing, forcing it and her fist up against Tammy's windpipe. Her action was so swift that Tammy stumbled backwards. 'Are you going to go and get dressed or do I have to throw you out in the fuckin' street in what you're wearing?' she threatened.

'All right, keep your hair on!' said Tammy.

Adele let go of her and the woman scuttled off into the bedroom.

'What the fuck's got into you?' asked Peter.

'I'll tell you what the fuck's got into me just as soon as she's left!' said Adele.

'Can't it wait? My fuckin' head's thumping!'

His admission that he was the worse for wear because of drink only made Adele more annoyed as she recalled his drunken state the previous night and the show he'd made of himself in front of the police.

For a few seconds they sat glaring at each other across the living room. But Peter didn't have to wait long to find out what was wrong with Adele. Tammy soon reappeared fully clothed and dashed through the apartment and out of the front door without so much as a goodbye.

'Let's get one thing straight,' said Peter. 'What I do in my private life is none of your fuckin' business. You might be my sister but you're not my fuckin' keeper! You frightened the fuckin' life out of that poor cow.'

'Maybe she should be a bit more choosey in future, then,' Adele barked back.

'What is your fuckin' problem?' Peter asked. 'You've obviously come here for a row so, come on, out with it.'

'Oh, yes, you can be sure of that,' she said between gritted teeth. 'Did you know that young lad died of an overdose last night?'

She watched as Peter's face blanched. Then she could almost see the cogs in his brain desperately grinding away as he rushed to defend himself.

'How was I supposed to fuckin' know that? I wasn't there, was I?'

'No, you weren't, Peter. Because you buggered off with that tart and left me to sort everything out, including the police who, by the way, are conducting an investigation.'

But Peter wasn't ready to concede. 'Look, I didn't fuckin' know he was going to die! Right? And why are you going on at me as though it's my fuckin' fault? I didn't give him the fuckin' drugs, did I?'

'No, but it's your club, Peter. That makes you responsible.'

'No, it doesn't! Anyway, it's not me that's been fuckin' running the place lately, is it? Nothing like that ever happened when I was in charge.'

'You *are* in charge!'

'Give me a fuckin' chance! I haven't been back five minutes. How can I be responsible for what's gone on while I was inside?'

'What are you trying to say, Peter?'

'Well, look what's happened to the place, for Christ's sake! You've changed the staffing arrangements, promoting barmaids and sacking people. You even had someone working in my fuckin' office.'

Adele knew he was referring to Margaret, who Adele had quickly transferred back into her office, which she now shared with her. She'd been hoping he wouldn't have been any the wiser. But, of course, Glynn would have told him. She was about to defend her decisions but Peter's tirade wasn't over.

'We've had staff seriously injured because some fuckin' lunatics were running riot through the club and the useless bastard doormen that you employed couldn't stop them. And now we've got a fuckin' overdose on our hands and I find out there's drug dealing in the club!'

Peter's words cut through her. She was dumbfounded. How dared he criticise her when she had run the club for him to the best of her ability despite all the problems that came with it? But, as well as being annoyed, she felt a sense of guilt. Maybe she had let him down and also Anna, who would never be the same again.

Adele didn't speak for a while. His words had stung and she was shocked by them. Her mind was in turmoil as despair, worry and a sense of failure besieged her.

When she did speak, her temper had eased a little and there was a crack in her voice.

'OK,' she said. 'If that's all the thanks I get, you can shove it. Let's see if you and your twisted sidekick can do any better.'

Then she left the apartment, fully intending never to set foot inside the Golden Bell again. Peter and Glynn deserved each other. She'd leave them to run the club without her and see how they coped with it all. But she'd made a hasty decision because, without the Golden Bell, she had no idea how she would earn a living.

35

It didn't take Peter long to arrive at Adele's flat full of apologies the next day. Neither did it take him long to persuade her to stay at the Golden Bell, but only because she'd been doing some serious thinking in the meantime. She knew that her chances of finding alternative employment were still slim because of her prison record. Besides, she'd miss the place.

After a serious heart-to-heart and shared apologies, they eventually agreed that Adele would help Peter to run the Golden Bell until he was fully up to speed with all the new procedures. Then she'd take a back seat and concentrate on the financial side of things once more. In some ways she was relieved that she would eventually be saying goodbye to all the problems associated with managing the Golden Bell, although she couldn't anticipate how difficult it would be for her to fully relinquish control.

Adele was the main line of contact with the police. Together she and Peter had decided that it was for the best since he'd made a bit of a show of himself on the night of the overdose. She followed all of Caroline's advice and assured the police that she and Peter wanted to stamp out drug dealing in the club and would do anything necessary, including reinstating the bag searches. After some persuasion Peter agreed to the latter.

Although Adele assured the police that they had no links to any drug dealers in the club, she secretly believed that Glynn and Mike were still letting them in. Unfortunately she was at a loss as to what she could do to stop them, as her brother still insisted on retaining their services.

It was only two days later that her PA, Margaret, brought something to Adele's attention. They were working in the office together, Margaret opening the post while Adele was checking over the finances for the Golden Bell.

'I think you'd best take a look at this,' said Margaret, passing a letter to Adele.

Adele took the letter from Margaret, immediately noticing the official local government heading and the department that the letter was sent from. For several seconds she scanned the letter's contents, her breath catching in her throat and her heart hammering as the words hit home. When Adele had finished reading the letter she kept hold of it, her eyes staring at the words as she tried to take it all in.

'Are you OK?' asked Margaret.

'Yes, I'm...' but she couldn't think of any words to back it up. She wished Margaret hadn't seen the letter. It would be best if the staff didn't know anything about this. 'Margaret, I need a few minutes. Would you go and make us a coffee, please?' she asked.

'Certainly,' said Margaret, getting out of her seat, her face full of concern.

Straight away Adele picked up the phone and dialled Caroline's number. 'Caroline, I'm sorry to trouble you,' she said, 'but you'll never guess what's happened now.'

Caroline remained silent and listened patiently while Adele confided in her about her latest troubles. 'We've had a letter from the council, licensing department,' Adele said. 'They're going to review our licence because they're not happy about public safety inside the club.'

Then she quoted from the letter. 'It says, "in light of recent incidents". And then it says we'll have to go to a hearing,' she babbled. 'Jesus, Caroline! What am I going to do? I can't tell Peter. Things are bad enough with him as it is. I already feel as though I've let him down.'

'OK, OK, calm down,' she heard her friend say on the other end of the phone. 'They're reviewing the licence, Adele, not revoking it. It doesn't necessarily mean they'll shut the place down.'

'Oh, God, I hope not,' said Adele in a panic. 'I don't know what we'll do if the club gets shut. Peter would never forgive me and all the staff would be out of jobs. And what the hell would *I* do for work?'

Caroline silenced her again. 'You're letting your imagination run away with you, Adele,' she said. 'It might not come to that.'

Adele continued to babble. Despite Caroline's calm words, Adele was still in a state of shock because of the contents of the letter. While she babbled she noticed Margaret approach the office door then turn away again. She had obviously heard the panicked edge to Adele's voice and decided to make herself scarce for a while longer.

It took several minutes before Caroline could calm Adele down and make her see reason. 'Look, Adele, you've got a while before the hearing, which means you can do something to prevent closure.'

'What?' asked Adele, at a loss. Then she listened while Caroline outlined an idea.

'No, I couldn't do that,' she said. 'Peter would never agree to it.'

Her friend's voice came back on the line, strong and self-assured. 'Then don't tell him.'

'OK, I'll have a think about it,' said Adele, noticing Margaret hovering near the office door again. 'Look, I'll have to go,' she said. 'But thanks, Caroline. Like I say, I'll have a think about what you've suggested.'

She put down the receiver and beckoned Margaret back into the office.

'Are you OK?' asked Margaret as she took her seat at the desk, opposite Adele.

'Yes,' replied Adele automatically before switching the conversation. 'Look, I need a favour,' she said. 'I want you to forget that you saw that letter. Please, can you keep it to yourself?'

'Certainly,' said Margaret, whose loyalty had remained with Adele ever since she'd given her the job. 'My lips are sealed,' she added, before using her fingers to imitate pulling a zipper across her mouth.

'Thank you,' said Adele.

While she sat at her desk, still staring at the letter, Adele mulled over what Caroline had advised and, as she did so, her confidence grew. Yes, it could work, she decided, and she could feel her heartbeat steadying in response to her decision.

She'd do what Caroline suggested. After all, what alternative was there? She couldn't just stand by and watch while she and Peter lost the club that meant so much to them. But she decided not to tell Peter straight away. As she'd said to Caroline, he would never have agreed to her plan.

36

Peter soon got used to being back on the outside and within a few weeks he was visiting all the businesses that he and his men looked after as well as the businesses he owned. He wanted to reacquaint himself with his customers although he left the actual collecting to Glynn, Mike and some of his other men. Peter was still enjoying spending many of his evenings celebrating his release so he was also leaving Adele to take care of most things relating to the club.

Currently he was driving to the George and Dragon just outside the city centre to speak to the landlord and landlady, Pat and Mary. He came off the roundabout at Ardwick and carried on past Ardwick Green, which had for a long time been a popular hangout for vagrants. Then he crossed the Mancunian Way and carried on up London Road past Piccadilly Station. Here he got caught up in traffic and the one-way system and seemed to drive around for a good while before reaching the pub on the other side of the city centre.

As he approached the front of the George and Dragon he was disturbed to see a man putting boards up to the windows.

'What's going on?' he asked as he drew level with the man.

'Ask him,' said the man, nodding towards two men who were standing close by.

Peter followed the man's eyes and noticed that one of the two other men was Pat, the pub landlord. He quickly hurried towards him.

'What's going on, Pat?' asked Peter, ignoring the other man.

'We're shutting up,' said Pat. 'We can't do it any more. Mary's nerves are torn to shreds with it all and we've fuckin' had enough.'

'What do you mean? Had enough of what?'

'The bleeding gangs, that's what. I might be paying you but that doesn't stop the others giving me grief. They'll do anything to try and fuckin' scare us. They were here again last night, and they tore the bleeding place apart. It was the last straw for me and Mary. She's been living on her nerves for months as it is.'

Peter noticed that the other man was listening keenly to the conversation. 'Come to the car, Pat. Let's have a chat.'

Pat instructed the man to carry on with the boarding up while he reluctantly followed Peter.

They got inside Peter's new Jag, and Peter sat in the driving seat with Pat sitting across from him in the passenger seat.

'Right, Pat. I wanna know what the fuck's been going on so we can fix this,' said Peter.

'There's no point,' said Pat. 'My mind's made up. You'll never stop them.'

'Who is it? Is it that fuckin' Alan's lot?'

'I don't know their names,' said Pat 'but it's not always the same people. Last night it was a crowd of young uns. They seemed all right at first till they started tear-arsing around the place ripping everything to fuckin' shreds. Me and a few of the locals saw them off the premises but half an hour later a few heavies arrived. They told me there'd be more to come if we didn't pay them to protect us.'

'How much did you pay them?'

'Nothing yet. They gave me till Tuesday but said that if I didn't pay by then I might regret it when the place got wrecked again. It was a definite threat. They were making out that they were trying to protect us because they'd heard about the trouble but it was fuckin' obvious what they were really about.'

'What will happen to this place? Have you found a new owner?'

'Not yet but I'm not hanging on till we do. I just want out. I doubt whether anyone will take it on as a pub though. Too many people round here know about the trouble. It'll probably end up being a nursery or summat, like a lot of the old pubs.'

Peter could hear the resignation in Pat's voice and for a fleeting moment he felt guilty at what he and others like him were doing to the once vibrant night scene of Manchester. But he didn't want to let his touch of conscience show.

'OK, you might as well go,' he said, already starting the engine as Pat fiddled with the door handle.

As soon as Pat stepped from the car, Peter sped away. His momentary touch of conscience was immediately replaced by anger at the other gangs who were trying to muscle their way in, and concern about the number of businesses he was losing.

That same night Glynn and Mike were standing in the foyer of the Golden Bell keeping an eye on things when Spinner walked over to them. He had been doing a roaring trade since Glynn had put his men back on the doors, and Glynn and Mike were benefitting from the mark-up on drugs sales.

As Spinner approached, Glynn could see that he looked agitated, his movements even more jittery than usual. He sidled up to Glynn then put his mouth close to Glynn's ear and whispered.

'You see that bloke over there?'

Glynn followed Spinner's eyes. 'The one in the blue shirt?' he asked.

'Yeah, him. He's a fuckin' plain-clothes cop, I'm sure of it. And I've spotted a couple more in here tonight too. Straight up, mate, I think they're fuckin' working undercover.'

Glynn blanched. 'You sure?' he asked, but even as he asked the question he could see that the man in the blue shirt was taking everything in. He didn't look like your average punter so Spinner might well be right.

'Fuck! This is all we need,' he cursed.

Mike looked at him with a confused expression on his face.

'Fuckin' old bill,' Glynn whispered to him. 'Over there in the blue shirt and there's a few more in the club according to Spinner.'

'Shit!' said Mike.

'OK, Spinner,' Glynn said, once he had had a chance to come up with a plan of action. 'Thanks for letting me know. You'll have to knock it on the head for tonight.'

'But I'll be well out of fuckin' pocket!' Spinner complained.

'Don't worry, I'll see you right,' said Glynn knowing that Spinner would spend the rest of the evening searching for customers elsewhere, but also knowing that he was one of his best pushers and he might come in handy in the future.

When Spinner had gone, Glynn said, 'Right, Mike, we need to round up the rest and get them to fuck off out of it. We can't take any fuckin' chances with the old bill sniffing around. I know they've agreed to take the rap but you never know with fuckin' junkies; you can't trust most of 'em.'

'Sure,' said Mike, already looking around the club to pinpoint all the drug dealers so he could tell them to leave.

Glynn did likewise and after almost an hour they met again in the foyer.

'Do you think that's all of them?' asked Mike.

'Fuckin' hope so. I've been round the club three times to make sure. I even made up an excuse so I could go and check the ladies.'

'Bet that was fun,' sneered Mike.

'Not really, just a bunch of pissed-up tarts putting the warpaint on and slagging off their boyfriends. By the way, I've left a message with the guys on the doors to make sure they don't let any more dealers in tonight.'

'OK,' said Mike. Then after a moment he spoke again. 'I wonder who put 'em onto us.'

'No fuckin' idea but if you ask me it's definitely an undercover operation. It's no fuckin' coincidence that they've all come to the Golden Bell separately on their night off. I saw a couple of potential plain-clothes cops on my way round; snidey bastards, you can spot 'em from a thousand fuckin' paces.'

'I know what you mean. I didn't spot any of 'em coming in but once Spinner pointed it out, you start to suspect every fucker, don't you?'

'Dead right.'

'So, what do we do after tonight, Glynn?'

'I think we'll have to lie low for a while. We'll bring Spinner in for a few nights so he can have a look around and tell us whether he thinks there's any coppers in the club. There'll be no dealing though and we'll have to pay him for his services. We'll be well out of fuckin' pocket.'

'Yeah, we will. How long will we have to lie low?'

'No idea, mate. But I'm not taking any fuckin' chances. We've had a narrow escape tonight but it was far too fuckin' close for comfort for my liking.'

By the end of the night Glynn was in a foul mood. He knew they were already losing money from the security side of things. And now this. It was the last thing they needed. As the night drew to a close and Glynn watched the revellers leaving the club he wondered who it was that had given the police the tip-off. The obvious suspect was Alan but it might have been one of the other gangs. He wasn't sure, but there was one thing he was sure of: if he ever found out who it was he'd string them up by their bollocks.

37

It was a Monday afternoon almost four weeks since Adele had received the letter about the hearing. She was in Peter's office, feeling fidgety, flicking through files then putting them back on the shelves as she tried to put off the inevitable revelation.

'For fuck's sake, Adele! Is summat bothering you?' said Peter. 'Cos if there is I'd rather you spat it out than carried on fiddling about with the files. You're doing my fuckin' head in.'

Adele took the seat opposite him, her face serious. It was no use putting it off any longer; she'd have to tell him.

'We've had a letter,' she began tentatively.

'What kind of letter?'

'From the council,' she said. Then, noticing the dark shadow that passed across her brother's handsome face, she quickly uttered the rest. 'The club's under review. There's gonna be a hearing.'

'Fuck! Why? When did this happen?'

'The letter came a few weeks ago,' she said.

'Then why the fuck didn't you tell me?'

'I didn't know how to. They said it's because they're not happy about public safety inside the club following recent incidents. I thought you'd go spare. And I felt like I'd let you down seeing as how most of the shit happened under my management.'

'Well, you were dead fuckin' right about that! I can't believe you didn't tell me about something as important as this. When is this fuckin' hearing anyway?'

'This Thursday.'

'You're fuckin' jokin', aren't you?'

'I wish I was… Sorry, Peter, but there never seemed a right time to tell you.'

Peter butted in before she could say anything else, his voice now edged with panic.

'What the fuck are we gonna do? This is serious, Adele! I might lose my fuckin' licence, then where would we be? Things are already bad enough as it is. I'm losing money hand over fist with the security and the other businesses. It's only the fuckin' nightclub that's earning a decent wedge.'

Adele sighed and met his gaze. 'I think we might be OK,' she said.

'Well, I wish I felt the fuckin' same. What makes you so confident anyway?'

Adele took a deep breath and looked towards the office door to make sure no one was outside listening.

Then she lowered her voice while she divulged what had been happening in the club since they'd received the letter from the council.

Three days later while Adele and Peter rushed to attend the hearing, Glynn and Mike were outside the Grey Mare. They were standing well back from the pub, on the flagged area that led to the crumbling blocks of council houses. It was too hot to stand any closer. They watched in disgust as lurid amber flames danced about the building, consuming everything within.

Just in front of them a crowd of people had gathered, their eager faces displaying a mix of excitement, shock and horror at the spectacle. Glynn could hear a tense muttering from the crowd as people speculated about the number of bodies trapped inside and how the blaze had started.

As the fire gathered momentum and ravaged hungrily through the building, the windows shattered, causing a loud gasp from the onlookers. The drone of the crowd, combined with the roar of flames and the sound of breaking glass, created an auditory overload of despair.

With the windows now smashed, the flames broke free, rising up from the building like a raging beast, the blaze giving off a pall of thick black smoke with an intensity that was suffocating. Meanwhile, the fire crews fought valiantly to keep the inferno contained.

Glynn's immediate thoughts weren't for the innocent people trapped inside, but for the loss of business now that they could no longer collect protection money from the pub. 'Fuckin' disgrace, this,' he said to Mike, who nodded solemnly.

He and Mike remained standing for a few moments, watching the tragic scene unfold before them. When a group of PCs began to circulate the crowd, asking if anyone knew anything about how the fire had started, Glynn decided it was time to go.

'Come on, let's fuck off out of it,' he said to Mike. 'Last thing we need is them fuckers interrogating us.'

As they headed back to Glynn's car, he could feel the rage building within him. This was one step too far and he'd had enough.

'Who d'you think did it?' asked Mike.

He bore the brunt of Glynn's fury as he snapped back at him, 'Who the fuck d'you think did it? There's only one fuckin' gang that would have the nerve to do that as far as I'm concerned.'

'What, Alan Palmer, d'you mean?'

'Yes, Alan fuckin' Palmer. That tosser!'

'I couldn't stand the bastard when we were in the nick.'

'Yeah, I know. You've fuckin' mentioned it!'

'All right, keep your hair on!' Mike snapped back.

Glynn managed to stop himself biting back. It wasn't Mike's fault when all was said and done so it wasn't fair to take it out on him. But he was still raging inside. Alan's gang seemed to be stepping up the action and he was beginning to feel as though things were getting out of his control. He wished, not for the first time, that he was running the firm instead of Peter; then people would think twice before they crossed him.

'That cocky bastard, Alan, and his lowlife crew think they can take fuckin' liberties with us!' he ranted. 'Pete's such a soft cunt that they just do what the fuck they want.'

'You're not gonna let them get away with this, are you?' asked Mike.

'No, I'm not! As soon as we get back I'm gonna fuckin' have it out with Pete and find out what he's gonna do about it.'

Mike stayed quiet for a while as they both got inside Glynn's BMW, and Glynn slammed the driver's door shut before turning the key in the ignition and treading hard on the accelerator.

As they sped away from what remained of the Grey Mare, Mike looked back over his shoulder, taking in the scene of devastation one last time before they were out of view. 'Pity, really.' He sniffed. 'Jim wasn't a bad landlord really.'

'Shut the fuck up!' ordered Glynn. 'And let's concentrate on how we're gonna deal with the twats that did this.'

38

It was the first time Adele had set foot inside Manchester town hall although she'd seen the grand exterior many times. Dating back to the late nineteenth century, it was a grade one listed building of neo-Gothic design; impressive from the outside and formidable on the inside.

As she entered the doorway with Peter she barely had a chance to gaze around at the ornate carved wooden doorways, impressive stained-glass windows and elaborate chandeliers before she and Peter were met by a security guard.

Adele handed him the letter she had received from the council about the hearing. She noticed her hands sweating, causing the letter to become damp at the edges where she had handled it, and she was conscious of the security guard's look of scorn.

'Lift's over there. You want level one, room 132,' he barked officiously.

As Adele and Peter made their way to the lift she became conscious of the sound of her heels tapping on the marble floor and could feel her heart beating frantically. She looked at her brother as they waited for the lift to arrive but he didn't speak.

The ping of the lift startled Adele and they waited patiently while a bunch of council employees made their way out. It seemed that no sooner were they in the lift than it had arrived at the first floor. They walked along the corridor in search of room 132. To Adele it felt as though her heart would burst through her chest, it was beating so erratically.

When they arrived at the room, they both stopped. Adele looked across at Peter once more. 'Fingers crossed,' she said but again he remained silent. Then she took a deep breath and pressed the buzzer to room 132.

Once inside the room, everyone there immediately scrutinised the two new arrivals. Although Adele and Peter were ten minutes early, it looked as though the other people had been there a while and were all keenly waiting to get on with business.

The lady who had answered the door led them to two seats, which were facing three people, two men and a woman, who Adele presumed to be council officials. They all wore smart suits, and each of them had a handful of papers in front of them.

To one side of the officials were two uniformed police officers, a younger one and an older man who looked official yet approachable. Adele recognised the older of the two, who was a police inspector, but he didn't acknowledge her. There was also a lady sitting near to the council officials with a pad and pen in front of her, and a few more people dotted around. Adele guessed that the lady was some form of secretary who was there to record the meeting.

The oldest of the three council officials seemed to be the one in charge. He was a man in his fifties or sixties, who bore a stern expression while he eyed Adele and Peter suspiciously. As soon as Adele and Peter were seated, he began to address the meeting, explaining why the hearing had been called and briefly outlining the background that had led to the hearing. His voice was monotone, his bearing rigid.

While he spoke Adele tried to focus, frightened that she might become overwhelmed by the formality and enormity of it all. She practised taking deep breaths, hoping to calm her racing heart and steady her shaking hands, but her breath seemed to jar in her throat and she could feel the first stirrings of panic.

She shook it off and listened while the council official invited the police inspector to speak. The inspector rose from his seat. Standing tall, he pulled his shoulders back before addressing the council officials calmly and authoritatively, pausing intermittently to peer at the notes he held in his hand.

'We decided to apply for a review of the licence of the Golden Bell due to the number of incidents there recently.'

Adele tried to concentrate while he detailed all the disruption that had taken place at the club over recent months and the dates they had occurred. When he referred to Anna's injuries along with all the others that had been sustained that night, she fought to contain the tears that threatened to erupt.

After what seemed like a lifetime, the inspector finished speaking, rounding off his speech by detailing the actions that had been taken since the council sent the letter, such as the undercover police operation. The council leader thanked him for his input, then addressed Adele.

'I believe you have something to add,' he said.

'Yes,' said Adele, her voice trembling.

'Could you stand, please, and address the hearing?' he requested.

Adele stood unsteadily. As she did so, she took a sidelong glance at Peter, noticing the expression of astonishment on his face. She hadn't told him she was going to speak. His look of shock brought home the importance of what she had to say and her panic threatened to reignite. What she said now could mean the difference between them keeping the licence for the Golden Bell or having it revoked.

As she spoke to the three officials her voice sounded small and shaky. 'When I received the letter from the licensing committee I rang Inspector Burscough,' she began, gazing across at the inspector for affirmation and receiving an encouraging nod. 'I explained to him my concerns about drug dealing in the club and told him that I was as keen as the police to stamp it out. We have an anti-drug policy at the Golden Bell and I was obviously upset at what had occurred.'

She paused, noticing the encouraging nod from the inspector, before clearing her throat. Then she looked down at the notes she had made, at Caroline's suggestion, and tried to ignore her quivering hands while she continued.

'We came up with a plan of action, aimed at stamping out any further occurrences of drug dealing in the club.'

Adele's throat dried up and she was finding it difficult to voice her next words so the head official gave her a moment to calm down. 'It's all right. Take your time,' he said.

Adele took yet another deep breath before continuing.

'I agreed with the police to carry out an undercover surveillance operation. I also arranged to reinstate the bag searches so that all female customers of the Golden Bell are searched at the doors on their way in. My door staff also search all males entering the club by patting them down.

'Two of our bouncers patrol the club each evening specifically looking for anybody who seems to be involved in drug dealing. Up to now they have found two people in possession of drugs and we have reported them to the police.

'I've also discussed future actions with Inspector Burscough, such as employing a mixed team of doormen with some having local knowledge and others coming from outside the Manchester area.'

Adele looked at her notes again, and scanned the words till she got to the end, making sure that she had covered all of the points she wanted to make. 'Er, I think that's it,' she said.

'Very well,' said the council official. 'Could you sit back down, please?'

Adele did as asked then let out a gasp of air, relieved that her speech was over.

'Has anyone got anything to add?' asked the official, looking around at the other people in the room. Adele could hear them mutter *no* and she noticed a couple shake their heads. 'Very well,' he said. 'We will now take some time to reach a decision. Perhaps you would like to go for a coffee in the upstairs canteen and meet us back here in an hour's time.'

Everybody apart from the council officials shuffled out of the room and Adele and Peter made their way to the canteen. While they waited for the lift with the other people from the hearing, nobody spoke. Once they arrived at the canteen, Adele and Peter grabbed a table away from everyone else. Adele knew they needed to talk.

'What the fuck's been going on, Adele?' asked Peter. 'You never told me you were behind that fuckin' undercover operation. And when did you find two people dealing drugs? You never fuckin' told me about that either!'

'OK, calm down,' said Adele, looking around her then lowering her voice. 'To be honest, Peter, you did take your eye off the ball a bit so I decided to do what had to be done.'

'But why the fuck didn't you tell me?'

Adele shrugged. 'I suppose I felt guilty in a way for everything that had happened while I was managing the club. I thought the onus was on me to put it right.'

'But that still doesn't explain why you didn't tell me what you were planning, for fuck's sake!'

'And if I had done, would you have agreed to an undercover police operation?' she asked. 'We both know how much you hate the police!'

'I might have done, I dunno. I didn't get the fuckin' chance to decide, did I? When did you nab the two dealers anyway?'

'A couple of weeks ago. You weren't in the club.'

Peter seemed lost in thought for a moment before

he said, 'I wondered why you brought those two new bouncers in. Are they the ones who have been patrolling the club?'

'Yes… Anyway,' she said, switching the emphasis, 'it's done with now. We just have to hope we've done enough to keep the licence.'

For a few moments there was silence between them. Adele knew Peter was annoyed with her but, in her view, she'd done the right thing by cooperating with the police. Apart from Peter's dislike of the police, she also secretly thought that she had handled the situation better than Peter would have done.

Although Adele had initially been alarmed when she'd received the letter from the council, what Caroline had suggested had made a lot of sense, and Adele was glad she had followed her advice. Besides, there was another reason she had acted alone without consulting Peter; if she was honest with herself, she was still finding it difficult to relinquish control of the club. She just hoped to God she had done enough to keep hold of the licence.

39

They trudged back inside room 132 and took their seats. Adele gazed across at the council officials but they were all stony-faced, making it impossible to read their expressions. She noticed that the inspector was no longer present; he obviously had more pressing matters to attend to, but the other officer was in the room.

The head of the council officials waited until they had all taken their seats, then stood up to address his audience. Adele felt the heat rush to her face as his eyes hovered over her and Peter. *Please let it be good news,* she repeated over and over in her head in time to the pounding rhythm of her heart.

'We have reached a decision,' he said, formally. 'We will not be revoking the licence for the Golden Bell.'

'Yes!' roared Peter, punching the air with his fist.

Adele felt a breath of air escape from her lungs, which had been like a taut, over-pumped balloon for the past few minutes. 'Thank God,' she whispered.

The head official raised his voice. 'Before we get carried away,' he said, 'we have attached several conditions to retaining the licence. These are as follows...'

He then went on to detail how Adele and Peter must continue to cooperate in full with the police. The door searches were to continue, as was the regular patrolling of the club by doormen and the reporting of any suspects to the police. They were also instructed that they must employ more doormen from outside the area to make up a total of six. That presented them with a bit of a problem as they would have to lay off some of the existing doormen but, aside from that, Adele and Peter were overjoyed with the news.

'Fuckin' great news, that,' said Peter as soon as they had left room 132, ignoring the scowls and tuts from a lady who had overheard his bad language.

Peter was so pleased with the outcome of the hearing that he seemed to have forgotten his earlier cross words with Adele. 'Let's go and have a drink to celebrate,' he suggested, peering at his watch. 'The pubs will be open now.'

'Not for me this early in the day,' said Adele. 'Maybe tonight. I want to get back to the club. I've got some mail that wants dealing with.'

'OK, tonight, then,' said Peter as they entered the lift that took them to the ground floor. 'I'll come back to the club with you. I've got a few things that I could do with seeing to myself.'

Adele was glad to get out of the town hall. It might have been a beautiful building but it was also the place where the future of the Golden Bell had hung in the balance. As they walked away, Peter turned to Adele.

'Right, sis,' he said. 'Now that's out of the way, I want you to promise me summat.'

'What?' asked Adele, looking back at him.

'That in future you won't do anything without running it by me first. That was a fuckin' close call, and you took a big chance without telling me about it.'

'OK,' said Adele, smiling.

Despite Peter's feelings, they both knew she had done the right thing. She was glad that she had saved the club from closure, no matter what lengths she had gone to in making sure of it. And now, hopefully, all would go well.

Adele and Peter's joy was short-lived. As soon as they walked back inside the Golden Bell and saw the look on Glynn's face they knew something wasn't right.

'Hey, we've just come back from that hearing I told you about,' said Peter.

'Oh, yes, I'd forgotten about that,' said Glynn. 'How did it go?'

Peter thought it was strange that Glynn could forget something as momentous as a hearing to decide on the future of the club, but nevertheless he answered him.

'Great! We get to keep the licence, apart from a few conditions that we have to keep to but they're no big deal. I can tell you about them later.'

'Good,' said Glynn, but his speech was flat, as though he couldn't care less either way. 'Can I have a word with you upstairs?' he asked, looking disparagingly at Adele to let Peter know this wasn't something she should be a party to.

'Sure,' said Peter, his earlier euphoria already beginning to wear off.

'What's up?' Peter asked when they arrived inside his office. 'You look well fucked off. Anyone would have thought I'd just told you I was going for a piss, the way you reacted. We've just saved the club from being shut down, for fuck's sake!'

He was about to tell Glynn all about how Adele had saved the day by arranging an undercover police operation but a sixth sense told him to keep schtum. Glynn didn't like the police any more than he did and he knew Glynn had never liked the fact that he'd left Adele managing the club while he was inside. Although Glynn had never said so outright, Peter knew that he had expected to run the Golden Bell.

'Yeah, I know, mate,' said Glynn, 'and I'm dead chuffed for you but there's other shit been going on while you've been away.'

'Go on,' said Peter.

'The fuckin' Grey Mare's been torched.'

'What? You're joking!'

'Wish I fuckin' was, mate.'

'Will they be able to repair it?'

'No fuckin' chance! It's burnt to a cinder. The landlord and his family were still inside, according to the locals.'

'You're joking!' Peter repeated, although he knew this was anything but a joke.

Glynn didn't reply to Peter's comment, knowing it was just his way of expressing his shock. Instead he said, 'I reckon' it's that fuckin' Alan and his crew again. We need to do something about it. We can't fuckin' let them get away with this.'

'OK,' said Peter, raising his right hand. 'Give me a chance. I've only just come back from a fuckin' hearing to make sure we've kept our licence. One thing at a time, mate.'

'Look, we can't afford to wait too long,' said Glynn. 'We're losing business right, left and centre, and it's only gonna get fuckin' worse.'

'Don't you think I fuckin' know that?' snapped Peter, feeling the pressure. 'I need time to think. I know we need to do summat but it's no fuckin' good rushing at it.'

'We need to hit the bastards hard!' raged Glynn.

'I know we need to do summat,' Peter repeated, 'but if you think I'm gonna raid their clubs and end up serving a fuckin' stretch again, you've got another think coming.' Peter was recalling the prison sentence he'd just served when the police had caught him raiding two of the clubs protected by Alan's gang, in retaliation.

'Right,' said Glynn, slapping his hand on the desk. 'Well, don't take too fuckin' long over it. They're making mugs of us and it's got to stop! And if you won't fuckin' do anything about it, then I'll make sure *I* will.'

Peter didn't get a chance to come back at Glynn as he stormed straight out of the office, leaving Peter feeling disturbed. Glynn's display of anger worried Peter. He'd never seen him lose his temper to that extent before, let alone question his authority so openly.

But, at the end of the day, Glynn wasn't in charge; he was. And there was no way he was going to let Glynn pressure him into a decision he might regret. That had happened before and he'd spent time inside while he was paying the price for it.

As he stood staring at the empty place where Glynn had stood, Peter reached a decision. He'd been thinking about it for some time but these latest events had affirmed it in his mind. He would let the security business go and concentrate on other areas of business instead. It just wasn't worth the hassle.

He knew Glynn wouldn't welcome the news. After all, the protection business was his baby and he'd been instrumental in helping to build it up from nothing. But that was before so many other gangs had started to get in on the act. Now it was a different ball game altogether. You had to move with the times, and Peter was already thinking of other business areas he could move into in the future.

Once he'd made up his mind, he decided to find Glynn and break the news. It was better to get it out of the way as quickly as possible. Bollocks to what Glynn thought. The days of Peter being pressured into doing something he didn't want to were long gone. Now he was going to do things his way and Glynn would just have to accept it.

40

Glynn and Mike were on their way to a job. Glynn had just picked Mike up from his home and they were now sitting inside Glynn's BMW.

'Another of our fuckin' pubs got torched last night,' said Glynn.

'You're fuckin' joking! Which one? Who did it? Do we know?'

'The Monkey. I don't know who was responsible but I could make a fuckin' good guess.'

'You think it's that Alan's lot?'

'Yeah, deffo. The twats had been putting pressure on the landlord for a few weeks. I tell you, Mike, it makes my fuckin' blood boil! Those bastards think they can get away with anything.'

'So, what's the plan?'

'What, to hit 'em back, d'you mean?'

'Yeah, what's Pete planning to do about it?' asked Mike.

'Fuck all! That's the other thing I've not told you yet. Pete's gonna let the security business go. He says it's not worth the hassle now that so many other gangs have got on the bandwagon.'

'Are you fuckin' serious? What's got into him?'

'I don't know but I'm not fuckin' taking it lying down, I'll tell you that. Why are we pissing about waiting for his permission? I can run the fuckin' security business without him. But I'll do it my way.

'That's two fuckin' pubs that have gone up in smoke now, not to mention the ones that have shut because of the intimidation from other firms. They've even been beating the bouncers up at one of the clubs we look after. People like Alan need to know that they can't fuckin' get away with it and we'll be the ones to teach them a fuckin' lesson.'

While Glynn delivered his diatribe, Mike sat patiently and listened. Glynn was now red in the face, his voice raised and his words rushed.

'I agree with you,' said Mike when Glynn stopped for breath before continuing again.

'And another thing, I reckon it was that Alan's lot that set the fuckin' coppers on us at the Golden Bell. That twat's got a lot to answer for.'

Glynn slammed the brakes on his BMW as they arrived at one of the pubs they looked after. 'Come on, we've got work to do but when we've finished our rounds we need to talk some more. From now on me and you will decide what happens with the security business but I ain't fuckin' letting it go, and Alan's firm are gonna get what's coming to them.'

Peter walked inside the city centre pub on Deansgate. It was a step above the usual pubs he visited when collecting protection. The old converted bank still had the high ceilings, dramatic archways and original stone pillars. Peter walked over to the well-stocked bar, the front of which was finished in padded leather upholstery. He ordered an overpriced brandy and soda, and sat down on one of the plush leather Chesterfields that were dotted about the place.

While he sipped his drink he gazed around him. The lighting was subtle but still sufficient to bring out the best features of the place. It was also light enough for him to see who stepped inside the pub even though he was sitting well back from the entrance, away from prying ears and eyes. It wasn't long before his visitor entered the pub and walked over to the area where Peter was sitting. Peter immediately stood up to greet his visitor, who announced himself.

'Hi, I'm Chris,' he said, holding out his hand.

Peter had known it was him as soon as he entered the pub. He fitted the description perfectly: around six feet tall, blond and in his early thirties. He seemed a friendly sort of guy, but professional too.

Peter shook Chris's hand and returned his greeting. 'Let me get you a drink,' he said, before rushing back to the bar.

While Peter was waiting to be served, he admonished himself for appearing too keen. It didn't pay to be overeager in business. So, while he would let Chris know that he was interested in doing business with him, he'd try to play it cool.

Peter walked back over to Chris and made himself comfortable. For a few minutes they made polite chit-chat before they got down to the real matter in hand. Peter found it easy to relax with Chris. He was a likeable guy with one of those amiable faces that instilled trust.

For the next hour they discussed the state of the property market in Manchester. Peter was impressed by Chris's knowledge; he certainly knew his stuff. He noticed, however, that Chris stopped short of detailing the illegal gains to be made. But Peter could read between the lines and he already knew this was a potential goldmine as he'd had a tip-off from a friend of his. He tried not to get too carried away by his enthusiasm.

Eventually the meeting finished and Peter shook hands with Chris again before arranging a follow-up meeting at his office at the Golden Bell. As he left the pub Peter reflected on the past hour. It had gone well, and this might just be the perfect sideline to inject some profit back into his ailing businesses.

He also felt that Chris was someone he could work with. He seemed a trustworthy guy but then, you never knew. He'd put his trust in people before, people who he'd thought were all right, such as Alan and David, and he'd been badly let down. He just hoped that this could be the lucrative lifeline he needed and that Chris's amiable persona wasn't concealing a devious character.

41

Two days later Peter was having his second meeting with Chris in his office at the Golden Bell. Peter had thought over everything they had discussed since that first meeting, and the more he thought about it, the more he knew it was a goer. Although Chris hadn't detailed how the illegal scam would work, Peter had enough contacts to enable him to find out more. By gathering information here and there he eventually joined the dots so that he could see the bigger picture.

During the meeting they agreed that Chris would start work for Peter as soon as possible. Peter had been impressed with Chris's knowledge, his positive attitude and his professionalism, and he couldn't wait to get started. He led him out of the building, eager to do some more research about the points they had discussed.

*

Adele was on the way to her office when she bumped into Peter in the corridor. He was with another man and Adele was immediately struck by how good-looking the man was. Tall, blond and slim, he was nothing like Glynn, who was thick-set and had stern, chiselled features. Instead, this man had a friendly face, the type of face that drew people to him.

'Adele,' said Peter, with a big grin painted across his face. 'Meet Chris. He's going to be working with me on my new business venture.'

'Hello,' said Adele, looking sceptically at Peter while Chris shook her hand enthusiastically.

'What business venture is that?' she asked, trying to ignore the effect Chris's charming smile was having on her.

'I'm going into property,' Peter gushed.

'Property? You didn't tell me that.'

'I've only just reached my decision. I'll tell you about it later. I'm just showing Chris out, but you'll be seeing quite a bit more of him in the future now he's going to be working with me.'

'Oh, right,' said Adele, deliberately remaining stand-offish with Chris.

She continued to her own office, leaving Peter and his new associate, but the brief meeting had left an impression on her. *Just what the hell is Peter up to now?* she thought. She dreaded to think but, whatever it was, she preferred not to get too involved. Knowing Peter, it was something shady.

Her thoughts switched to the handsome stranger who was to become Peter's new business associate. He was certainly a looker, that was for sure. But, despite his friendliness, she doubted that he would be any different from any of the other people her brother associated with in the course of his underhand dealings.

In fact, his amiable persona probably hid a whole heap of trouble. At least with Glynn you knew where you stood. He had rugged good looks and a hard edge to him that hinted at trouble, but which women couldn't resist anyway.

Chris, on the other hand, was a tricky one to fathom. But she'd give him a wide berth. Her relationship with Glynn had ended so badly that there was no way she was going to make the same mistake again. Despite Chris's charming manner and good looks, she was determined that this time she wouldn't be swayed.

42

'So, run that by me again,' said Glynn, swirling brandy around in the glass Peter had handed to him.

It was early evening and they were sitting in Peter's office chatting. Despite their previous stern words they were now back on friendly terms, even though an underlying tension still hung between them. It was nothing that Peter could define, more a feeling that things just weren't right with Glynn.

'Right,' said Peter, trying to explain the property scam that he was now involved in. 'What happens is, we get someone to buy a run-down terraced house that's been repossessed. He'll get it for a knock-down price with it being run-down. Then we get someone to revalue the house. He'll pump the price right up so it's a lot more than market value.'

'And do you know someone who'll do that?' asked Glynn.

'Oh, yeah. I know a couple of bent surveyors, one's an alcy and the other one's got massive debts. They'll do anything for a few extra quid.'

Peter stopped short of telling Glynn who his contacts were. Although he was prepared to let Glynn help with the running of the property scam, he wasn't going to fully put his trust in him. Glynn had been a great employee but Peter still had a niggling doubt about him. It seemed he was getting a bit too big for his boots lately and, if Peter was honest with himself, he wasn't sure he fully trusted him any more.

'OK, so what happens then?' asked Glynn.

'Then, and this is where you come in, one of us buys the house by applying for a mortgage using fake ID.'

'OK, no problems getting hold of that,' said Glynn.

'Yeah, then once we've got the mortgage we pocket the difference between the knock-down price and the value our surveyor has come up with. The person who bought it originally will get his money back and we'll have plenty left for ourselves.'

'Sound,' said Glynn, his enthusiasm beginning to show as he got to grips with the specifics of this new illegal scam.

'Yeah, good, innit?' said Peter, grinning. 'And we can put tenants in the houses too. We can charge 'em rent. They'll be paying that with their housing benefit so we can more or less charge what the fuck we like. And the building society won't be able to come at us for the mortgage because the person who took out the mortgage doesn't exist. By the time they realise that and take action to repossess the house, we'll have been earning rent from the tenants for fuckin' months.'

'Nice one,' said Glynn, returning Peter's grin and high-fiving him. 'So, where does this new guy, Chris, come into it?'

'He's just one of the cogs. He's got a lot of knowledge of the property business so he's useful to have around. Seems a good bloke too but there's only one thing about him that bothers me: he doesn't seem to want to get his hands dirty himself.'

'Crafty bastard,' said Glynn. 'I've come across people like that before. They wanna be part of it but if it all goes tits up they can cover their tracks and make out they didn't know about the illegal side of things. I'd keep an eye on him if I were you.'

'Don't worry. I'm not daft.'

'Other than that, it sounds like a good number.'

'Yeah, I reckon it'll be a great earner,' said Peter. 'It should make up for some of the losses we've been making recently. I tell you, I'll be glad to wave goodbye to the fuckin' protection. This is a much better way of making money.'

'Well, now you've brought it up, I was gonna talk to you about that,' said Glynn.

Peter raised his eyebrows inquisitively so Glynn continued speaking. 'I know your feelings about the protection, mate, but I'm not prepared to let it go. Me and Mike have worked fuckin' hard to build it up and I don't see why we should let it go to some other tossers who've decided to jump on the bandwagon.'

'No, Glynn. I'm not running it any more. It's gone to shit.'

'You don't have to,' said Glynn. 'I'll take it over; Mike will help. No offence, mate, but you have been a bit of a soft cunt with the other gangs. Me and Mike will make sure they know who's fuckin' running the show.'

'Have you still been collecting for the last couple of weeks?' asked Peter.

'Yeah. I can let you have everything up to today if you want but from today I wanna run it.'

'No, that's OK,' said Peter. 'You're welcome to it. Do whatever you think you need to do but I don't want any fuckin' comeback from it. If you're gonna go in hard then the other gangs will retaliate and start hitting the club and the sunbed shops again. I've had enough of my people getting hurt. You need to make sure they know I'm not connected to it.'

'Don't worry,' said Glynn. 'I'll put the word out. Every fucker will soon know that I'm running the protection in Manchester.'

Glynn held his glass up to chink it against Peter's and, although Peter responded, it didn't really feel like a celebration. He felt betrayed. Since he'd told Glynn he wanted to let the protection business go Glynn had carried on collecting, and yet he'd only just bothered telling him.

Peter felt as though he'd been backed into a corner. He didn't really want Glynn to take over the protection; he was too closely connected to him, and Peter would have preferred to sever all ties with the protection business. But, somehow, he got the feeling that if he hadn't acquiesced, Glynn would have taken it anyway.

Glynn had told him to keep an eye on Chris, and Peter would. It was something he had already decided to do. But after this meeting with Glynn, Peter felt even surer that there were other people he needed to keep an eye on too. Once again, Glynn had questioned his authority and Peter didn't like it. He didn't like it at all.

43

It was over two weeks later and Caroline had stopped by the club to see Adele. They were currently seated at the bar helping themselves to a drink before the night staff came on shift. It was good to talk to Caroline. She had a way of always making things seem better. Caroline had just come back from a trip visiting Anna, and Adele was eager to find out how their old friend was doing.

'So, how was Anna when you visited her?' asked Adele.

'Pretty much the same,' said Caroline, 'although she does recognise me now, and she remembers you. I didn't get that much chance to talk to her though. Her mother seemed eager to see the back of me.'

'I bet she did. She wasn't very friendly with me either when I saw her at the hospital. I think she doesn't like anyone who Anna knew from prison.'

'Well, it was a bloody long way to travel just to grab a few minutes with Anna.'

'I bet it was. I was thinking of going myself but I just haven't had the time.'

'I wouldn't bother if I were you. I think Anna's mother wants to forget about Anna's insalubrious past and, although I'm sad to say it, I think we need to move on too.'

'It's a pity,' said Adele.

'I know, but that's just the way it is, unfortunately,' Caroline said, putting her arm around Adele's shoulders in a comforting embrace. Then she pulled away and changed the subject. 'Anyway, how are things going for you otherwise?' she asked.

'Well, where do I start? Things have been a bit different since Peter came back on the scene. I must admit, I'm finding it hard to hand things back over to him. I'd kind of got used to being the one in charge.'

'Power can do that to you,' Caroline teased.

Adele smiled. 'It's not so much that,' she said, becoming serious. 'I don't like how he does things. While he was inside I did my best to keep things on the right side of the law but now I'm worried about what goes on behind my back.'

'Do you really think he'd do anything to jeopardise the future of the club after you almost lost your licence a few weeks back?'

'I'm not sure. I think he's forgotten how close we came. I know he's worried about how much money his businesses are losing, which might lead him to make unwise decisions. And I'm also worried about how much influence Glynn has on him.'

Adele thought back to the time when she'd caught Glynn involved in drug dealing inside the club. She'd told her brother all about it but Peter had still been reluctant to sack him. That thought worried her. Then she recalled the night Glynn had shot a man in cold blood when he'd broken into her office and held a knife to her throat. The memory made her shudder involuntarily, and her facial muscles tensed.

'Are you all right?' asked Caroline.

'What?' asked Adele as she drifted back into the present. 'Sorry, I was miles away.'

'You can say that again. You looked troubled.'

'No, I'm fine,' said Adele. 'I was just getting a bit carried away with my own thoughts, that's all.'

'Try not to worry. As long as you do everything they suggested at the hearing, you should be OK,' said Caroline.

'Yeah, I know. We're still doing the searches and patrolling the club. Oh, and we've taken on some new bouncers from out of the area as well. They all seem decent guys, especially the one called Bear.'

'Bear? That's a funny name, isn't it?'

'It's because he's like a big, cuddly teddy bear. He looks soft and he's so lovely to get on with, but you wanna see him in action; he won't stand any messing from the punters.'

'He sounds like the sort of man you need to be employing. Am I sensing a soft spot here, by any chance?'

'Bear? Oh, no! If you saw him you'd know what I mean. No, he's just a nice person to get on with.'

'So, what else has been going on?' asked Caroline.

'Oh, just some other business that Peter has decided to get involved in. To do with property. I don't know what it involves, exactly, but I don't think I want to know. He's taken on some guy called Chris to help him with it but I'm not sure how he fits into things yet.'

'Well, you never know, this might be a legal business. Maybe Peter's seen the error of his ways at last.'

'Pffft,' said Adele. 'I'll believe that when I see it.'

'Anyway,' said Caroline, looking at her watch, 'it's time I was going.'

'Come on, I'll lock the doors after you,' said Adele, getting up from her bar stool.

As they moved away from the bar Adele saw Chris approaching. He beamed a smile at them, displaying his usual charm.

'Is Peter in?' he asked Adele.

'In his office,' she replied curtly. Then she continued past him without introducing Caroline.

'Bloody hell!' said Caroline, when they were out of hearing range. 'You might have introduced me. Who is he?'

'Chris. Peter's new business partner I told you about,' said Adele, hoping Caroline couldn't detect her blushing.

'Well, he seems like Mr Charm himself and, if you ask me, he's got a bit of a soft spot for you,' Caroline teased. 'And,' she added, scrutinising Adele's reaction, 'I think you might have a soft spot for him too.'

'No!' said Adele. 'It's not like that. I mean, he's been very nice and friendly to me since he started working with Peter but there's nothing more to it.'

'You sure?' Caroline asked.

Adele took a deep breath between gritted teeth, showing her irritation. 'Look, Caroline, there's no way I'm going to get involved with another one of Peter's cohorts. He might seem a nice guy, but he's probably running something illegal with Peter. My experience with Glynn has put me off bad boys for good.'

'OK, OK,' said Caroline, holding up her hands in mock surrender. 'Still, it's nice to have a bit of eye candy while you work, isn't it?'

Adele smiled at her friend's audacity. 'I suppose so,' she said. Then, opening the doors for her friend, she added, 'I'll see you soon. Thanks for coming.'

She shut the doors, reflecting momentarily on what her friend had said, but then quickly dismissing it. No, there was no way she was going to get involved with another bad boy, no matter how much she might be attracted to him.

44

It was late at night and Glynn was sitting in a car outside a three-bedroomed council semi in Gorton. The house was in a cul-de-sac off the main road and Glynn had parked the car facing the open end of the street, ready for a quick getaway. It would have been a nice cul-de-sac if it hadn't been for the litter, the decayed state of the houses and the overgrown gardens.

Glynn was on his own; he didn't even want Mike to witness what he was about to do. He hadn't brought the BMW today, opting instead for a recently stolen Audi that still had the smell of new upholstery. He didn't like it as much as his BMW but he didn't want his own car to be spotted at the scene. Like his BMW, the Audi could shift and had tinted windows, and those things were important. When he'd done what he came here for, he'd dump the Audi and jump back into his BMW, which he'd left parked in Reddish.

What he was about to do was needed as far as Glynn was concerned. In fact, he didn't know why he hadn't done it ages ago. He was sick of people taking the piss. Sick of taking orders from Peter. Sick of watching it all go to shit while Peter sat back and did nothing. It was about time he took control and let everyone know who was boss.

Although there'd be no witnesses, Glynn knew that people would put two and two together and know who was responsible. But no one would squeal; nobody ever did in the gangland fraternity. Still, it was best to do this alone just to be on the safe side. You never knew when the police might get to people. And he couldn't risk that.

While he waited he watched an elderly lady knock at the house where his target lived. Shit! That was all he needed. He wouldn't have expected many people about at this time of night. The woman was wearing a dressing gown, her hair messy. As she waited for someone to answer the door, she was muttering incoherently to herself.

He sat watching her, hoping she would soon disappear. If she hung around then he'd have to put things off till another day. But, despite her knocking on the door several times, there was no answer.

Eventually she seemed to give up and turned around. Her eyes gazed swiftly about her but didn't settle on anything. Then she gave a whimper and shuffled back into her own home, where she'd left the front door wide open. Glynn guessed she wasn't the full ticket. Who else would ignore the shiny new Audi, considering it looked so out of place on the run-down council estate?

A few minutes later Glynn was rewarded by the sight of a taxi pulling into the cul-de-sac. His target emerged, slung some money at the driver then wobbled precariously in the direction of his home obviously the worse for wear. The taxi sped away. *How ironic,* thought Glynn. This guy, who professed to be a so-called gang leader, still lived in a poxy three-bedroomed council semi with his mam and dad, and caught a taxi home from the pub. Not only that, but he went home alone without any protection.

Alan's drunken state played to Glynn's advantage. He failed to take any notice of the Audi as he stumbled towards his home, stopping to grab a bunch of change from his pocket, which he then began flicking through. Glynn guessed he was looking for his door key and had forgotten where he'd put it.

As he watched him, Glynn's focus sharpened. He had to get the timing right. He needed to wait a few seconds till the taxi was out of the way, but he couldn't afford to wait too long. Then Alan seemed to spot something amongst the loose change and looked up at his front door, ready to head towards it.

This is it! thought Glynn. It would be easier to get him before he was on the move again. He quickly wound down the car window till there was a narrow gap at the top. It was just big enough to stick the barrel of a gun through. Then he aimed. But Alan turned around, alerted by the sound of metal hitting glass. For a few moments he stood prone, looking confused.

Now! thought Glynn. *Before Alan realises what's happening and dashes away.* Briefly registering the shock on Alan's face, he pulled the trigger then watched Alan drop to the ground in a pool of blood. Satisfied, he started the engine and fled.

It wasn't until Glynn had left the cul-de-sac that lights were switched on, the residents curious as to what had caused such a loud bang. It was Crazy Mary who found the body. Wandering out to see what the noise was, she was oblivious to any danger. The sight of Alan caused her to rush forward and drop to her knees over the body, her distressed screeches reaching the ears of the other residents as Alan's blood saturated her dressing gown.

Glynn didn't see the devastation caused by that one shot from his gun. Crazy Mary, howling and inconsolable. The shock of the dead body disturbing her already fuddled brain. Or Alan's parents, numb with shock at the horrific sight of their dead son. It was a shock that would manifest itself in the weeks, months and years to come.

As he zoomed away a feeling of euphoria came over him. He'd done it! He'd taken Alan out of the game.

One of the most astute and ruthless gang leaders was now gone, and Glynn knew there was no one in Alan's gang capable of taking over. A couple of them were handy but they didn't have the brains to run things. He might just take advantage of that and take a few of the better guys on himself. He wouldn't bother with David though, not that loser.

He drove through Gorton and headed towards Reddish and his beloved BMW. His mind was buzzing with the endless possibilities now Alan was gone. He'd be able to build the protection business back up, and they were no longer in danger of losing the Golden Bell to Alan's gang.

Glynn had taken the first step in building his reputation as one of the big names in Manchester. And this was only the beginning. He was fed up with taking orders from Peter when he knew he could run things better himself. It was about time Peter learnt to respect him.

In fact, before long he'd have the respect of everyone in the Manchester gangland community. He smiled as he thought about the opportunities mapped out before him. Yes, there was no doubt about it; Glynn Mason had just secured his future as one of Manchester's biggest and meanest faces. And, from now on, there'd be no stopping him.

45

Adele was troubled. Ever since Peter had told her about Alan's death two weeks previously, she'd been nervous. The fact that he'd been shot in the street made his death even more alarming. To think that someone she and her brother had known for years could suffer such a brutal killing was beyond belief.

The police were calling it a gangland killing and there was a lot of speculation about who could be responsible. Talk was rife in the club too, although nobody mentioned any names. They were all too frightened of reprisals if they were found to be the source of any rumours. And with nobody willing to point the finger, the police had very little to go on.

Adele had never liked Alan, ever since Peter had teamed up with him and David as a youngster. He and David had been known around the local area as a pair of tearaways, and Peter's crimes had escalated once he was in their company.

But then, for some reason, Peter wasn't friends with them any more. Adele didn't know the full story about what had happened to sever their friendship. But the fact that Alan and David had become Peter's enemies made Alan's killing all the more disturbing. It was just too close to home as far as she was concerned.

All these thoughts were swirling around in her head as she stood next to the outer perimeter of the Golden Bell watching what was going on. Although her attention wasn't fully on what was happening around her, she was brought to her senses when she spotted a familiar face amongst the crowd of revellers. Tall and good-looking with dark hair. Yes, it was definitely him.

It had been a long time since she'd seen him, but now, as she watched him casually standing at a table and glancing around the club, her mind shot back to their last encounter. He had been dealing drugs in the club and when she'd approached him about it he'd lost his cool and intimated that Glynn was in on the deal. His presence in the club confirmed her suspicions that Glynn was still allowing drug dealers in despite her efforts to put a stop to it.

Deciding that she needed to take action, she gazed around for backup. She could see Bear but he was walking away. Adele rushed to catch up with him but before she got there she spotted Peter chatting with two attractive women wearing short skirts that showed off

HEATHER BURNSIDE

their long, toned legs. Adele rushed over and excused herself while the two women tutted and murmured their irritation.

'Come over here,' Adele said, leading Peter towards the door marked 'Private' and away from the sound of the music.

'I've just spotted someone,' she said, trying to keep her voice to a whisper but failing to be heard as it was still loud even here. She leant over to him and whispered in his ear, 'A dealer.'

Then she drew away and walked a little further inside the club. 'Over there,' she said, nodding furtively. 'Tall, dark hair, wearing a blue shirt and standing on his own with a pint next to him. I've seen him in here before, ages ago. He was the one that said Glynn was OK with it.'

'OK,' said Peter. 'Leave it with me.'

'Do you want me to fetch some of the bouncers to help you shift him?'

'No, it's OK. Everything's under control. Don't worry.'

Adele stared at him, confused. 'What do you mean?' she asked. 'D'you mean... you *knew* about him?'

'Yeah, stop worrying,' he said, failing to meet her eyes. 'I've got things under control now. You don't need to worry about it.'

Then realisation dawned on her. 'Just what the hell is going on, Peter?' she demanded.

'Shush!' he said.

'Don't you shush me!' she raged, her raised voice drawing attention from some of the bystanders. 'I want to know what the hell is going on here.'

'All right, all right,' he said, taking her by the arm and leading her towards the door marked 'Private' again. 'Not here. There's too many people listening.'

Peter dashed through the door then shut it behind him once Adele had come through. He rushed up the stairs with Adele trailing after him, demanding answers. It wasn't till he got to the top corridor that he stopped and turned to face her.

'Will you keep your voice down, for fuck's sake?' he said. 'We don't want everyone knowing!'

'Then tell me what's going on, Peter. I have a right to know. My future is invested in this club just as much as yours and I don't want it jeopardising because of some low-life drug-peddling scum!'

'OK, if you must know, we're controlling any dealing that goes on in the club now.'

For a few seconds Adele stared at him, open-mouthed. She couldn't believe what she was hearing after all she had done to save the club when it had come under review.

'Look, Adele,' he continued. 'You can't get rid of the fuckin' dealers. They're everywhere. So the best we can do is control it ourselves.'

'Are you fuckin' serious?' she yelled. 'Is that why I went through weeks of worry leading up to the hearing, trying to convince them about our anti-drugs policy? Just what was the fuckin' point of all that, Peter?'

'Calm the fuck down,' he said. 'You saved the club, didn't you?'

When she responded, she spoke slowly, loudly enunciating each of her words. 'Yes. I. Did.' Then she glared at him. 'So what was the point of it all?'

'You're not listening to me, Adele. You've managed to convince them that we're not dealing so now we're off the radar. Believe me, this is the best way to handle things. We only let in the dealers who we know because we have an agreement with them. If they get caught by the police, they take the rap and we deny all knowledge.'

Adele had heard similar words before, spoken by Glynn, and it confirmed her suspicions that Glynn had got to her brother. It also enraged her even more to think that Glynn had had a hand in this.

'And I suppose the mark-up that you take from every deal comes into play as well, does it?' she asked sarcastically.

'Yeah, we do get a mark-up. But, I had to do something, Adele. My businesses were losing money hand over fuckin' fist!'

'Spare me the fuckin' sob story,' she growled. 'There are legal ways of making money, y'know.' But she wasn't finished. 'I can't believe you, Peter. It wasn't so long ago that you were opposed to drug dealing in the club. Was that before Glynn got to you?'

'Why do you always have to fuckin' bring him into it? No, no, it wasn't. It was before I knew the lie of the land. It makes sense, Adele. Why risk being done for drug dealing in the club when we aren't even fuckin' gaining anything from it?'

'That's a warped justification and you know it!' she snapped.

For a while they remained standing in the corridor, Adele breathing heavily following her rant, and staring angrily at Peter while his eyes flitted around him. Eventually he spoke.

'Look, if you've finished, I'm going back down to the club,' he said.

'No, wait a minute,' said Adele, her tone now calmer. 'You said you did it because you needed the money, didn't you?'

He nodded.

'Well, what about the new business? Isn't that earning you an increased income?'

'It will do, yes. Once we get things properly set up.'

'Then you won't need the drug dealers any more. Please, Peter, can't you see? All it takes is for one of them to go against their word and tell the police about your involvement, and we'll be shut.'

'They won't be able to prove it.'

'That doesn't matter,' she argued. 'Just a hint of suspicion will be enough to get us shut. Don't forget, we only managed to stay open by the skin of our teeth as it is. Believe me, Peter, the best way is to have nothing to do with the dealers. Then there will be no comeback.

'The only reason they're in our club is because Glynn's bouncers let them through the doors. But we've got enough good security around to make sure they don't get in and we can have more staff patrolling just in case the odd one gets through. In fact, if it was left up to me, I'd sack Glynn's men and fetch some others in.'

'Oh, yeah, and look what happened last time you did that,' he said.

His words cut through Adele like a dagger. She still felt guilty about what had happened when she'd changed the doormen. The image of Anna in a coma was never far from her mind.

But, despite his sharp words, Peter seemed to spend a moment thinking about what she had said. Then he shrugged his shoulders. 'OK,' he said. 'I'll think about it.'

Adele nodded and watched him walk away. She hoped to God that he would agree to do as she wanted because, for her, there was more than the club's future at stake. She was morally opposed to drugs on every level. She detested the damn things and the damage they did to young lives.

But as she recapped on their conversation she wondered whether Peter would do as she asked. After all, if he was going to change his policy on dealing with drug dealers then he would have to stand up to Glynn. And Glynn was a formidable adversary.

After her encounter with her brother Adele took a few moments to compose herself before going back downstairs to the club. She nipped to the ladies on the first floor and rinsed her face, which was still flushed with anger. Although she wasn't as annoyed as earlier, the adrenalin continued to course around her body and she knew it would be a while before she calmed down fully.

Driven by a desire to get back to her post in the club and her curiosity about what was going on downstairs, she wasn't fully concentrating when she swung open the door to the stairway. There standing in front of her was the large figure of a man. She jumped back and automatically clutched her chest, the shock of a surprise visitor alerting her already primed senses. It was unusual for people to be upstairs at this time of night.

As soon as she realised it was Chris and spotted his smile of amusement, she felt foolish and tried to mask her shock. Suddenly self-conscious, she overcompensated for her dramatic reaction, becoming stiff and formal.

'Sorry, excuse me,' she said, stepping forward to where Chris was holding the door open for her.

A look of concern replaced his boyish smile. 'Adele, are you OK?'

'Yes,' she said. 'You took me by surprise, that's all.' She could feel the heat returning to her cheeks at her accidental choice of ambiguous wording.

He smiled again and flashed his eyes in recognition of the double entendre. Adele tried to ignore his response and went to pass him. The gap between Chris and the door jamb was tight and she hovered doubtfully until he moved slightly to one side.

'Sorry,' he said. 'I didn't realise I'd not given you much room.'

Despite Chris's movement, the gap was still small and as Adele squeezed through she could sense him. She felt his body heat and smelt his aftershave. It was a woody, earthy aroma, which screamed of his manhood, and she felt her knees go weak. Becoming clumsy, she bumped her head against his arm then tried to duck, throwing herself off balance so that her steps were faltering and self-conscious.

Once through the gap, she dashed to the top of the stairs, almost missing her footing in her haste to get away.

'Adele!' he called to her, and she turned to face him again while her heartbeat switched up a gear.

'Are you sure you're OK? Only, you seem a bit flustered, that's all.'

His face showed that lovely, kind expression that she had noticed before. But she wasn't going to be fooled. He wasn't getting round her that easily.

'Yes, I'm fine,' she snapped, rushing down the steps and away from him.

Damn him! Why did he have this effect on her? She wished he didn't. Getting involved with another of Peter's so called 'business partners' could only be a bad thing. She couldn't deny that she was attracted to him. But she'd fight it all the way. She had enough to deal with right now, and the last thing she needed was a repeat of her disastrous relationship with Glynn.

So, she walked away, determined in her mind that a relationship with Chris wasn't on the cards. But her body was telling her something different. Adele loved the way his blond hair shone under the club lights. She was drawn to his slim yet manly physique, his broad shoulders and his toned arms. His boyish good looks and impish smile made her insides turn to mush. And, at the moment, Adele was finding it very difficult to fight against her most basic impulses.

46

It was a week later and Peter was sitting at the bar of the Golden Bell deep in thought. He was surprised to see Adele sitting with Chris further along the bar, and it looked as though they were getting along. There were lots of smiles, fluttering eyelashes and coy head movements. Around Peter, young attractive females vied for his attention, drawn by his good looks and the fact that he was the club's owner. But tonight he wasn't interested; he was troubled.

He'd been doing a lot of thinking since his set-to with Adele the previous week. What she had said made a lot of sense. Although he'd previously agreed with Glynn to allow drug dealers in the club, now he wasn't so sure. At the time he'd been glad of the extra income. But that was then and this was now.

Things were looking good with his new property business, which should prove very lucrative. The mark-up from drugs would be a fraction of what he could earn in the property market. And, the more he thought about it, the more he decided that the drugs mark-up just wasn't worth the risk of losing the club if the police found out.

But the problem was how to tell Glynn. Peter knew he wouldn't be happy when he told him they were stopping the dealers. In fact, judging by his recent behaviour, he'd go ballistic. So, although Peter agreed with Adele, he hadn't made any changes yet.

The more he thought about Glynn, the more he realised that he was becoming a threat and at the moment Peter didn't know what to do about it. If he sacked him, that would make matters even worse. Glynn was bound to put a gang together and they might even try to take control of the Golden Bell.

Despite her better judgement, Adele was enjoying Chris's company. She'd gone to the bar to have a few drinks after working late on Friday. When she'd had a couple of drinks and a chat with the bar staff, Chris had appeared alongside her.

'Mind if I join you?' he'd asked.

She'd been about to protest but couldn't think of anything to say without offending him so he'd slipped into the seat beside her and ordered them both a drink. She looked at him, at his boyish good looks and cheeky grin, and the way his blond hair dazzled under the club lights. He was wearing a short-sleeved shirt, exposing the toned muscles of his arms.

Adele wanted him, she knew she did, but she remained determined to fight it. Still, they were only having a few drinks together after a hard day at work. What harm could that do?

She'd never spoken more than a couple of words with Chris before as she'd always been eager to get away. But now, as he started to make conversation, she found herself becoming even more drawn to him. He had a lovely, affable way about him and regaled her with amusing anecdotes. He was also a good listener and seemed genuinely interested in getting to know more about her. And he was a massive flirt!

While she was sitting at the bar being entertained by Chris, Adele saw Peter approach. But he subtly left them alone, choosing a seat further along the bar instead. After that she didn't really notice what her brother was doing; she was too busy enjoying herself. It was the beginning of a shift in her affections towards Chris, and she was powerless to resist.

Adele was having such a good time that she failed to see what was going on behind her. It was Peter that brought it to her attention. All of a sudden she became aware of him by her side, and then noticed that the atmosphere in the club had changed. Conversations stalled, and laughter was replaced by cries of alarm.

'It's a raid! The fuckin' coppers are all over the place,' said Peter, shuffling from foot to foot, his eyes scanning the club.

Adele turned around. 'Oh, shit!' she said as she watched the police charge through the club, stopping to search people and quiz them.

She noticed that one of the police officers had a German shepherd on a lead, which was hurriedly dragging its master. Its nose was dipped to the ground, eagerly sniffing around.

Unlike the undercover operation, this time Adele had known nothing about the raid. She was as shocked as Peter by this impromptu visit from the boys in blue. What she couldn't understand was why the police would organise a raid after she had been so cooperative with them.

'I think you'd best make yourself known to them,' she said to Peter.

She watched Peter walk away in search of the senior officer and for a few moments she sat gazing around the club, not really sure what to do.

'Don't you think you'd better go with him?' asked Chris. 'After all, Pete can be a bit hot-headed at times and you wouldn't want him to say anything out of line to the police, would you?'

Adele hesitated for a moment, unsure whether or not to trust Chris. But his suggestion made sense so she went in search of her brother. She found him at the other side of the club, furiously demanding an explanation from a stony-faced plain-clothes officer.

It was soon easy for Adele to see that Peter's protestations were getting him nowhere. The only response he received from the police was that they had reason to believe that drugs were being sold on the premises. Adele took hold of Peter's arm.

'Peter, come here,' she said, gently pulling him towards her. 'You're not going to find out any more from them,' she said. 'There's nothing we can do but wait and see what happens.'

Peter looked around him, his face a picture of fury as he watched hordes of police with sniffer dogs tearing through the place. Adele's focus also switched to the pandemonium going on around them. The police had locked the doors so no one could get out and some of the club-goers were becoming distressed. She noticed the panicked expressions on some of their faces, the cries of outrage from others and the indifference from those too drunk to care.

For the next few minutes they had no choice but to stand and watch while the police did their job. Adele tried to calm Peter down, telling him it didn't necessarily mean the end of the club. It all depended how the search went. Then they saw a policeman dragging a man towards the senior police officer, and they stepped closer to find out what was happening.

'I caught this one in possession,' said the policeman. 'I'm taking him to the van.'

The senior officer nodded just as Adele spotted a brief look exchanged between Peter and the drug dealer. She stared at Peter, her face a picture of indignation, and he shuffled about uncomfortably. When the drug dealer kept quiet, Peter's relief was palpable. She only hoped the police officers hadn't noticed it too. But then, unlike Adele, the police didn't have the advantage of knowing about Peter's arrangement.

Eventually the senior officer declared that the raid was over, and he turned to speak to Peter.

'Sorry to have troubled you,' he said.

'Is that all you've got to say after all the hassle you've caused tonight?' asked Peter.

'It's all part of our job, I'm afraid,' said the officer. 'And we've caught one dealer on the premises so it wasn't a complete waste of time.'

He had that air about him that suggested he was disappointed with the result. It was as though he had expected to find much more and Adele was relieved that they hadn't found whatever it was they had been looking for. Judging by the look on the drug dealer's face, he would keep quiet about the arrangement with Peter. She therefore hoped that it would be the end of it. But she couldn't be sure.

'Fuck! That was a close call,' said Peter once the police had left the building.

'We don't know that, Peter. There might be some comeback,' she said, her worry evident. 'We'll have to stop the drug dealing now. It's too much of a risk. What if that man tells the police that you agreed to it?'

'Don't worry, he won't,' said Peter, but his words were more confident than the tone he used to convey them. She glared at him till he spoke again. 'OK,' he said, his slumped posture displaying his resignation. 'We'll do it. We'll put a stop to the pushers. Straight away. I'll let everyone know.'

'And Glynn?' she asked.

'Yeah, course. Glynn as well. In fact, I'll go and tell him now. No point waiting, is there?'

His words were full of bravado but Adele could see the fear in his face. It was at that moment it dawned on her that her brother was just as unnerved by Glynn as she was. And, even as he searched for Glynn, he could probably feel the trepidation. It would sit in the pit of his stomach like a lead weight.

47

It was the following day. Peter hadn't been able to find Glynn that night, although he could have sworn he'd seen him in the club earlier. So, he'd grabbed the chance to have a word with him at the first opportunity and Glynn was now sitting across his office desk from him.

'What the fuck d'you mean, we can't let the dealers in any more?' demanded Glynn, his face red with anger, and the veins in his neck protruding.

'It's too risky,' said Peter. 'We came fuckin' close to losing the club not so long ago and I don't wanna risk it again. And we might not even be in the all clear yet.'

'Course we fuckin' will!' yelled Glynn. 'The coppers haven't been back today, have they? That means our dealer's taken the rap, and not told the coppers we were in on it.'

'I don't care, Glynn. It's still too risky,' said Peter, finding it difficult to maintain control of Glynn, who was livid by now.

'No, it fuckin' isn't!' stormed Glynn. 'This way there's less risk. The dealer didn't let us down, did he? So that fuckin' proves we did the right thing!'

Glynn slapped his palm on the desk to emphasise his point.

'He wouldn't have been in the club in the first fuckin' place if it wasn't for our arrangement!' said Peter, his voice also rising.

'Maybe not but there's plenty of others who fuckin' would. If you think you can stop them then you're a bigger fuckin' mug than I thought!'

'I'm no one's fuckin' mug!' shouted Peter, getting out of his chair.

'Aren't you?' asked Glynn, his question mocking and his face forming a scowl as he also stood up and bent over the desk towards Peter.

For a few moments they stood glaring at each other across the desk. Glynn was breathing heavily and his eyes were bulging in his scarlet face. Eventually, Peter sat down and said, 'I've got work to do. I don't wanna discuss this any more. I've made up my mind and that's final.'

'Right, suit your fuckin' self!' roared Glynn, slapping the desk again then adding, 'But you're making a fuckin' big mistake.'

He then stormed out of Peter's office, leaving Peter shaken. It seemed that Glynn was making a habit of storming out of his office lately. There was no doubt in

Peter's mind that Glynn was becoming too difficult to handle.

Although Peter tried not to let it show he found Glynn's displays of temper intimidating. But you couldn't afford to let someone like Glynn bully you. It was best to let him know who was boss. Lately, though, Peter was finding it more and more difficult to keep Glynn in line. As he reflected on this latest confrontation, Peter had a feeling that he had a serious problem on his hands where Glynn was concerned.

When Glynn met Mike he was still angry following his meeting with Peter.

'Come on, let's get in the fuckin' car,' he ordered, stomping through the club.

Mike followed after him but didn't manage to keep pace until they reached Glynn's BMW. 'What the fuck's got into you?' he asked as he got into the passenger seat.

Glynn started the engine and roared off up the road. There was no question of whose car they were going to take. Glynn loved the feeling of power his BMW gave him, and he liked to be in the driving seat. It made him feel in control and gave him a way of expressing his temper as he drove at speed, cutting up other motorists and yelling at anyone who got in his way.

'That fuckin' bastard Pete's only putting a stop to the dealers,' he fumed.

'What, cos of last night?' asked Mike.

Glynn nodded. 'Yeah, he's a fuckin' dick. I've told him the dealers won't sell out on us but he won't fuckin' have it.'

'It's not a problem, mate,' said Mike. 'We can still fuckin' do it without him. He doesn't need to know. And it means our cut will be bigger.'

'Course we'll still fuckin' do it. The trouble is, with all these new bouncers they're bringing in, they've got eyes and fuckin' ears all over the place. And I can't risk him getting rid of us cos if he does it'll make it harder to take over the Golden Bell.'

'I didn't know you were still after taking over the club,' said Mike.

Glynn hadn't mentioned it to Mike recently. It was a long time since he'd organised a raid and tipped off the police so that Peter got caught. His intention at that time had been to take over the Golden Bell but then Peter had put his sister in charge. Despite this, Glynn still had designs on the club and he knew that one day it would be his. He just hadn't figured out a way yet.

'Course I fuckin' am and I'll do it one day. Pete won't know what's fuckin' hit him! He makes me fuckin' sick. Just cos he's got his shitty property business, he thinks he's doing all right now, and bollocks to the rest of us.'

'No worries, mate,' said Mike. 'We've still got the protection business, haven't we?'

'Yeah, only cos Pete's too fuckin' precious to dirty his hands with it.'

Mike continued trying to pacify Glynn but for Glynn it was about more than money. He was sick to death of Pete pulling his strings. The man was a fuckin' coward, and Glynn didn't see any reason why he should keep answering to him.

'All right, shut the fuck up!' spat Glynn, when he became sick of hearing Mike trying to counter his arguments.

Mike didn't speak straight away. Even he was wary of Glynn when he was in one of these moods. For a few minutes the tension hung in the air between them until Mike eventually asked, 'Where are we going anyway?'

'I'll tell you where we're going,' said Glynn, his voice still full of anger. 'We're going to let everyone know who's the fuckin' big bollocks around here. And we're gonna start with that dickhead Dave Scott. By the time I've finished they'll all fuckin' know my name.'

He glanced across at Mike and noticed the corners of his mouth turn up in a half-grin. Glynn knew what Mike was thinking. He'd smelt blood and he couldn't wait to get started. Mike turned his head, meeting Glynn's gaze, a full smile now lighting up his face.

'Fuckin' bring it on,' he said.

48

They didn't wait around for David. The mood Glynn was in, he wasn't prepared to wait. Instead they went straight to David's home and hammered on the front door. As soon as David answered it, in his stockinged feet, they dragged him out of his house and shoved him roughly into the back seat of the car.

Glynn jumped into the driving seat, locked the doors and fired up the engine while Mike sat in the back with David and kept a tight hold on him.

'What the fuck are you doing?' yelled David in protest.

Nobody answered him, but Mike rewarded him with a sharp blow to the chin. David gripped his chin with his right hand, yelling in pain.

'That fuckin' hurt!'

'It was supposed to fuckin' hurt!' growled Mike. 'Now shut the fuck up if you know what's good for you.'

But David wouldn't shut up. He continued protesting. Each time he spoke Mike thumped him again until he eventually bullied him into submission and David sat quietly whimpering on the back seat.

Within no time they had reached their destination and one of Mike's favourite places: the Ancoats warehouse where they carried out all their tortures. The relevance of their destination wasn't lost on David. Why else would they want to visit an abandoned warehouse? And hadn't Todd mentioned a warehouse when they'd punished him? As soon as David realised why they were here he started yelling again but Mike soon shut him up by raining a volley of punches about his head and face.

Glynn switched off the engine and came round to the back of the car to help Mike haul David out. As they crossed the tarmac to the warehouse entrance, David kicked and screamed and tried desperately to break free. But they kept a tight grip on him until they had him inside.

'Tie the fucker up!' ordered Glynn, and they dragged him across the warehouse floor till they reached one of the old, rusted pillars. While Mike struggled to keep David pinned to the pillar Glynn secured his hands and feet to it using some rope they kept in the warehouse.

'Right, this time I'm starting it,' said Glynn.

He still hadn't calmed down from his encounter with Peter and the adrenalin was coursing around his body. He felt an impulse to do something to release his pent-up anger. Something physical. Something drastic. Something violent!

He walked a few yards and selected a hammer from the tools and weapons they kept stored at the warehouse. Mike looked at him and nodded, a sly grin forming on his lips.

'Yeah, go for it.' He chuckled.

David's screams now sounded like the desperate yelps of a frightened animal. He fought against his restraints, twisting and contorting his body till the rope left lacerations on his ankles and wrists.

Glynn swung the hammer and brought it down swiftly onto David's knee. A piercing shriek filled the air amidst a crunching sound as the hammer smashed against David's bones. Glynn repeated the action again and again.

A dense thud. Crunching. An agonised wail.

A dense thud. Crunching. Another agonised wail.

Over and over till the bone disintegrated and blood pumped from the torn flesh, running in rivulets down David's shin, diluted by his own urine.

When Glynn had exhausted himself he stood tall and launched the hammer across the warehouse floor.

'Your turn,' he said to Mike, a smile of amusement gracing his lips as Mike eagerly raced to retrieve the hammer.

Glynn waited till Mike had finished torturing David before he spoke. He didn't want David's screeching to drown out his voice. When David's screams had died down to a painful whimper, Glynn said what he had to say.

'Just in case you might have been thinking of taking over Alan's gang, don't fuckin' bother. In fact, I don't think you'd be capable of it now anyway,' he mocked, looking at David's shattered kneecaps.

'And make sure you put the word out to anyone else who might be thinking of having a go. Now your mate's out of the picture, we're the top firm in town. Not Pete Robinson's firm. Glynn Mason's fuckin' firm!'

He laughed at the expression on David's face, recognising that David now knew for certain who had killed Alan. But David wouldn't go squealing to the police. He wouldn't dare!

Glynn marched up to David and roughly gripped his chin. 'Who are we?' he hollered into his face.

'The top firm in town,' whispered David.

'Say our name. Say it!' shouted Glynn, twisting the flesh of David's chin between his fingers.

'Glynn Mason's firm,' David whimpered.

'Say it again!' ordered Glynn.

'Glynn Mason's firm,' David repeated.

'Louder!' Glynn yelled, twisting David's chin again until tears sprang to his eyes.

'Glynn Mason's firm,' cried David, his eyes pleading for mercy.

'That's better,' said Glynn, beginning to gain satisfaction from his handiwork. Then he turned to Mike. 'Untie him.'

Mike looked at him, puzzled. He had been expecting them to leave David dying a slow, painful death in the cold, desolate warehouse.

'You heard,' said Glynn. 'We need him to deliver a message, don't we?' Then he turned back to David. 'But don't expect a fuckin' lift. I don't want the blood of a scumbag like you messing up my car. You can hitch a fuckin' lift or else hobble back.'

When Mike untied David he slumped to the ground, the pain of his injuries too much to bear. They left him weeping on the dusty floor of the abandoned warehouse.

'Come on, let's get out of here,' said Glynn. 'I never could stand the sight of that little wanker.'

'Where are we going now?' asked Mike once they were back inside the car. He reminded Glynn of an eager puppy, his face full of glee now his bloodthirsty cravings had been assuaged.

'We're going collecting,' said Glynn. 'And, just so we're clear on this, I'm taking no shit from anyone. It's time we let them know that we're the only fuckin' firm that gets paid. I'm the boss around here now!'

He knew that Mike would be only too eager to oblige. After all, he'd had to keep him in check on many occasions. Mike's blood cravings were troublesome at times. But when there was shit to be done he knew Mike wouldn't balk at it. He was a sick fuck who wouldn't have any problems in getting handy with the customers. In fact, Mike wouldn't just carry out his instructions; he'd have a smile on his face while he was doing it.

The car skidded to a halt outside the Lord Nelson.

'We've been having problems with this one for fuckin' months,' said Glynn. 'Sid's such a cowardly little twat that he'll pay anyone who comes calling just to keep 'em off his back. But it's about time he learnt that there's only one firm he should be fuckin' paying around here.'

They marched into the pub, ignoring the look of astonishment on the barmaid's face as they strode through the bar area and into the back room. There they found the landlord, Sid. At only five feet two, and slight in frame, Sid was small for a landlord. He was also getting on in years and lately he was finding it more and more difficult to handle the more risky side of running a pub.

When it came to troublesome customers Sid knew he could depend on his regulars to help him out. He wasn't a tough guy, and mostly relied on his friendly nature to keep the peace in the pub. He'd been running the pub for years and had built up a strong rapport with the locals, who always came to his aid on the rare occasions when things threatened to get a bit out of hand.

But when it came to the gangs it was another matter. Even his handiest customers gave them a wide berth. Knowing that the gangs were ruthless and often used weapons rather than fists, the locals made themselves scarce when the gangs came calling. It just wasn't worth the risk.

This was where Sid had a problem. For months he'd been paying protection to Peter's gang and also to Alan's. Nobody else had approached him, knowing that the pub was under the control of two of the toughest firms in Manchester. But Glynn wasn't happy with Sid paying double. As far as he was concerned Alan's gang had been taking the piss and it was time to address the situation in case any other gangs were thinking of trying it on now that Alan was out of action.

As they walked into Sid's living quarters Glynn spotted the alarmed expression on Sid's face, which he quickly replaced with an obsequious smile.

'I've got your money,' he said, racing over to the sideboard and pulling a wad of notes out of a drawer. 'It's all there,' he said, holding the bundle out.

Glynn snatched the wad of notes and passed them to Mike. 'Check it,' he ordered. Then he addressed Sid. 'You been paying anyone else?' he asked.

'Well, yeah, but I'm still paying you,' Sid said, his voice as timid as his appearance.

'I don't give a fuck if you're still paying us. I've told you before not to pay anyone else,' he shouted, smacking Sid across the face.

Sid recoiled and covered his smarting cheek with the palm of his hand. 'But they were gonna smash the place up,' he pleaded.

'I don't give a fuck what they threatened!' yelled Glynn, punching Sid about the head till he fell to his knees.

He could feel Mike hovering by his side so he turned and glared at him. He didn't need his help this time. He wanted to handle this himself. Reaching down, he bunched his right hand into a fist as he grasped the front of Sid's shirt and hauled him to his feet. Then he rammed him against the wall, hearing a satisfying thud as Sid's head made contact.

Sid stared at him, his eyes pleading for mercy. But Glynn wasn't in the mood for mercy. He forced his fist hard against Sid's throat until he could hear a choking sound and could see Sid fighting for breath, his face ruddy and his eyes protruding.

'Next time anyone comes asking for protection, you fuckin' send them to me. OK?'

He released his fist slightly so Sid could speak.

'But,' Sid began until Glynn forced his fist back into his throat.

'What was that?' Glynn demanded, easing his fist again as Sid gasped for air.

'Y-yeah. I'll tell them,' Sid babbled, his face contorted with pain and distress.

'That's better,' said Glynn, letting go of Sid and watching him slump to his knees once more. 'As far as you're concerned there's only one firm in town. Alan's firm are out of business now, and if anyone else tries it on they'll be out of fuckin' business too. So you tell 'em that from me!'

Sid nodded avidly, his eyes wide with terror.

'Oh, and by the way,' he added, 'we're not Peter Robinson's fuckin' firm any more. I run the show now. So if anyone comes calling, you give 'em my fuckin' name. Is that clear?' he asked, aiming a sharp kick at Sid's thigh.

'Yes, yes, it's clear. I'll tell them,' gushed Sid, grasping his bruised leg.

'Right, that's better,' said Glynn, turning to Mike. 'Right, we're done here. Let's go.'

The landlord of the Lord Nelson wasn't the only one who received an unwelcome visit from Glynn and Mike that day. Over the coming days Glynn made sure they covered every business under their protection, and added a few more to their list. At every one they carried the same message: Glynn Mason's firm was the number one protection firm in Manchester now.

For Glynn it was as though someone had flicked a switch. He'd had enough. From now on he wasn't going to put up with people taking the piss. And he wouldn't be taking orders from Peter or anyone else for much longer either. He'd finally decided he was ready to be the Mr Big of Manchester.

And nothing and nobody was going to stand in his way.

49

It was one of those nights for Adele; a night when she had intended to have just one or two drinks in the club after work but had ended up getting carried away. Deep down she knew it had a lot to do with her present frame of mind and the worries she had been carrying around with her for the past few weeks.

For a start there was the issue of drug dealing in the club. Ever since Peter had clamped down on the dealing of drugs she had an unsettling feeling that it was still going on. Even though she was assured that Peter was no longer playing a part in it, she had a feeling that Glynn and Mike were still involved. But catching them was another matter.

Another thing that was worrying her was Glynn's attitude towards Peter. Again, it was since Peter had agreed to put a stop to the drug dealing. He had assured her that he'd told Glynn of his intentions, and to her it seemed that Glynn's attitude had now changed towards

Peter. Although Glynn stopped short of snubbing him altogether, his tone was now curt and his manner disrespectful.

What she found hard to handle was the fact that Peter wasn't pulling him up on it. She had a feeling that Peter was becoming increasingly intimidated by Glynn and that thought worried her. The man was becoming cockier by the day. What would he do next now that he seemed to have lost all respect for Peter? She dreaded to think.

It was now nine o'clock on a Friday night and Adele was nursing a brandy and soda, having already downed two as well as two glasses of red wine. She had intended to stay for only an hour or so, then go home for something to eat, but somehow the time seemed to fly by. When Chris found her sitting on a bar stool she was already well on her way to being drunk.

'Hi, how's things?' he asked, taking the stool next to her.

Adele's face lit up on seeing his handsome face smiling disarmingly at her. Despite her previous reservations about Chris, she was becoming drawn towards him and in her present state she had dropped her guard even further.

'Good, thanks, and even better now you've arrived,' she said, flirtatiously.

Chris seemed to notice that she was getting a bit tipsy so he asked, 'Have you eaten?'

'No. I was intending to go home soon and have my tea.'

'I know a nice Chinese restaurant we can go to,' said Chris. 'Let's get some food down you, sober you up a bit.'

Without exercising caution, Adele immediately agreed to go with Chris to the Chinese restaurant. After all, it was only a meal. What harm could it do? And a bit more flirtation with the delectable Chris could be just the pick-up she needed. Adele slid off her stool, gulped down the remainder of her brandy and soda and let Chris take her by the arm and lead her out of the club.

She was expecting Chris to take her to Chinatown, an area of central Manchester densely populated by Chinese restaurants and supermarkets, but instead he led her to a restaurant that was situated down a side road off Cross Street.

'The China Village. I've never heard of this one,' she said.

'It's good, believe me, the Peking duck is to die for,' said Chris.

He pulled the door open for her and placed his other hand on the small of her back, gently nudging her in the right direction. Adele tottered down the stairs that led to the restaurant, noticing on her way how sumptuous the interior was.

The lights were suspended from the ceiling and formed clusters, their honey-coloured shades fashioned like ornate Chinese lanterns. Each one was decorated with a crimson tassel, which hung beneath it. The lanterns gave off just enough light to accentuate the intricate gold designs on the shades while bathing the restaurant with a subtle glow.

Around the room silk screens hung from the walls, their vibrant designs capturing the essence of Chinese culture. The room was divided up into private booths, each one separated by a gold filigree panel, again depicting Chinese design. The seating was plush and the dark wood tables were polished to a high sheen. Elsewhere, dark wood latticework divided one section of the restaurant from another.

Overall the impression was one of opulence designed to indulge a discerning clientele. Adele noticed that most of the tables were occupied by people who she would consider well-heeled.

'Wow!' said Adele, her jaw dropping. 'This is lovely.'

'You ain't seen nothing yet. Wait till you taste the food,' said Chris.

An attentive waiter led them to a table, which was set with expensive-looking glasses and cutlery. He handed them a menu each and a drinks list, then left them to make their selections.

'Bloody hell! It's a bit pricey, isn't it?' said Adele, looking at the menu.

'Don't worry about it,' said Chris. 'Order what you want.'

Adele began to scan the menu but before she had the chance to decide what she wanted a waiter arrived to take their drinks order.

'We'll just have water, thanks,' said Chris.

'No,' said Adele, grabbing the drinks list from the table. 'Let's have some wine.'

'I don't think that's a good i—' began Chris but Adele cut him off.

'Don't be daft!' she said, louder than intended, to the consternation of a prosperous-looking lady on the next table who tutted noisily.

'This one will do,' said Adele, pointing to the wine list.

The waiter took down the number and went to fetch it.

'Are you sure that's a good idea?' asked Chris. 'After all, you've had quite a bit already.'

'Don't be daft!' said Adele, deliberately speaking even louder to annoy the lady on the next table. 'We're here to enjoy ourselves, aren't we?'

For the next few minutes they concentrated on the menu until the waiter arrived with their wine and passed Chris a sample to taste.

'That's fine, thanks,' said Chris and the waiter bowed politely.

Once the waiter had left the table, Adele grabbed the bottle of wine and poured a copious amount into her glass. Noting the expression on Chris's face, she said,

'Ooh, sorry, excuse my manners.' Then she leant over and poured an equally large measure into his glass, spilling part of it onto the pristine white tablecloth.

By the end of the meal Adele had ordered a second bottle of wine, having downed most of the first bottle herself. When they stood up to go, she lost her footing and landed in a heap on the floor. Chris bent down and grabbed hold of her arm to help her back onto her feet.

'Come on, we'd better get you home,' he said.

Adele spent the taxi journey voicing her concerns about Glynn to Chris, any attempt at secrecy now lost in her alcohol-fuddled state. When she arrived home she was only too happy to allow Chris to lead her to her front door and help her search for her key. He let them inside and Adele staggered into the living room.

'Do you want a drink?' she asked, swaying slightly from side to side.

'It's OK,' said Chris. 'I was more interested in making sure you're all right.' He sat down on the sofa. 'Why don't you sit down before you fall over again?' he asked, with a hint of amusement in his voice.

In response Adele plonked herself next to him, her drunken state making her oblivious to the concept of personal space as her leg squeezed up tightly against his.

'D'you know?' she slurred. 'You're a lot nicer than I thought.'

'Glad to hear it.' Chris laughed.

'No, I mean it,' she said. 'You've really looked after me tonight.' Then she drifted for a short time before resuming conversation, the topic slightly disjointed. 'I've fancied you for ages, y'know,' she said, draping her arm around his neck, her lips seeking his.

Chris took hold of her arm and lowered it down to her lap. 'No, not now,' he said.

'Why not? I thought you fancied me too.'

Then she leant forward and began kissing him till he responded but after a few seconds he pulled away and held her back.

'What's wrong?' she asked. 'Don't you want to?'

'Not now,' Chris repeated. Then he sighed, 'Look, Adele, you're right, I do fancy you but it would be wrong to do anything about it while you're in this state.'

'What state?' she snapped. 'I might be a bit pissed but I know what I'm doing.'

'I don't think you do,' said Chris, but then he was silenced as Adele lunged forward again, and grabbed his crotch while kissing him.

For a while they let their passions run away with them until Chris pulled away again.

'No, Adele, this isn't right,' he said.

'You...' she slurred '... can try to deny it all you want but I know you fancy me. And guess how I can tell?' She giggled, grabbing hold of his crotch again until she was rewarded by the feel of him swelling beneath her touch.

She began to work her fingers, gaining satisfaction from the sound of Chris groaning with pleasure. Then she undid his trousers and slid her hand inside, working her fingers again until his penis was fully erect. Withdrawing her hand, she then lowered herself onto his lap and thrust her hips backwards and forwards, simulating the sex act while still wearing her underwear.

'Come on, let's go upstairs,' she said, rising from the sofa and walking unsteadily towards the door.

'Wait!' called Chris. 'Are you sure about this, Adele?'

'As sure as I've ever been,' she said, walking from the room and knowing that Chris would be following closely behind.

Now she had him he was powerless to resist. She was consumed with passion for this man whom she had grown to both like and desire over the past few weeks. Where her sober self would have fought her feelings, her drunken mind acted out her desires. For the moment that was all that mattered.

But tomorrow, once she had sobered up and regained possession of her senses, it would be another matter entirely.

50

Peter hadn't seen Adele leave the club but he knew she'd been sitting with Chris, who had also left. He was sure she'd be all right; Chris was a good guy. But if she was going to start anything with Chris then he hoped it didn't end as badly as her relationship with Glynn had.

Peter thought back to the fallout from that relationship. Adele had got too close to Glynn and had freaked out on discovering that he was a killer. It had shaken her badly and it had taken Peter all his resolve to calm her down and stop her delving deeper into his business dealings.

Ever since Adele had finished the relationship she hadn't had a good word to say about Glynn, who'd subsequently worked his way through a bevy of attractive females. It wasn't easy watching Glynn flaunt other women in front of his sister and seeing the hurt on Adele's face. Peter had spoken to him about it once or twice but Glynn's reaction was that he wasn't with Adele any more so he could do as he pleased.

Although Peter knew what Glynn was, he had put up with it. To his mind Glynn was a good man to have on your side. Yes, he had a ruthless streak but he was also smart and efficient. Peter had therefore decided to take the rough with the smooth but at the same time keep an eye on him to make sure he didn't step out of line.

Glynn had always respected Peter's authority in the past but lately things had changed. As he sat alone at the bar, Peter went through this in his mind. As far as he could see there were two things that had sparked the change in Glynn. The first had been when Peter had let him take over the protection business.

Peter had heard about Alan's death and about what had happened to David, and there was no doubt in his mind that Glynn and Mike were responsible. He'd also heard about how brutal they were behaving with the customers. But Peter had kept out of it. He wasn't running the protection any more and he knew it wouldn't benefit him to dictate to Glynn how he should do things.

But there was more than just that going on. The second thing that might have been a catalyst to Glynn's behaviour had been when Peter had put a stop to the drug dealing inside the Golden Bell. Glynn's immediate reaction had been aggressive and confrontational and, from that moment onwards, there had been a definite shift in Glynn's attitude towards him. Glynn mainly avoided him but when Peter had cause to speak to Glynn he found his responses curt and hostile.

But the more Peter thought about it, the more he realised that Glynn's change in behaviour probably went back even further. Since Peter had been released from prison he had noticed that Glynn was different from how he was beforehand. He wondered whether Glynn had spent all this time harbouring a resentment at the fact that he had left Adele in charge of the Golden Bell.

Not only that, but Mike had changed towards him too. Nowadays Glynn and Mike were nearly always seen together. Mike usually had a knowing look about him as though they were cooking something up between them; it was something that Peter couldn't quite figure out but, nevertheless, it was there. And while Glynn spoke sharply to Peter, Mike would replace his knowing look with a satisfied smirk.

But Peter was at a loss as to what to do about it. He was wary of challenging Glynn, knowing that any form of confrontation might lead to Glynn finally stepping over the tenuous line between cooperation and rebellion. And that was something Peter wanted to avoid. If he was honest with himself, the consequences of such an insurgence worried the hell out of him.

*

When Adele awoke the following morning her head was pounding. She pulled the covers up tightly around her, not intending to go anywhere while she felt so rough. Then she turned over, letting her right arm spread over the other side of the bed. But as she did so she felt a presence. She opened her eyes, noticing at once the outline of a body under the duvet and the back of a head of shiny blond hair.

Oh, shit, no! What was I thinking? she thought to herself. 'What the hell?' she cried, waking Chris up.

He turned around and beamed a big smile at her. 'You all right?' he asked.

'No, I'm not all right,' she said, gritting her teeth. 'Please tell me I didn't—'

'Yes, you did,' said Chris, smiling. 'Don't worry. We both had a good time, didn't we? What's the problem?'

Despite her headache Adele sprang out of the bed and quickly threw on a dressing gown, regardless of the fact that it was a bit late to preserve her modesty. 'How dare you?' she screamed.

'Eh, hang on!' said Chris. 'What the hell am I supposed to have done?'

'You know!' she said but her memories of the previous night were vague, and she couldn't find the words to back up her statement.

'No, I don't know, Adele. In fact, I'm pretty bloody confused! What's the matter with you?'

Battling with her inner turmoil, Adele marched over to the chair on which Chris had slung his clothes the previous night. She picked them up in a bundle and shoved them at him.

'Just get dressed and go, will you?' she raged, turning her back on him, and resting her chin on her bunched-up fist, her teeth gnawing at her knuckles as she fought to contain her temper.

For a while she remained standing with her back to Chris, hearing the sound of him getting dressed and willing him to hurry up. Then she heard him stepping towards her. Refusing to budge, she remained where she was, hoping there was a chance he might just say nothing and leave. But then she felt his hand on her shoulder and he swung her round to face him.

'Get your filthy hands off me!' she yelled. 'Just go, and leave me alone.'

Chris held out his hands in a placatory gesture. 'Right, I'm going. But before I do, just remember that you were up for this just as much as I was.'

'No, I wasn't! You took advantage of me when I was drunk,' she shouted.

'Oh, no!' said Chris, his face becoming stern. 'Don't you dare play that card with me, Adele. It was you that made the first move. And I kept asking if you were sure, but you insisted.'

'OK, OK, you got what you wanted,' she said. 'So now you can go.'

She stormed through the flat until she reached the front door then held it wide until he caught up with her. As he walked out she kept her head bowed low, frightened he might see the tears in her eyes.

'I'll see you around,' he muttered as he walked out of the door.

In the few minutes since she'd got out of bed, Adele's recollections of the previous night were already coming back to her, causing a mix of shame and regret. Deep down she knew she was wrong for accusing Chris of taking advantage. She remembered instigating their night of passion and she hated herself for it. Because no good would come of it.

Once he had gone she berated herself. Chris was one of Peter's cohorts. Had she forgotten that in her haste to bed him? He was probably involved in all sorts of illegal activities, acts of violence and God knew what else. Just like Glynn!

Her mind drifted back to her time with Glynn and how that had ended. And, although Chris had been a much more considerate lover than Glynn, she couldn't help but compare Chris with him. They were both bad boys and she'd sworn off them for good.

Knowing that last night had been a big mistake, she promised herself that it would never happen again. And the next time Chris tried to sweet-talk her she'd let him know exactly what she thought of him and his type.

Despite her resolve, she knew she still wanted him. But she couldn't have him. It was no good. It just wouldn't work. And as she realised that a relationship with Chris was never going to happen, she wept with despair.

51

It was Saturday night and Adele was again sitting at the bar inside the Golden Bell, and chatting to Paula. But this time she was determined not to have too much to drink; just a bit of a pick-me-up after her excesses of the previous night.

She'd calmed down since that morning and had reflected on what had happened. Chris was right, she had instigated it, and it wasn't fair to take it out on him just because she'd made an error of judgement. So, when Chris approached her at the bar she was more receptive than she had been that morning. Paula had gone to serve somebody so Adele was currently alone.

'Adele, I just wanted to have a word with you about last night,' he said, checking around to make sure no one was listening. Adele went to speak but he held up his hand to stop her. 'Hang on,' he said. 'Before you bite my head off again, I just want to say that, although you think it was a mistake, I have no regrets. I realise that nothing is going to happen between us but perhaps we can just stay friends and be civil to each other.'

Adele nodded. 'I'm sorry. I was a bit out of order this morning. It was just such a shock to see you in bed beside me when I woke up.'

'Why was that such a bad thing?' he asked.

'I – it's nothing personal... and I am attracted to you, Chris, but it's just that... well, I've made too many mistakes in the past... and I don't want to have a relationship with someone who is connected to Peter's businesses.'

'Aah, now I see where you're coming from,' he said. 'You don't want another bad boy, is that it?'

Adele nodded, feeling her face colour at the perceived insult to Chris's character. 'I'm sorry but I was drunk and irresponsible. I shouldn't have come on to you like that.'

Chris held up his hands again and smiled. 'Y'know, I'm not such a bad guy when you get to know me.'

As he smiled at her Adele felt a tingle run through her body but she tried to remain impassive. She shrugged. 'Look, can we please just forget last night happened and leave it at that?' she asked.

He looked crestfallen. 'OK, then, if that's what you want. But let's stay friends, eh?'

She nodded again but stayed silent as she watched him walk away. She didn't have the chance to dwell on it because shortly afterwards Peter came to join her at the bar.

Peter waited till he saw Chris walk away before he went over to speak to Adele. He was curious about what had happened between them.

'Hi, sis, how's it going?' he asked, tapping her affectionately on the back.

Adele looked up from the bar area where she had been nursing a half-pint of lager. 'I'm good, thanks. How are you?'

'Not bad, y'know.'

'Good. Peter, I've been meaning to ask you… what's going on with you and Glynn?'

'What d'you mean?'

'I noticed he's been a bit off with you lately. Well, more than off, he seemed pretty bloody aggressive when I saw him talking to you the other day.'

'Oh, that? Yeah, he's not been too friendly recently.'

'Is it because you won't let him allow dealers in the club any more? He doesn't seem to have been right since then. Lately, though, he's been even worse for some reason. There's no love lost between me and Glynn, as you know, but he was always all right with you, wasn't he?'

'It's OK, sis, nothing for you to worry about. I can handle it,' said Peter.

There was no way he was going to share all his concerns with his sister. It was best she didn't know about some things. He wondered whether she had made the connection about what had happened to Alan but he hadn't discussed it with her at the time.

Peter didn't want to reveal his suspicions about Glynn and Mike to anyone, least of all Adele. He couldn't risk her going spouting off to the coppers. Chances were they wouldn't find any proof so all that would succeed in doing would be to piss Glynn off even more. And Peter wanted to avoid that. He knew that, where Glynn was concerned, he was treading on very dangerous ground.

To switch the emphasis away from Glynn, he quickly asked, 'Anyway, what's going on with you and Chris?'

'What d'you mean?'

'Oh, come on, sis, I know you left with him last night.'

'So what if I did? We went for a meal, that's all. End of story.'

'OK,' said Peter, holding up his hands in mock surrender. 'I was just asking, that's all… You don't make a bad couple actually.'

'No! That's never gonna happen,' she retorted sharply.

'Why not? Chris is all right. He'd treat you properly.'

'Unlike your other friend, Glynn, you mean?'

'Look, sis, fair enough, you had a bad experience with Glynn. But don't you think it's about time you put that behind you? Not every man is the same as Glynn, y'know.'

'Peter, leave it. I'm not interested.' She quickly downed the last of her drink. 'I'm off home. I don't want to end up drinking too much like I did last night.'

'OK, see you,' he said, but she had already jumped down from the bar stool and was on her way out of the club.

She hadn't told him much about her and Chris but Peter guessed that there was a clue in her last statement. She'd drunk too much last night when she was in Chris's company. And now, for some reason, the relationship was a non-starter. Oh well, if she didn't want to talk about it, there wasn't much he could do. Besides, he had much more pressing matters on his mind.

He glanced around the club, surprised to see an old acquaintance standing further along the bar. Pat O'Reilly, former landlord of the George and Dragon. He hadn't seen him for a while, in fact, not since the pub had been boarded up when Pat and his wife had decided they'd had enough of gang intimidation.

Just as Peter spotted him, Pat made eye contact and walked over.

'Hi, Pat, how's it going?' asked Peter, giving him a friendly tap on the shoulder.

'All right. I've heard a lot about this place so I thought I'd call in and see what you get up to. I'm not so bad, y'know.'

Peter grinned. 'Yeah, this is the infamous Golden Bell.' Then he asked, 'So, what are you and the missus up to these days?'

'We're running a newsagent's,' said Pat. 'It's not so bad. The early mornings are a bit shit but we take turns each with that.'

'Right, so I'm assuming it's Mary's turn tomorrow, is it?' Peter asked on noticing that Pat was a little worse for wear.

'Dead right,' said Pat. 'You've gotta make the most of a lie-in while you can. Anyway, it beats running a pub any day of the week.'

'I bet it does,' said Peter, feeling a twinge of guilt when he recalled how much grief Pat and his wife had suffered at the hands of his firm and many others. He soon dismissed his guilty feelings though; business was business when all was said and done and you couldn't afford to let sentiment stand in the way.

But there was no stopping Pat now he had started on the topic. 'It broke my fuckin' heart when we had to shut down the George and Dragon, y'know,' he said.

'I know,' said Peter. 'But, like you said, you're happy with what you're doing now, aren't you?'

'Aye, it's not so bad but I still miss the old place, y'know. It was all right before everyone started muscling in. I mean, I was already struggling when you put the rent up by a hundred pounds but then we had the other firms coming round too.' He sighed, looking into his beer before raising his head and adding, 'Five hundred quid a week's a lot of dosh to cough up, y'know, Pete. And that other bloody firm were after four hundred off me too. They'd already smashed the place up once—'

'Hang on,' said Peter, cutting him short. 'What did you just say?'

'What? About that other firm?'

'No, before that. How much did you say you were paying?'

'Five hundred a week,' said Pat.

'No, it was four hundred a week, Pat. You were paying four hundred a week when we put the price up.'

'The first time it was, yeah. But when you put it up again it was five hundred.'

A look of concern flashed across Pat's face and Peter could tell he was wary of him. He tried to calm his tone when he spoke to Pat again so he wouldn't freak him out.

'When was this?' he asked.

'What, the second time you put it up?'

'Yeah.'

'Erm…' Pat then seemed lost in thought for a few seconds before he said, 'Not sure of the dates but it was while you were inside. Glynn said you were putting up the payments for all your businesses.'

'Ah, right,' said Peter, not wanting to lose face in front of one of his former customers. 'Yeah, that would be it. I left Glynn to look after things while I was inside and let him make all the decisions. I never even noticed the difference in payments when I came out. I was more interested in the overall profits.'

Pat nodded then changed the subject. For the next few minutes they discussed topics of mutual interest until Pat announced that it was time for him to go.

'Nice seeing you anyway, mate,' said Peter, slapping him on the back again. 'See you around.'

Once Pat had gone, Peter thought about the conversation he'd just had. At first he'd thought that Pat had got a bit confused, seeing as how he'd had a few too many to drink. But then, he did seem a bit insistent that it was definitely five hundred pounds per week he'd been paying.

So, Glynn had put up the protection costs while he'd been inside? Fair enough, he had left him in charge when all was said and done. And just because he hadn't noticed the new figure in the books, it didn't necessarily mean Glynn hadn't banked the full five hundred pounds.

Peter thought back to when he had come out of prison. He'd been a bit irresponsible at first, living the high life while celebrating his release. And then he'd had a lot to focus on, getting back up to speed with all his businesses. By and large he'd left the collections to Glynn and Mike and some of his other men, and it hadn't even occurred to him to check how much they were banking. He tried to reassure himself that he'd have a look through the books on Monday and he'd probably find that Glynn had been banking the new amount.

But, if that was the case, then why hadn't Glynn told him that he'd put up the cost? Maybe Pat had got mixed up after all? But another thought was gnawing away at him. What if Pat hadn't got mixed up? What if Glynn and Mike had been charging extra and ripping him off by pocketing the difference themselves?

He didn't even want to think about that possibility. The consequences that would arise from it were too dire to contemplate. So, while he tried to put it out of his mind, he promised himself that once he was back in the office on Monday he'd have a good look through the books and find out the facts for himself. Then he'd have to decide what to do about it.

52

It was Monday morning. Peter was flicking through the old ledger that he had kept for the protection business. He'd always kept it hidden separately from all the other files and he was glad that Glynn hadn't asked for it when he'd taken over the protection business. He seemed to prefer his own way of doing things.

Peter's conversation with Pat, the former landlord of the George and Dragon, had been on his mind for most of the weekend. He'd been tempted to rush into the office on Sunday to check out the facts but then he'd told himself not to be so stupid. It was nothing that couldn't wait until Monday. Besides, he'd had his hands full on Sunday with an over-amorous blonde who he'd picked up in the club later on Saturday night.

He came to the page in the ledger where the entries for the George and Dragon had been made and he quickly scanned the rows of figures. No, four hundred pounds a week was definitely the figure that had been entered right up until the George and Dragon had shut down. That could only mean that either Pat had got confused about the figure or Glynn had taken five hundred pounds and kept the difference hidden from him.

Peter was reluctant to challenge Glynn. After all, he only had Pat's word for it. But he still felt uneasy about the whole business because, if Glynn had been pocketing the difference, then he couldn't afford to let him get away with it. Then a thought occurred to Peter that if Glynn had been taking a mark-up for the George and Dragon, then he could have been doing the same for some of the other businesses.

In the end Peter decided to ring around some of his old customers to check. He'd be careful though. He would only ring those he thought he could trust and he'd concoct some cock and bull story about an accounts audit and needing to double-check the figures.

After three phone calls Peter had all the evidence he needed. Every one of the businesses he contacted told him that Glynn had put up the price for protection not long after Peter had gone inside. He checked the ledger for each of the businesses he had rung and for each of them it was the same story. The amount entered in the ledger was the previous amount. In all of these cases Glynn hadn't entered the new figure.

Peter wasn't just disappointed in Glynn, he was angry. He knew deep down that Glynn and Mike must have been pocketing the difference and, although he wasn't looking forward to challenging Glynn about it, he felt he had no alternative. He couldn't afford to let Glynn make a mug of him.

It was bad enough hearing about the ruthless way in which Glynn and Mike were running the protection business. Then there was his brusque attitude towards him. Worse still were Peter's suspicions that Glynn and Mike were behind the death of his one-time friend, Alan, and the torture of David. But this latest revelation was one step too far. Peter knew that it was time he did something about it.

While Peter was anxiously flicking through the ledger, Adele was in the office next door. Margaret was off for a few days and Adele was sitting staring at the open door that Chris had just walked through. He'd called on some pretext or other but Adele had known straight away the real reason why he'd come to her office to see her.

It hadn't been long before he'd come to the point, trying to reassure her again that they'd make a good team. But he hadn't pressurised her. Instead he'd left it with her, telling her to let him know if she changed her mind. Then he had gone. She'd heard him have a quick word with Peter before the sound of footsteps followed by a slamming door had told her that he had left the top floor and made his way downstairs.

He'd been so nice about the whole thing and Adele could feel herself becoming increasingly drawn to him again. Come to think of it, he hadn't really done anything towards her that could be considered inconsiderate or unkind. She had based her mistrust of him solely on the fact that he was one of Peter's business associates. Maybe he wasn't such a bad guy after all. But then again, Glynn had seemed nice towards her at first.

As she sat there daydreaming she replayed Chris's words in her head. Then she found herself reliving the events of Friday night before the sight of Peter in the doorway made her snap to.

'Hello, daydreamer,' he said.

Embarrassed, Adele shuffled some papers around on her desk, bowing her head in the hope that he wouldn't see her blushing furiously. She was dreading him mentioning Chris again, frightened that the look on her face would give her thoughts away. But Peter seemed to have other things on his mind. He pulled out the chair opposite her, causing Adele to look up from her desk. The expression on his face was grave.

'What's the matter?' she asked.

Peter sighed. 'It's about time you knew,' he said. 'I'm not happy with Glynn at all. What you said the other day about his attitude; well, I agree. It stinks. But I was prepared to let it slide, thinking that perhaps he'd come around eventually, knowing that it was just because he was pissed off about me putting a stop to the drug pushers.

'But there's more than that. He's been really cocky since he took over the security business, and I don't like the way he's been going about things.'

'What do you mean?' asked Adele.

'Well, he's been a bit too keen where the customers are concerned.'

'And what else?' asked Adele.

She had her suspicions about Glynn and Mike where Alan's death was concerned but she'd put it out of her mind, somehow telling herself it was just too bad to be true. But now, seeing the worried look on her brother's face, she had a feeling he was thinking the same thing. When he didn't reply straight away, she asked. 'You think they had something to do with Alan's death, don't you?'

Peter shrugged but his face gave him away.

'You do, don't you?' she pressed.

He sighed again before speaking. 'I don't know. Maybe. I just don't know. But there's one thing I do know... Him and Mike have been ripping me off.'

'Really?'

'Yes, when I was inside they put up all the costs for security. Pat O'Reilly told me when he was in the club on Friday night, and I've just checked with some more of my old customers. He started taking an extra hundred quid a week off all of them when I went inside. Only, he didn't bother telling me about it and he didn't enter the new amounts into the ledger either.'

'Shit!' said Adele. 'What are you gonna do?'

'There's only one thing I can do, Adele. I'm gonna fuckin' have it out with him. I can't afford to let him get away with that or everyone will think I'm a right fuckin' mug.'

'And what if he admits it?' she asked.

'Then he'll have to go. Him and Mike. I can't afford to have men working for me if I can't trust them.'

'I told you what he was like, Peter.'

'Yeah, I know, and I've had my suspicions for a while. But I didn't want to think the worst of him. After all, he's had my fuckin' back enough times. And he is an asset to the business. I don't want to let him go really but I might have no choice. I can't just sit by and watch them make a fuckin' mug of me.'

'I agree, Peter.' Then she held out her hand. 'But don't just think this is sour grapes,' she said. 'I was over Glynn a long time ago. Now it's just about business. And I don't actually think he's an asset, like you do. I think he's poison and I'm just glad you've seen through him at last.'

For a few seconds she looked at him across the table. His expression had switched from gravity to resignation.

'OK, do what you have to do, Peter,' she said.

He got up to go but Adele called him back just before he made it through the door. 'What?' he said, his tone one of irritation.

'Just… be careful. That's all,' she said before Peter walked away.

53

After Peter had left Adele's office she heard him return to his own. Perhaps he had gone to collect some things because he was only there for a few minutes before she heard the outer door shut. Adele assumed, after their earlier conversation, that he was on his way to see Glynn. She hoped to God that their meeting would work out all right for Peter.

Her brother's revelation about Glynn had made her curious about other things. For a while she'd suspected that the property business wasn't all legal and above board, and this was one of the reasons why she wouldn't put her trust in Chris. With thoughts of Chris still in her mind as well as the conversation she'd had with Peter, she decided to do some checking of her own. It was an ideal opportunity while Margaret was off and nobody else was about.

She started by looking at the property deals that her brother had entered into recently. Like the security business, this information wasn't kept on the computer. Instead Peter kept a separate ledger, and Adele wondered whether this was so that the information could be hidden to prevent the police tracing his dealings. There were certainly a lot of property purchases listed, but although they were listed under Peter's property business they had been purchased by different individuals.

She carried on wading through the ledger, noticing the various house purchases listing the name of the buyer and the address of the property. Adele didn't recognise any of the names of the people who had made the purchases, which wasn't unusual in itself. But what she did notice was that the houses were highly priced. She looked at one, a three-bedroomed semi in Gorton. The price seemed a bit steep to her so she checked the local paper to see what price similar properties were selling for. Sure enough, they were all priced a lot lower than this particular one.

With her curiosity piqued she decided to delve even deeper. She scrolled through the ledger looking for further mention of any of the properties that these people had bought. As she waded back a few pages she found some of the same properties. They had been bought only a few weeks previously by different people but this time their price was well below the market value. *How strange!* she thought. There was definitely something amiss but what exactly that was she wasn't quite sure.

Next, she turned up the pages for property sales. There she found the same properties listed yet again. The sale was by the buyer who had bought the property only a few weeks previously but in each case the buyer was selling the property on at a vast profit. *Just who were these new buyers?* she wondered. *And why would they all want to buy a property worth substantially less than they were paying for it?*

She couldn't think of a reason why this would be and, still dissatisfied with what she had found, she turned over a few more pages in the ledger. This time she stopped at one of the pages for property rentals. She couldn't believe her eyes! All of the properties that had been sold on were now being rented out and the rental income was astronomical. There was definitely something not right.

Adele shut the ledger and pondered for a few moments. It just didn't make any sense to her at all. She couldn't figure out what was going on but she knew that she needed answers. As an employee of the business she had a right to know just what she was involved with. So she decided that she needed to ring Peter to find out.

She also realised that if the property dealing was illegal then Chris might somehow be involved with it. She wasn't quite sure what his role was but the very fact that he might be involved in something illegal wasn't good. It reinforced in her mind that she was doing the right thing in not taking her relationship with him further and yet again she realised that her one-night stand with Chris had been a bad mistake.

For the rest of the afternoon Adele was busy doing the bookkeeping. She knew that Peter had left the office with the intention of meeting Glynn so she decided to wait until that evening before she spoke to him. While she was on the phone she'd find out how his meeting with Glynn had gone too.

It was evening and Adele was back home. She didn't wait long before she picked up the phone and called her brother. Peter seemed to take forever to answer the phone and as she waited for him to pick up Adele became increasingly irritated.

'Oh, you're there, are you?' she asked brusquely when she heard her brother's voice on the other end of the line.

'Yeah, what's wrong?' he asked.

Adele decided to come straight to the point. 'What's going on with the property business, Peter?' she asked.

'What d'you mean?'

'Why are properties being bought cheaply then sold for a fortune to someone else a few weeks later?'

'Have you been checking up on me?' he asked, sounding put out.

'Not exactly, no,' she answered automatically.

'Then how the hell would you know that?'

'I have a right to know, Peter. If you're involved in something dodgy then I don't want it coming back on me when you get caught out.'

'There's nothing dodgy. What are you on about? That's the way the property market works. People buy and sell properties at a profit.'

'But why would people want to buy them at more than market value?'

'Who says they're more than market value? These are fuckin' high standard, Adele! We do them up.'

'Why would you do them up to such a high standard if the new owners are only gonna rent them out?'

'For God's sake, Adele! I haven't got time for this shit. I've got Glynn calling round any minute and I've got to have my fuckin' wits about me if I'm gonna tackle him about ripping me off.'

In her haste to get to the bottom of what was happening with the property business Adele had overlooked Peter's meeting with Glynn, but hearing Peter mention it put her senses on alert again. 'Have you not spoken to him yet?' she asked.

'No. Well, only to arrange for him to come round. I've only just been able to get hold of him on the phone.'

'Oh, I see,' she said, suddenly feeling guilty for putting her brother under further pressure. 'In that case I'd better let you go but I'll be coming to see you at work tomorrow. I'm not convinced about these property deals, Peter. I want to know just what the hell has been going on.'

She heard Peter sigh down the phone in that all too familiar way of his. He often sighed when he was presented with something that made him uncomfortable. 'OK, I'll talk to you tomorrow,' he said. 'But don't worry, it's all kosher.'

Peter put down the phone and loosened his shirt collar. It was moist with perspiration. Jesus! This was all he needed. Adele had cottoned onto his property scam and he had to think of something to tell her to get her off his back. Somehow he needed to convince her that it was all legal and above board.

He knew it was a good number and there was no way he was going to let his sister wreck it for him. She was very bloody close to figuring out how it all worked though even if she hadn't quite fully got to grips with it.

For months he'd been successfully operating the scam. Using his many contacts he'd get a property speculator to buy a run-down house that had been repossessed. Then one of his corrupt surveyor friends would revalue the house at a price that was above market value. The property speculator would get his initial outlay back once the house was sold, plus a little extra for his trouble.

When it came to selling the house on, somebody such as Glynn would apply for a mortgage using fake details and Peter would recompense them for their services. But Peter would pocket the bulk of the profit himself, which was usually a substantial difference between the original price and the new over-inflated price.

Peter would then put tenants into the property as soon as possible. As the tenants were usually in receipt of housing benefit, he'd set an unrealistically high rent and claim it back from the authorities. By the time the mortgage provider took any action against the errant customer, Peter would have received months of rent plus a considerable mark-up from the resale.

It was foolproof. There was no way the authorities would cotton onto it unless somebody put them in the picture. He just had to think of a way to stop Adele doing that. But at the moment he had more pressing matters to attend to.

He looked at his watch. Glynn was already late. He said he'd be there twenty minutes ago. Maybe he was deliberately keeping him waiting to gain a psychological advantage. Perhaps Glynn had an idea of why he wanted to meet him.

Peter loosened his collar again and noticed how much his hands were shaking. He grabbed the glass of brandy he'd poured and sipped at it for Dutch courage. He was dreading how Glynn would react when he confronted him. Then Peter looked at his watch one more time, willing Glynn to arrive so he could get this meeting over and done with.

54

When Peter heard the sound of the doorbell, he felt as though his heart had shot up into his throat. He tried to swallow down the feeling of trepidation that besieged him, telling himself to stay calm. After all, it wasn't the first time he had met with Glynn. On the other hand, it *was* the first time he'd had to tackle him about ripping him off.

'Come in,' he said, pulling the door wide for Glynn to pass through.

Peter followed Glynn into the living room. He didn't offer him a drink or a seat. Instead he picked up his own brandy and stood facing Glynn, gripping the glass tightly to steady his shaking hands.

'Well, I might as well come straight to the point, Glynn,' he said, trying to stay calm. 'I've found out from some of my past customers that you started charging them extra for protection after I went inside. Do you mind telling me why you didn't enter the full amount in the books?'

Glynn shrugged. 'Who's been telling you that?' he asked.

'It doesn't matter who,' said Peter. 'I've asked a few people and they've all told me the same. You charged a hundred quid a week extra to all of them. What happened to that money, Glynn?'

Glynn shrugged again. He wasn't making this easy.

'Right, so do you agree that you were charging them extra?' Peter persisted.

Glynn seemed deep in thought for a moment. Then, failing to come up with a defence, he went on the attack instead. 'What the fuck does it matter?' he said. 'You're not involved in protection now!'

Peter was shocked and, despite his trepidation earlier, he felt himself becoming annoyed. How dared Glynn try to play it down? 'Course it fuckin' matters!' he snapped. 'Any money you collected from my customers should have come to me. So why the fuck hasn't it?' he demanded.

'I owe you fuck all,' said Glynn but, although his words were harsh, his tone remained calm.

Peter found Glynn's cool demeanour unsettling. It told him that Glynn didn't give a damn what he thought. It was obvious that any respect Glynn had previously held for him was now gone.

Peter was flabbergasted. He'd expected Glynn to lie
or come up with a convincing argument as to where
the money had gone. And he would probably have
chosen to believe him rather than have to deal with the
inevitable fallout. But now he had no choice but to fight
his corner.

'You do fuckin' owe me!' he shouted. 'You've taken
a lot of fuckin' money from my customers since I went
inside. And it's not just money you owe me either.
You've betrayed me, Glynn, and I can't let you get away
with that.'

'I owe you fuck all!' Glynn repeated, but now his
voice had taken on a sharper tone. 'I was the one doing
all the fuckin' running around and sorting people out,
not you; me and Mike. Anyway, in this business you do
whatever you have to do.

'That's where you've always gone wrong, Pete,' he
continued, his tone now mocking. 'You're just not
fuckin' ruthless enough. I tell you summat: I don't piss
about with the customers like you did. They pay me
what they fuckin' owe me if they know what's good for
them. I don't take shit from anyone, including the other
firms. They'll all know my fuckin' name by the time I've
finished.'

'So, you think you're the big bollocks now you're
running the fuckin' security, do you?' asked Peter.

'I should have been running it from the start.
You've been out of your fuckin' depth for a long time,

mate. You let the other gangs walk all over you. But they're not fuckin' doing it with me, are they? And me and the lads are doing well out of the protection now. So, yes, you could say I'm pretty fuckin' proud of myself.'

Peter stared at him in stunned silence for a few moments until a disturbing thought came to him. 'So the rumours were true,' he said. 'You killed Alan.'

Glynn sneered. 'Like I said, you do what you have to do in this game. And I tell you summat: I'm getting a lot more fuckin' respect from the other gangs since I put Alan out of the picture. Anyway, there was no love lost between you and Alan, was there? Or between you and David, for that matter? Not since David double-crossed you all that time ago.

'And what was it David was supposed to have done exactly?' Glynn asked, his tone still mocking. 'Let me remind myself. Oh, yes, the Binkley warehouse job. He double-crossed you, didn't he? By tipping off the Millers. That was it, wasn't it? The Millers knew everything about the job you had lined up, didn't they? The day and time you were going to hit the warehouse, and the method of entry. No wonder they found it so easy to beat you to it.'

Peter didn't reply. He just stared at Glynn, a dazed expression on his face. Glynn was now grinning as he carried on speaking. 'Well,' he laughed, 'you assumed that David had double-crossed you but maybe you were wrong. Fancy having so little trust in yer old mates that you'd just accept my word for it.'

Peter was so shocked by what he was hearing that he let go of the tumbler. It crashed to the floor, spraying his legs with brandy and splinters of glass. But he was oblivious to the damage, his mind was so focused on what Glynn was saying.

Glynn was gloating now and Peter could feel the rage building in him. 'You bastard!' he yelled. 'It was you, wasn't it? You tipped off the fuckin' Millers about the Binkley warehouse job then had me thinking it was David.'

Peter had a disturbing flashback to the punishment they'd doled out to David on Glynn's say-so. The sight of his bloody, swollen face after Glynn had finished walloping him. His agonised screams as Peter had continued Glynn's handiwork. And the way in which David had still pleaded his innocence, even when they'd left him swollen and blood-soaked.

As he thought back to that time, he questioned his own poor judgement. Why, for God's sake, hadn't he believed David? He had judged David on his reckless behaviour when he was addicted to drugs. And because of that he had been too quick to believe everything Glynn had said.

No wonder David and Alan had turned against him! Who could blame them when he'd chosen to believe

Glynn over David? And now he realised that David had been telling the truth all along. He'd been such a fuckin' fool!

Suddenly he became aware of Glynn surveying him as his face reflected his conflicting emotions. Confusion. Recognition. Anger. Despair!

Glynn laughed raucously. 'I bet you feel a right cunt now, don't you?' he taunted. 'See, you think you're the fuckin' big shot around here, Pete, but I've always been a step ahead of you. Like that time when you raided Angels. I can't tell you what a fuckin' laugh I had watching you being led away by the police.'

Peter glared at him, the realisation written all over his face. Glynn had set him up all along. No wonder Glynn had decided to pull out of the nightclub raids. Peter recalled the bullshit excuse that Glynn had come up with at the time: something about having to rush to hospital to visit a sick relative. He should have known then not to believe him.

'Yes, that's right, Pete,' Glynn continued to mock. 'I called the coppers. Oh, and I tipped off the bouncers at Angels too. After all, I wanted them to be in with a fighting chance against you and the guys before the coppers came to arrest you.'

By this time Peter was fuming. He couldn't do anything about Glynn's double-crossing where David was concerned. The damage was already done. And he'd had to stand by and watch his two childhood friends go against him. Now he knew why: because he'd chosen to believe Glynn instead of David. What a mug!

Neither could he do anything about the fact that Glynn had set him up with the nightclub raid. He'd served his sentence for that and he'd never get that time back. But now, as he stood festering, his thoughts were on revenge. He was damned if he was going to let Glynn get off altogether.

'You double-crossing, dirty fuckin' scumbag!' he cursed. 'You'd better fuckin' give me what you owe me if you know what's good for you!'

Glynn laughed at him, his attitude scornful. 'Your Mr Big Shot act doesn't fuckin' wash with me any more, Pete. I'm the one who calls the shots around here now.'

The derisory expression on Glynn's face, together with Peter's despair at what he had now discovered, was too much for him to handle. With all thoughts of caution now forgotten, Peter charged towards Glynn. He was driven by an intense hatred against this man who had been the instigator of his downfall. He was livid to think that someone he had trusted could repay him like this and he was angry with himself at being taken for such a fool.

But before Peter could get to Glynn, he spotted something that pulled him up short. He stared in horror at the gun Glynn was holding. He'd swiftly pulled it out of his jacket and was now aiming it straight at Peter.

'You wouldn't,' Peter said, hoping he was right but afraid he wasn't.

'Wouldn't I?' said Glynn, whose scornful expression had now become menacing. 'Just fuckin' try me!'

'Come on, Glynn, drop the fuckin' gun,' said Peter. 'There's no need for that. We can sort things out between us.' But despite his brave words, inside he was quaking.

Peter continued to watch Glynn, his heart beating rapidly and his stomach churning. And to think his own gun was tucked away in another room. He cursed himself for not being more prepared. But then, he hadn't known what to expect.

As he stared down the barrel of the gun, Peter realised just how much he had underestimated Glynn. And now, he desperately needed to think of a way to persuade his ruthless nemesis not to pull the trigger and leave him for dead. He saw the determined look on Glynn's face and knew he had to beg for his life. It was the only way.

'OK, Glynn. Keep the money,' he said, his voice quivering. 'Nobody needs to know. Like you said, you're in charge of protection now and you can run it any way you like.'

He didn't mention that Adele already knew about Glynn and Mike creaming the top off the takings from protection. That didn't matter right now. All that mattered was trying to convince Glynn not to fire the gun.

Glynn came back at him. 'Do you really think I'd have confessed everything if I was gonna let you live?' he asked, sneering. 'And have you plotting your revenge? You must think I'm fuckin' stupid! You'd have me taken out at the first fuckin' opportunity. You know you would.'

'No, I wouldn't,' Peter pleaded. 'I'd always remember that you let me live and I'd be grateful for it.'

He was rambling, the words spewing out of him in his desperation to save himself. But looking at the resolute expression on Glynn's face, Peter felt as though his words were wasted. Then he noticed Glynn give one final evil smirk as he prepared to pull the trigger.

55

Adele was in the office early the next day. She still wanted answers from Peter and she was determined that, one way or another, she was going to get them. For a while she listened out for her brother arriving but when it got to 9.30 and she had still seen no sign of him she decided to go into his office and check if he had sneaked in quietly.

But he wasn't there. Adele remembered his planned meeting with Glynn and a feeling of disquiet settled in the pit of her stomach. She returned to her office and picked up the phone but there was no reply when she rang Peter's apartment. For the rest of the morning she kept ringing him at intervals, her feeling of unease growing.

As lunchtime approached, Adele toyed with the idea of going to Peter's apartment but then a supplier rang with an urgent query and she became distracted. The supplier hadn't been paid. A quick check through the books verified that the payment had been overlooked but despite her profuse apologies he demanded that she pay him straight away.

It was a while after she'd dealt with the angry supplier before Adele thought about Peter again. By this time it was early afternoon, and Adele still hadn't eaten. She tried his phone again. Nothing.

As she was beginning to feel faint with hunger, Adele decided to grab herself a sandwich and coffee from a local shop. Then, once she had eaten, if she still hadn't heard from Peter she'd decide what to do about it. She was busy chomping on her sandwich when she heard someone walking down the corridor. She looked up just in time to see Glynn and Mike breeze into her office.

'We've come to put the takings from one of the sunbed shops in the safe,' said Glynn.

Adele was alarmed to see him, her mind on his meeting the previous evening.

'Wh-wha…?' She was about to question him about the meeting with Peter but then thought better of it so she quickly disguised the question. 'What are you doing collecting it in the middle of the day?' she asked.

'Don't ask,' said Glynn. 'Some idiot forgot to collect last night so it's been fuckin' sitting in the till at the sunbed shop until now.'

'What, you mean it's been there all night?' she asked, feigning interest.

'Yeah, anyone could have come in and nabbed it. I'll have to have a word with Pete to keep a check on things in future. Where is he anyway?'

Adele tried to disguise the look of confusion that threatened to give her away. Surely Glynn would know more about Peter's whereabouts than anyone, having visited him last night. Either he hadn't called round after all, or he was an even bigger trickster than she thought. With her usual mistrust of Glynn she suspected the latter and a sixth sense told her not to let him know that she was aware of the meeting.

'I don't know,' she said. 'I've been ringing his apartment but there's no reply.'

'Crafty bastard,' said Mike. 'I bet he's got a bird there again and doesn't want to be disturbed.'

'Shush,' said Glynn. 'His sister doesn't want to know that.'

Adele tutted. 'No, you're right. I don't.' Then she said, 'Let me know if you hear from him, will you? I could do with a word with him myself.'

When they had left her office, Adele reflected on the exchange. How strange! Did Glynn really know nothing about Peter's whereabouts? If so, where was he? Had Glynn not gone to Peter's apartment after all? Or maybe he had gone... She began to get carried away in her thoughts but then stopped herself. The alternative was too awful to contemplate.

But sitting here wasn't going to give her any answers. After ringing Peter's phone for the umpteenth time that day and still getting no reply, she began packing away her things ready to finish work. It might be a bit early to knock off but she couldn't settle. If she wanted to find out anything about her brother's mysterious disappearance then the only way to do that would be to call round and see him.

It was mid-afternoon by the time Adele arrived at her brother's apartment. The front door was locked and for several minutes she alternated between ringing the bell and hammering on the door knocker. But neither of those things brought a response.

She had a spare key inside her purse. It had been there ever since she had stayed with him years previously. When she'd tried to return it he'd told her to keep hold of it as it was always handy to have someone with a spare. Now, as she stood outside Peter's front door growing increasingly anxious, she was glad she hadn't handed it back.

Adele rooted inside her bag for her purse, surprised to find that her hands were trembling. She pulled out the key, her fingers fumbling awkwardly inside her purse till she managed to grip it. Her clumsy movements reminded her of just how worried she was about her brother and as she put the key in the lock a feeling of intense dread flooded her mind and body.

She paused for a moment and took a deep breath. Then she began to turn the key in the lock. Her movements were slow. It was as if she were putting off the inevitable.

As soon as she opened the front door, Adele spotted faint patches of blood on the hall carpet. Her dread turned to panic and she rushed through the hall, leaving the front door wide open in her haste to find her brother. She pushed open each of the internal doors as she sped through the hall, taking a cursory glance into each room before rushing on to the next.

The blood patches were thicker near the lounge door telling her that this was where she would find the answers. So she pushed the door hastily and peered inside. But nothing could have prepared her for the sight that met her on the other side of that door.

Lying only a few metres from her was a body, coated in thick, viscous blood; it was difficult to discern whose body it was. But she knew. She dashed over to her brother, hoping in vain that he was still alive. But as soon as she caught sight of him fully, she realised there was no way he could have survived those injuries.

Half his face had been blown away, his handsome features now destroyed. Adele gasped in horror at the blood-strewn crater that had once been her brother's face. She felt the bile rise in her throat and reached up to cover her mouth. For a few seconds all she could do was stare in disbelief. Then her loud piercing screech filled the air.

Adele stepped back but as she did so she felt the room sway. And then she tumbled to the floor. When she came to she could feel a pair of strong, manly arms holding her. She was now in a different room and she wondered fleetingly whether it had been a bad dream.

'Are you OK?' asked a voice she recognised, and she looked up to see Chris peering down at her. He must have carried her out of the lounge.

At first she was alarmed to see him there; her mistrust still evident. But as she saw the look of concern in his eyes, she felt strangely comforted.

'What are you doing here?' she asked.

'I've been keeping my eye on things,' he said.

'B-but—' she said.

'Shush,' said Chris, caressing her brow. 'You've had a very bad shock. Let's get you out of here.'

Adele was so traumatised that she let Chris lead her away without question, despite her mistrust of him. She sat weeping in the passenger seat of his car while he took her home. Once they were there he fussed around her, sitting her down and making her a strong cup of tea for the shock.

'I-it was Glynn,' she said. 'It was Glynn that did it. We need to tell the police.'

'I know,' he said. 'I need to make some phone calls. Will you be OK?'

She nodded, confused, but still too traumatised to question him. In her vulnerable state she willingly put her trust in this man. It didn't even occur to her whether it was wrong of her to do so. She was too far out of her mind with distress and grief to think straight.

When he came back into the room she said, 'Did you ring the police?'

'Yes, don't worry. They'll be here soon.'

Then she kept repeating, 'It was Glynn. He did it. He was there last night. It was Glynn. Did you tell the police it was Glynn?'

Chris stepped over and kissed her gently on her forehead. 'Don't worry. They'll be here soon.' Then he took her hands in his. 'I need to go,' he said. 'I'm really sorry but I've got urgent things to tend to and I don't want to be here when the police arrive. Will you be OK?'

She nodded solemnly and Chris walked away. As he reached her living room door he turned back and said, 'I'll be back to see you soon.'

Then she heard the sound of the front door shutting after him and she sat and waited alone for the police to arrive.

56

It was two days since Adele had discovered her brother's dead body, and they had been two of the worst days of her life. She'd barely slept and was eating very little. Every time she tried to eat she felt a gagging reflex as she thought about her brother's battered face saturated with his life's blood. She had shed so many tears that her eyes and throat felt raw, and somehow she just couldn't get her food down. Her face was pale and drawn, and her eyes were bloodshot, the lids droopy.

Since Tuesday the club had been shut and it was now Thursday. Although the weekend was fast approaching Adele had no intention of reopening the club yet. Not only was it a mark of respect for her brother but she also couldn't bear to set foot inside the place at the moment. For her it represented everything that had been bad about Peter's life. If he hadn't gone into the nightclubbing scene maybe he would still be alive.

She'd had a few visitors since Tuesday. The police had called round twice to question her, and Paula had visited that day bringing flowers and a card. Adele hadn't seen anything further of Chris though and it made her wonder whether he might have had something to do with her brother's death.

Adele was still mistrustful of him. Even though she was almost certain that Glynn was behind her brother's killing, something about Chris's behaviour just didn't stack up. She was tormented by the constant speculation going on inside her head. The person responsible for such a brutal crime against her brother was still out there and it made her suspect everyone.

Adele had no way of contacting Chris to find out what had been going on. Usually she bumped into him in the club, but now that the club was shut for the foreseeable future, there was no way that was going to happen.

As she sat there chewing over the facts she heard a loud knock on the door, which made her jump. Her first thought was that it might be Chris come to see how she was. Despite her sorrow she rushed to the door, eager to find out why he'd been at the scene of her brother's killing. A tiny part of her also wanted to see him anyway.

When she pulled the door open she was astounded to see Glynn. Not giving her a chance to recover from her shock at the sight of him, he brusquely pushed his way inside and stomped up the hallway.

'What the hell?' she shouted. 'What on earth are you doing here?'

He didn't reply so she took off after him. She found him in the lounge, standing by the fireside as though he had every right to be there.

'What the hell are you playing at?' she asked. 'You can't just barge into my home!'

'Well, I knew you wouldn't let me in otherwise so here I am.'

He smirked and Adele recoiled on hearing his words, which brought her to her senses. She now realised that she'd been foolish to follow him through to the apartment. After all, he was the person she suspected of Peter's murder. But if he had done it then why hadn't the police arrested him?

She gazed at him in astonishment as he spoke again. 'I'm sorry to hear about Pete,' he said matter-of-factly.

When she didn't respond he cleared his throat, then said, 'Look, I know it's a bad time for you but I'm here to ask when you're thinking of reopening the club.'

'You what?' she asked, incensed.

'Well, I can appreciate that you might not feel up to it at the moment but we owe it to Pete to keep things ticking over. And then there's the staff to think about—'

'Are you fuckin' serious?' she asked. 'My brother has just been shot to death and all you can think about is profit! Have you any idea what it was like finding him in that state?'

She thought she detected a slight shift in his stance at the impact of her words but he quickly hid it. 'All right, all right,' he said. 'I'm not expecting you to run the place. I can keep things ticking over for you while you take some time off. Take as long as you like. The club will be in safe hands.'

'Get out!' she yelled. Glynn held his hand out in a conciliatory gesture, ready to speak again, but she continued to yell. 'Get out! Go on, get out! You disgust me. How dare you try to pressure me to open the club after what's happened? Get out!'

'All right,' he said, dropping his hands and making his way slowly towards the door. 'I'll be back in a couple of days to see if you've changed your mind.'

'Don't fuckin' bother!' she shouted. 'I'll reopen the club when I'm good and ready and not a moment before. Now get out of my home and don't bother coming back.'

'Don't worry, I'm going,' he said. Then, as a parting shot, he added, 'Oh, by the way, in case you're wondering why the police haven't arrested me, it's because they've got fuck all on me. Well, apart from your word, and who's gonna believe a murdering ex-con?'

'Get out!' she screamed again and she carried on yelling at him until she heard the front door slam shut.

It was after he had gone that the full effect of his visit hit her and she retched as she realised the danger she had put herself in by following him inside the flat. She'd just been alone with her brother's potential killer! The police might not have enough evidence to arrest him but that didn't mean he didn't do it. To her mind he was guilty. And now he had learnt from the police that she knew about his meeting with Peter. What was to stop him killing her too?

As she thought about the consequences, panic took hold. Her heart beat rapidly, her breath coming in shallow gasps, and the whole of her body was trembling. She dashed around the flat checking that the front door and all the windows were securely locked. Then she helped herself to a measure of brandy to calm her shaking limbs and numb the pain of her brother's death.

Adele was distraught but she was also frightened. She'd seen Glynn's handiwork so she knew what he was capable of. What was to stop him coming back for her? But she had no one to turn to. Her mother was in an even worse state than her, and her best friend Caroline was currently abroad on holiday.

Adele didn't feel able to confide in Paula or anyone else about Glynn. They'd think she'd lost the plot. After all, it looked as though the police didn't believe her about Glynn so what chance did she have of anyone else believing her?

But if the police wouldn't arrest Glynn, what could she do? As she sat nursing the glass of brandy she began to rock backwards and forwards in her seat, trying to comfort herself as tears of sorrow and despair ran down her cheeks. Her brother had been snatched from her but that was only the start of her nightmare. How would she ever feel safe again while the man she believed to be Peter's killer was still walking free?

57

It was the day of the funeral and Adele and her
mother were sitting inside a funeral car on their way
to Southern Cemetery. Adele had had a lot of time
alone to think in the week since her brother's death,
and she'd finally decided to walk away from the club
altogether. She would put it up for sale. At least that
way her mother would benefit financially. Peter's death
had brought home to her the level of danger she'd been
under while working at the club and she didn't want to
live that life any more.

She would still live in fear of Glynn though. But,
having had a chance to think about it logically, she
realised that if Glynn was going to kill her he'd have
done it that day in her flat. For some reason he'd decided
against it. Perhaps it was because she'd done her worst
in reporting him to the police, and it hadn't made any
difference. Then again, perhaps it was because her death

would point the finger of suspicion more firmly in his direction.

The past week had been very traumatic. As well as having her own grief to deal with, she'd been trying to look after her distressed mother. Shirley had gone to pieces ever since the news of Peter's death, and Adele was worried about how she would get through the funeral.

Adele was worried about her own future too. She had no idea how she would cope financially. At the moment she didn't even feel up to work. Maybe Caroline would be able to help her find work when she returned from holiday. But that was all in the future. She had to get through today first.

Adele glanced through the window of the car as it passed through the open wrought-iron gates of Southern Cemetery, and the funeral procession slowly wound its way down the approach to the chapel. The place was serene and calming, and for a few seconds she focused on her surroundings until they drew closer.

Hordes of people were milling about the chapel. While her mother had wept quietly throughout the journey there, she now convulsed with great big wracking sobs. Adele turned away from the window and paid attention to her mother, putting her arm about her and drawing Shirley's head towards her breast in an effort to comfort her.

'Shush,' she cajoled, stroking her mother's hair, until Shirley's intense sobbing abated and was replaced by a low whine.

When the car drew to a stop Adele took a moment to calm herself then turned to her mother. 'You ready?' she asked, and her mother nodded.

Adele stepped out of the car and everybody's eyes immediately shot to her and her mother. She walked steadily towards the building, making a conscious effort to remain calm. Adele's arm was draped about her mother, her bearing resolute as she supported her. When they passed through the crowd all conversations quietened to a lull, the people nodding in silent acknowledgement of their grief. Then Adele noticed the number of gangsters amongst the crowd.

Although she had been expecting members of the criminal fraternity to attend her brother's funeral, she was surprised at just how many of them had shown up. Adele didn't know most of her brother's associates but they were easy to recognise – they had gangster written all over them. It was in their posture, their expressions, everything about them, and Adele thought sardonically what a derogatory tribute to her brother's life they were.

These men were there superficially; their duty delivered but wrapped with indifference. To Adele it seemed that they didn't really feel pain like normal people. Their faces were impassive, their eyes not revealing any hint of emotion. They remained stoic and unflinching even as Adele and her distraught mother passed by them.

They reminded her of the guards at the Tower of London who were trained to remain dispassionate. She had been there on a school trip once when her grandmother had stumped up the money knowing that she wouldn't have gone otherwise.

Adele and Shirley stepped inside the chapel and made their way to the front. The sight of the coffin brought fresh tears to her mother's eyes and for a few moments Adele watched helplessly while her mother's body juddered with the strength of woeful emotion that swept through her. It was too much for Adele, who felt the sting of tears in her own eyes and finally gave release to her grief.

The sound of the priest's voice seemed to bring a degree of tranquillity to those in attendance. When he gave the eulogy his words were touching. Adele had sat with him a few days previously, telling him about Peter's life and trying to emphasise the positive points as she did so. To her relief the priest had done her proud, glossing over Peter's nefarious activities and focusing instead on his achievements as a businessman despite his troubled upbringing.

While she listened Adele became lost in her own thoughts, her mind wandering back to their childhood and all that she and Peter had been through together.

She thought about the way Peter had always been there for her, and she for him. The bitter-sweet memories flitted through her mind:

Fighting together with the local kids.

Condescension in the corner shop.

Exacting revenge on Jessie Lomas.

Their excitement at seeing Grandma Joyce loaded with gifts.

Peter's brutal hidings at the hands of his father.

Visiting Peter in the detention centre.

Covering up their father's killing.

The thoughts spun around inside her head like a fast-forward replay of their life together. Then the funeral drew to a close, its ending signified by the closing of the dark, heavy drapes creating a shroud around Peter's coffin. Her mother's cries of anguish reached a peak as the coffin was shunted along the conveyor belt of doom.

They shuffled outside and stood around while the funeral attendees approached to offer their words of condolence. Adele put on a brave face to speak to them all while her mother collapsed sobbing into the arms of a friend and neighbour.

Eventually the crowd began to file away and Adele turned to her mother, ready to take her to the waiting car. But one man had yet to see Adele. He had hung back from the throng of mourners waiting for his chance. Now, as she stood alongside her mother she caught a glimpse of him through the corner of her eye: tall, slim and good-looking with a shock of shiny blond hair; she looked up to see Chris approach.

'Can you look after my mam for a minute?' she asked the neighbour.

'Course I can, love,' said her mother's friend, who was already cradling Shirley's head in her bosom.

Adele stepped away from her mother, towards Chris, her lips forming the letter W, ready to quiz him. But he spoke before she had the chance.

'Adele, I'm so sorry,' he said, taking hold of each of her arms. 'I didn't really have a chance to offer you my condolences last time I saw you. We were too busy... well... y'know...'

'But—' Adele began till he cut her off again.

'I know. You've got loads of things to ask me. And I've got loads to tell you. But it will take a while.' He looked across at Adele's mother before continuing, 'Maybe later we can chat. I'll explain everything then.'

'OK,' said Adele, and he squeezed her arms affectionately before forcing a smile and walking away.

Adele hadn't seen him since he had turned up at the scene of her brother's killing and she had so many unanswered questions to put to him. But she knew as well as he did that now wasn't the time. She was too aware of her distressed mother sobbing in the background and their need to attend the wake. So, together with her mother's friend, she helped her mother into the funeral car then joined her before they set off.

Adele's mind was in a quandary. Alongside thoughts of the funeral and memories of her departed brother, her mind kept switching back to Chris. He had been so good on the day she had discovered Peter's body. When she'd been overcome with shock and grief, Chris had offered her comfort. But then he'd rushed her out of Peter's apartment. And why had he again rushed from her flat before the police got there? And if he really cared for her then why hadn't she seen him until now?

But all her thoughts of Chris were pushed aside when the car drew up at the venue and her mother began to nudge her. She looked at her mother's tear-stained face. Although Shirley had stopped crying now, her grief was nonetheless visible through the ruddiness of her sodden cheeks and her red-rimmed eyes. Adele would have to wait till later before she found out what Chris had to tell her. For now, she had other things to concentrate on.

58

They held the wake in a country pub in the affluent village of Lymm, Cheshire, in preference to holding it at the Golden Bell. To Adele's mind it had seemed disrespectful to hold it there; the scene of so much turmoil and trouble during Peter's adult life.

This place seemed a million miles away from the type of pubs and clubs that Peter had frequented during his life and that was why Adele had chosen it. Her mother had been happy to go along with Adele's suggestion and, although it was expensive, they knew they could recoup the cost from the sale of the Golden Bell.

Located on a narrow country lane bordered by hedgerows, fields and mature trees, the Lamb Inn was an eighteenth-century pub with whitewashed walls, window shutters and a proliferation of colourful hanging baskets. A brook ran alongside the pub and was straddled by an old stone bridge.

As they stepped out of the funeral car, Adele's mother gazed in awe at the lovely building and the setting. Despite her upset, Shirley's face lit up for the first time that day and Adele knew she was pleased that her son's life was being celebrated in such lush surroundings.

'Ooh, it's lovely,' she said. 'You've done him proud, our Adele.'

Adele gulped as she tried to fight back the tears that were threatening to erupt again. Instead she focused on getting her mother inside.

The interior was just as appealing as the outside. It was what Adele would have described as cosy and olde-worlde. They stepped in to find a floor of stone slabs but, rather than making the room seem cold, the stone slabs added character because they were rustic in appearance and varnished. Beams ran along the ceiling, which was painted cream. The walls were also cream in colour and were adorned with stunning oil paintings. Around the room were solid oak tables and well-upholstered chairs, and above each table was an ornate chandelier.

The stone slabs led onto a carpeted area with a bar on the far side of the pub. This was where the mourners were. As Adele approached she could see that the bar itself was also of solid oak polished to a high sheen. Again her mother gazed in awe at the splendid surroundings and Adele was glad that they at least took her mother's mind off her sorrows, if only for a short time. But as soon as they began to mingle with the crowd of mourners the reality of their situation became all too apparent.

The evening was drawing to a close. Shirley's neighbours had already taken her home and there were just a couple of stragglers still finishing their drinks. Adele had stayed back to speak with Chris and to say a final goodbye to the guests.

Adele was glad the wake was almost over although she realised that it was only the beginning in terms of learning to live without her brother, who she had loved from the bottom of her heart despite the corrupt path he had taken in life. It had been a trying day, which had left her feeling drained both physically and emotionally. By the time the last of the guests had said their goodbyes and Chris came over to talk to her she wasn't in the best frame of mind.

As she watched him cross the pub and make his way towards her she became overwrought. She really could have done without this right now! At the moment all she wanted was to go home, sit alone drinking a toast to her brother's memory and release the emotions that she had been bottling up all day while she had been busy taking care of things. How dared Chris choose today of all days to come and see her when he had had a week since Peter died?

As soon as he was within touching distance she rounded on him angrily. 'I wondered when you were going to show your face again,' she snarled. 'Just what the bloody hell has been going on, Chris? Why were you so eager for the police not to see you when we found Peter's body? Is it because you had something to do with his killing? And where the bloody hell have you been since then?'

'No, no!' he said. 'You've got it all wrong, Adele.'

'Well, what is it, then, Chris?' she asked. 'I know you were involved in his corrupt property business.' She noticed him raise his eyebrows in surprise. 'Oh, yes. I knew about that,' she continued. 'I bloody well knew when I looked at the books that there was something not right. Why on earth would you be selling the properties at a much higher price only a few weeks after they'd been bought and then charging extortionate rents for them? I'm not bleedin' stupid, y'know!'

She was building herself up into a fury until Chris eventually butted in, raising his voice to grab her attention. 'If you'll just give me a minute to explain!' he said.

His sharp tone stopped Adele in her tracks. She had never seen him like that before and it shocked her into silence.

'Right,' he said, 'now I've got your attention, I'll tell you what's been going on.'

He took a deep breath as though this was going to be a protracted affair, then he began.

'The reason I didn't want the police to see me is because I was working undercover.'

'What, you mean…?'

'Yes, I'm a police detective.'

'I don't understand,' said Adele, staring at him in astonishment. 'If that's the case then why couldn't you stay around till the police arrived?'

'Because I was still working undercover at that point. If I'd blown my cover it could have compromised the whole investigation. I couldn't let you know either. We had to rule you out as a suspect first.'

'You mean, you suspected me of killing Peter?' she asked, feeling affronted.

'Not personally, no. But I had to follow procedure so we had to be sure.'

'So, what's changed?'

'Well, we've been gathering evidence. That's why I haven't been able to see you till now. It's been a bit full on.'

'Hang on!' she said. 'If you're an undercover copper then why were you involved in Peter's shady property business?'

'I wasn't involved in the illegal side of things and I took great care to keep it that way,' he said. 'Although it wasn't easy at times. I wasn't working alone either. One of the doormen is also an undercover officer.'

'Who?'

'Bear.'

This almost raised a smile to Adele's face, even though she was still feeling angry and confused. She'd always liked Bear so she wasn't surprised to find out that he wasn't one of the bad guys.

'He's been collecting evidence about some of the illegal dealings in the club, such as the illegal drug deals.'

Adele blanched on hearing this. It was frightening to think that people who had worked amongst them were collecting evidence all the while.

'Oh, don't worry,' said Chris. 'We've learnt enough to know that you weren't personally involved in any of the illegal activities, and Bear can back me up on that. It's a bit different where your brother's concerned, though. If he had been alive we'd have been throwing the book at him.'

'Well, he isn't, is he?' said Adele. 'So, why can't you just leave things alone? It's bad enough that we've lost him but hearing everything he's been involved in would destroy my mother.'

'Don't worry,' said Chris again. 'This isn't about Peter any more. In fact, it was never just about him. We've also had two other suspects under surveillance: Glynn Mason and Mike Shaftesbury. Initially we were concerned about the illegal activities that all three men were involved in. But then your brother was killed and the investigation switched emphasis.'

He paused, allowing Adele to digest his words before he continued. 'The good news is that we've uncovered some evidence linking Glynn to the murder of your brother.'

Adele gasped and Chris gave her a moment before going on to explain further. 'We've also gathered a lot of evidence on both Glynn and Mike in relation to the illegal side of the businesses. We've arrested both of them and we're confident that we'll have enough to charge them with.'

'B-but you haven't charged them yet?' asked Adele.

'Not yet, no. But hopefully we will be doing so very soon. I wanted to tell you that much though, which is why I'm here today. And, obviously, I wanted to pay my respects to your brother.'

Adele stood silently for a few moments, shocked by what she had just found out.

'I – I need to sit down,' she said, and Chris took hold of her arm and led her to a chair.

For a while she avoided his gaze, her eyes misty and her lips trembling as her mind tried to come to terms with what she had just learnt. It was one thing suspecting Glynn of her brother's killing, but it was another thing entirely to have it confirmed. Then Adele suddenly realised that she hadn't seen either Glynn or Mike at the funeral, and it all made sense. She hadn't even noticed their absence previously; she'd been too busy just getting through the day.

'I know it's a lot to take in,' said Chris. Then he put his hand on her arm in a comforting way. 'If it's any consolation, I liked Peter. If I'd met him in any other walk of life I'd have thought he was a great guy. And, well, he didn't deserve to die in such a way.'

His final words were Adele's undoing and she was suddenly hit by the futility of it all. She collapsed, sobbing uncontrollably, burying her head in her arms, which were folded on the tabletop. Her face was hidden from Chris's view but her shoulders heaved as each mighty sob shook through her body. Then he lifted her head and took her in his arms, holding her close and letting her cry out all the pain of the day.

It was some minutes before Adele recovered her composure and, as she lifted her head, Chris passed her a handkerchief from his pocket. 'Adele, I'm really sorry but I need to go now,' he said. 'As I explained, we're still holding Glynn and Mike. The investigation isn't over yet and I might still be needed.'

'All right,' she said, smiling meekly.

'Come on, I'll drop you at home on my way to the station,' he said. 'But, before I do, here's my number.' He pulled a pen from his jacket pocket and scribbled his phone number onto a beer mat. 'If you need me for anything, call me.'

'OK,' said Adele. 'But, before you go, promise me something. Next time I see you, please give me some good news, for God's sake, because I've had about all the bad news I can take for now.'

59

It had been two days since the funeral and Adele was sitting alone inside her flat feeling desolate and bereft. How she missed her brother, Peter! She'd just returned from her daily visit to her mother, a duty she had imposed on herself to make sure her mother was coping all right. But although she felt duty-bound, she didn't enjoy going to visit her at the moment. Shirley would become maudlin and weepy, and Adele would leave her for home feeling much worse than when she'd arrived.

Adele hadn't had any visitors since the funeral, including the people she had worked with such as Paula and Margaret. It seemed that they didn't want to associate with her since she'd decided to close the Golden Bell and put that life behind her. Instead they were focusing on moving on to another place of work and another life.

She'd thought a lot about Chris since the funeral. His revelation that he was an undercover police officer had surprised her and changed her perception of him. Adele wondered whether he might call round at some point but then she put that thought straight out of her head. He might seem caring but, at the end of the day, he was a policeman, and what would a policeman want to do with her, an ex-con?

Caroline was due home from her holidays that day and Adele couldn't wait to see her. At least then she'd be able to confide in someone about how she felt. Unlike the people at work, Adele shared an emotional connection with her best friend, Caroline. She was so understanding that Adele knew she'd have a way to make her feel better about things.

It was difficult not to dwell on the past and, no longer able to focus on reading a book, Adele had taken to watching TV; anything to try to take her mind off things. Now, as she sat watching something mind-numbingly boring, she heard a knock on the door. She sprang out of her seat, expecting it to be Caroline, and raced to answer it. She was surprised to see Chris standing there, but also pleased.

'Hi. How are you?' he asked.

Adele shrugged then said, 'OK, I suppose... Come in.'

'Do you want anything to drink?' she asked once they were inside the lounge.

'No, I'd rather just come straight to the point,' he said. 'We've charged Glynn and Mike. We're holding Glynn in custody till the case goes to trial but, to be honest, I think we've got enough evidence to make any jury convict him.'

'Thank God for that!' she muttered half-heartedly, sitting down on the sofa. Then, remembering her manners, she added, 'Have a seat.' She lifted her hand to indicate the chair across from her, and Chris sat down.

'I thought you'd be pleased,' he said.

'Oh, I am,' said Adele. 'But, it's just... well... nothing can bring Peter back, can it?'

'I realise that,' he said. Then he crossed the room and sat down beside her, taking her in his arms. 'I'm sorry for what you've been through and I just wish I could make it right for you, Adele.'

'I know,' she said.

For several minutes they remained silent, Adele drawing comfort from the feel of his arms around her. This was what she had needed: someone to comfort her and make everything seem better.

Eventually Chris loosened his hold and then spoke. 'I understand why you're not exactly turning somersaults. After all, you've been through a lot.'

Adele smiled. 'Thanks anyway for doing all you can.'

He smiled back then took hold of her arms and held her away from him while he gazed into her eyes. 'You're one hell of a woman, y'know,' he said.

Adele smiled and lowered her gaze, embarrassed at all the attention.

'I need to go now but I wondered if you'd let me call round and see you again,' said Chris.

'What would you want with the likes of me?' she replied, automatically.

'Adele, as I've already told you, you're one hell of a woman. When I said you'd been through a lot I wasn't just referring to losing Peter. I – I did a bit of research and, well… let's just say I know everything.'

'And you still want to see me?' she asked, thinking back to the night when she'd lost all control and brutally killed her father.

'I do. Adele, I understand why you did what you did. I know that you were pushed. Believe me; I've come across cases like this before. After years of abuse people sometimes just snap.'

'Jesus! You've really done your research, haven't you?' she sneered, using sarcasm to cover her shame.

'Sorry. I didn't mean it to come over like that. But what I'm trying to say is that it doesn't make any difference to how I feel about you. So, can I come and see you again?'

'Yes, if that's what you want,' she said.

Once he had left her flat she couldn't help but feel a frisson of excitement at the prospect of seeing him again, despite her grief. But then she tried to suppress it. She didn't want to get her hopes up and risk being hurt again.

60

True to his word Chris came to see her again and he continued coming to see her. But he didn't push her into anything. Mindful of her sorrow, he was respectful and gave her the space and time she needed to grieve. They got on well and Adele grew increasingly fond of him. She enjoyed his visits and gradually, over several months, they grew closer, and their initial friendship deepened into a loving bond.

Adele hadn't reopened the Golden Bell. She had sold it, and her mother had given her a share of the proceeds to keep her going until she found employment. With Chris's support Adele had grown stronger and she now felt ready to look for work.

They were currently lying on Adele's double bed, satiated after a night of passionate lovemaking, and entwined in each other's arms. Adele loved this feeling when they would lie there chatting about anything and everything. Chris was such a good listener and he was also an interesting conversationalist. They'd been sharing a joke when Chris suddenly became serious. He let go of her and moved away, creating a distance between them but looking intently into her eyes.

'There's something I need to tell you,' he said. 'I've got a post elsewhere; Macclesfield of all places.'

'Oh,' said Adele, stunned. 'When do you go?'

'I start next week.'

'Oh. That is sudden!'

'Well, I'd been planning it for a while but I had work to finish here, and I didn't know how you'd take the news.'

Adele didn't know what to say. She was astonished and, if she was honest with herself, disappointed too. He had been so kind and supportive while she had been grieving the loss of her brother, and she'd steadily grown to love him. But now this!

'It's a new start,' he continued. 'The crime rates there are nothing compared to Manchester and, to be honest, I'm looking forward to taking it a bit easier. And, after all you've been through, I thought that perhaps you might want a new start too.'

'Well, yes. I mean, that's why I got rid of the club and why I'm going to try to find work elsewhere. And once the trial is over I think I'll finally be able to move on with my life. It's not going to be easy but—'

He put his finger to her lips, silencing her. 'Shush,' he said. 'I wasn't talking about that; I mean a new start with me, Adele. I'm asking you to come away. Leave Manchester and stay with me.'

Adele was completely floored. Despite her desire to be with him she wasn't expecting him to take such a big step. 'I – I need time,' she said. 'After everything that's happened, I just need some time to think, and I want to make sure my mam's OK.'

'I understand that,' he said. 'But I don't want to lose you. Will you at least come and stay with me for some of the time while you're still living in Manchester? It's not a million miles away. You could still come and visit your mother regularly. And it's not too far to come back for the trial either.'

'Yes, I'd love to,' she said.

He smiled. It was a becoming smile that lit up the whole of his face. Then he took her into his arms again and Adele melted into him, content in spite of her sorrow.

This was the last thing she had expected but once she'd had time to come to terms with Peter's death and had helped her mother over the worst, she would definitely give his proposition a lot of thought. And maybe she would have some kind of a future after all.

EPILOGUE

1994

S teve Anthony, clinical psychologist, raised his head from the notes he had in front of him and peered at Adele as she walked into his office. He smiled, pleased at the sight of the attractive woman who he had come to know well over the past few months.

It was very gratifying for him when his patients could finally open up and share their innermost secrets. In some cases his patients had been holding everything inside for years and as they offloaded all their troubles he would gain tremendous satisfaction from witnessing the transformation in their personalities.

During the period in which Adele had been visiting him, Steve also found that he had come to like her as a person. Despite the things she had been through and the things she had done, she was an honest, caring woman, and she had earnt his utmost respect.

He was always sad to say goodbye to patients like Adele because he gained a lot of pleasure from helping them change their lives for the better. So, in a way today would be a sad day because he had to say goodbye. He already knew there was nothing more he could do for her. Therefore, it wouldn't be fair to keep taking her money.

For a while they chatted. Steve realised that their sessions had taken on a new emphasis and they were spending increasing amounts of time talking about things in general now that she was no longer in need of his help. Eventually he decided that he would reluctantly have to draw things to a close.

'So, if we can just recap before we end today's session,' he began, taking a quick peek at his notes. 'You've been seeing Chris for around a year and a half and are getting married next month.'

'That's right,' she said, her eyes sparkling.

Steve added a few words to his notes before saying, 'Well, as I've said before, Adele, I think he's good for you. And I'm pleased that you've managed to get a handle on your temper. Before you leave here, don't forget that if you ever feel your temper building in the future, you're to practise the exercises I set you.'

'Yes, I will,' she said. 'Don't worry, I'm determined that I won't let anything ruin what I've got with Chris. I know he's a good man and I don't want to lose him.'

'Very well,' said Steve, picking up his pile of papers and tapping them on the desk to straighten them up.

'Then there's nothing more to say other than goodbye, Adele, and I wish you well in the future.'

'What? You mean – this is the last session?'

He grinned. 'Well, unless you want to keep paying me to chat about the weather.' He read the expression on her face, a moment's alarm, but she soon recovered. 'Don't worry,' he added. 'You'll be perfectly all right. I have every faith in you. But if you ever need me in the future, you've got my number.'

Adele smiled and stood up. 'Well, I suppose that's it, then,' she said. 'Thanks. Thanks for everything you've done for me.'

'You're welcome, Adele, but you did most of it yourself. You're a remarkable young woman, you know. Take care.'

He also got up from his seat, walked across the room and gave her hand a brisk shake. Then he held the door open for her.

'Goodbye,' said Adele. 'And thanks again.'

'You are very welcome,' said Steve and he watched her walk away looking radiant and unfettered with her head held high. He smiled, thinking about the marked contrast between the beaten, stressed and emotional woman who had walked into his office all those months ago to the confident and self-assured young woman who was now walking away.

*

Adele left Steve Anthony's office for the last time, happy that she was finally moving on from her turbulent past. Although she'd felt for some time that she was now getting on top of things, it was good to hear it from Steve. And Adele knew that if she was going to cope with the next challenge in life she would need to keep a level head.

As she walked through the front door and into the street Adele gently patted her stomach and felt the first stirrings of new life respond to her touch. A smile played across her lips. Yes, she would definitely need to have her wits about her to face this next challenge. And she had a feeling that this little one was going to keep her busy. After all, he already seemed to be perfectly in tune with what she was thinking.

ACKNOWLEDGEMENTS

This book marks the end of my Manchester Trilogy and my first experience of working with a publisher. The Aria team have been a joy to work with and from the start I have felt as though I am in safe and very competent hands. So, big thanks to the entire Aria team who continue to be a great support. I'd particularly like to thank Sarah Ritherdon, Caroline Ridding, Nikky Ward, Geo Willis, Vicky Joss, Sue Lamprell and Sabir Huseynbayli, and Melanie Price for past support.

I recently had the pleasure of meeting my editor, Sarah Ritherdon, who, apart from being a lovely person, is so knowledgeable about the publishing industry and my writing genre in particular. I honestly don't think I could have chosen anyone better to work with, and I feel very privileged to have her support.

Big thanks to all the bloggers and reviewers who took time to read an early copy of the book and leave feedback. They do an excellent job for the writing community in general and are a gift to authors.

I'd also like to thank all the readers who have remained loyal and continue to read my novels. I've tried to make this book a fitting end to the Manchester Trilogy so I hope you'll enjoy it, and that you will carry on enjoying my books in the future.

Last but not least, I want to thank all of my family and friends for their support. It is lovely to hear all your words of encouragement and get feedback from all the friends and acquaintances who read my books.

ABOUT HEATHER BURNSIDE

HEATHER BURNSIDE spent her teenage years on one of the toughest estates in Manchester and she draws heavily on this background as the setting for many of her novels. She previously worked in credit control and accounts until she took a career break to raise her two children. After ten years as a stay at home mum, she decided to move away from credit control and enrolled on a creative writing course.

She started her writing career twenty years ago when she began to work as a freelance writer while studying towards her writing diploma. As part of her studies Heather wrote the first chapters of her debut novel, *Slur*, which became the first book in the Riverhill Trilogy. During that time she also had many articles published in well-known UK magazines.

Heather later ran a writing services business, and through her business, she has ghost-written many non-fiction books on behalf of clients covering a broad range of topics. However, Heather now prefers to concentrate on fiction writing and works full-time on her novels from her home in Manchester, which she shares with her two grown-up children.

If you would like to find out more about the author, you are invited to subscribe to her mailing list, which you can find by visiting her website at www.heatherburnside.com. As a subscriber you will be among the first to find out about forthcoming publications.

Hello from Aria

We hope you enjoyed this book! If you did, let us know, we'd love to hear from you.

We are Aria, a dynamic digital-first fiction imprint from award-winning independent publishers Head of Zeus. At heart, we're committed to publishing fantastic commercial fiction – from romance and sagas to crime, thrillers and historical fiction. Visit us online and discover a community of like-minded fiction fans!

We're also on the look out for tomorrow's superstar authors. So, if you're a budding writer looking for a publisher, we'd love to hear from you. You can submit your book online at ariafiction.com/we-want-read-your-book

You can find us at:
Email: aria@headofzeus.com
Website: www.ariafiction.com
Submissions: www.ariafiction.com/we-want-read-your-book

⬛ @ariafiction
🐦 @Aria_Fiction
📷 @ariafiction